THE CAIN CHRONICLES

The Seasons of the Moon Series
Book Five

SM Reine

BOOKS BY SM REINE

THE SEASONS OF THE MOON
Six Moon Summer
All Hallows' Moon
Long Night Moon
Gray Moon Rising
The Cain Chronicles

THE DESCENT SERIES
Death's Hand
The Darkest Gate
Damnation Marked
Dire Blood
Paradise Damned

SM Reine
Website: smreine.com
Email: smreine@gmail.com
Twitter: @smreine

Interior and cover design by SM Reine.

For my readers—
You've made all my dreams come true,
and you're pretty good-lookin' too.

PART ONE

New Moon Summer

PRELUDE

The White Dress

Moonlight shimmered in Gwyneth Gresham's unshed tears. Her gray braids had been combed out and tied in an elegant knot, and she wore the only dress she owned—a modest cotton sheath patterned with yellow flowers.

She fidgeted with her niece's sleeve, trying to smooth the satin flat.

"Why are you crying?" Rylie asked.

Gwyn picked up her shotgun and started loading it with silver bullets. "It's just—you look beautiful, babe. I wish your dad was here to see the way you look tonight."

Rylie swallowed around the lump in her throat. "I don't."

Her aunt jacked a round into the chamber. Propped the gun against her shoulder. "You ready?"

Rylie closed her eyes and imagined everyone waiting for her to step outside. Werewolves on one side. Plainclothes Union army on the other. A murderer hidden in their midst. And Scott Whyte waiting to officiate the wedding.

Music started to play outside the tent. Whether or not Rylie was ready, it was time to walk down the aisle.

She picked up the bouquet and used the blossoms to conceal the claws that had already replaced her fingernails. Her inner wolf was stirring.

Rylie took a deep breath and stepped outside for the wedding.

ONE

Eight Seasons

Two years earlier.

The forests of Gray Mountain were filled with shrieks and howls. Hunter was pitted against wolf. The soil absorbed splashing blood as gunfire echoed off of the rocks.

A woman, tall and dark-skinned with blazing eyes, dragged her son onto the rocks ringing the top of the mountain. Together, they approached the swollen moon.

"Where's your girlfriend?" Eleanor demanded, shaking Seth's arm hard.

"I don't know," he said through gritted teeth.

He was telling the truth. He really didn't know that Rylie was watching from the trees.

She circled the battle silently, searching for a way in without getting shot. Her pack was getting killed as she watched, but she couldn't do anything without risking Seth.

Her paws gripped the earth. Her nose tilted to the air.

The wind smelled of blood and bullets.

Eleanor shook her son again. "Rylie! Come and get him!" Her voice echoed over the yelping wolves.

The sight of Eleanor's hand on her son filled Rylie with cold fury.

She leaped.

The power of the wolf's muscles launched her from the trees and onto the rocks atop the mountain. Eleanor raised the shotgun, but Rylie bit before she could fire.

The feel of her teeth sinking into Eleanor's leg was fleeting, but satisfying. Rylie jerked the older woman off her feet, and another wolf jumped onto the rocks to help— Abel. He was out for his mother's blood.

But Eleanor wriggled free of them and smashed the shotgun into Seth's gut.

Both wolves froze.

"Get down, Abel," Eleanor commanded, and he could only obey or watch his brother get shot. When he slunk far enough away to satisfy her, she faced Rylie. "Change back."

She did.

A few moments later, she was human. Blond hair hung around her bare shoulders. Her heated skin steamed.

Eleanor pressed her gun harder into Seth's stomach and grinned an evil grin. "Walk to the top. Do it. Go on! Call your gods down, and tell them to save you!"

Rylie ascended, feet melting the ice. Late spring air kissed her bare arms with frosty wind.

Gray Mountain was supposed to be the seat of the gods, but Rylie never believed it. Not really. And yet, if she *was* the Alpha—the leader of the wolves, the one who could save them all—was it really so hard to believe there might be more than that, too?

She reached the top and stretched her arms toward the moon.

It was waiting. Expectant.

Her boyfriend watched her from below with desperate eyes, silently begging for her to save herself.

"Sorry, Seth," Rylie whispered.

And she jumped.

Later, Rylie would try to make sense of what happened after she plummeted off of Gray Mountain's peak.

She should have been bashed at the bottom of the cliff. She should have broken every bone in her body and died. But that obviously hadn't been the case. Her memory was pretty blurry on the facts, but her survival was undeniable.

She was also certain that *someone* had spoken to her. Rylie had only the vaguest sense of what they said, but she knew it was apologetic. Something about how the werewolf ability wasn't meant to be a curse.

Shouldn't there have been a face to go with that voice?

All Rylie remembered clearly was the moon hanging low in the sky. She remembered being bathed in silver light and a weight lifting from her chest.

She had been given a gift: the ability to change into a werewolf at will, rather than being chained to the cycles of the full and new moon. It was liberation from the monstrous hunger.

But years later, she still had no idea who had done her such a favor.

When Rylie climbed to the top of the mountain, she wasn't the same girl who had fallen.

She dragged Eleanor off of the cliff, and the woman died at the bottom of the rocks in the way that Rylie hadn't. The smell of her blood washed over the breeze.

Maybe she was imagining it, but the moon seemed satisfied.

She embraced Seth and Abel, went home to Aunt Gwyneth's ranch, and they worked together all summer to convert it into a sanctuary for the other werewolves who had survived.

Then they were supposed to live happily ever after.

Right?

Three months later.
Rylie sat on the side of the bed, struggling to hold back tears as Seth packed for college. He had been putting it off

for weeks, but he had to move into the dorms that weekend; there was no more time to delay.

He didn't have much to take—Seth was leaving his guns behind, so he only had a few outfits and the spiked plugs he kept in his pierced ear.

"I'll call you as soon as I have my new address," he said, stuffing a pair of jeans into his backpack. Wind chimes sang softly outside their open window. "We can write letters to each other again. It's going to be fun."

Fun? Rylie bit her bottom lip and picked at her thumbnail. How could being hundreds of miles away from her boyfriend be considered *fun*?

He caught her expression and dropped to his knees in front of her.

"Oh, come on, Rylie. Don't cry."

"I just don't think I can do this without you."

Seth kissed her. His lips tasted salty.

He cupped her face in both of his hands and pressed their foreheads together. "You're Alpha, Rylie. You don't need me to control all of the werewolves. You can do it alone."

"But I don't *want* to do it alone."

"Abel will help you," Seth said.

She sniffled. "Abel isn't *you*."

"Yeah. He's not. And don't you forget that." He flashed his lopsided smile. "You're going to be okay. I promise."

What was the point in arguing with him? He was leaving for college whether Rylie liked it or not, and she would have to finish off her last two years of high school responsible for two dozen werewolves—alone.

"I love you," she said.

His lingering kiss was all the response she needed.

Abel took his brother to the airport. It was a long drive into the city, and they didn't talk much. They hadn't really talked at all since they worked together to kill their own mother.

It felt strange, knowing that Eleanor wasn't out there anymore. After haunting them for so long—trying to kill Rylie, keeping Seth under her trailer, and stabbing Abel— he wasn't quite ready to believe the nightmare was over.

He worried, just a little, that saying her name out loud might bring her ghost back.

They parked in the airport garage.

Seth sat in the passenger's seat of the Chevy Chevelle, backpack in his lap, and didn't move. A long silence stretched between them.

When two minutes passed without Seth getting out of the car, Abel's lips spread into a forced grin. "You want me to walk you through security, bro? Need me to hold your hand?"

"You'll look after Rylie, right?" Seth asked.

Abel blinked. "That's the deal, isn't it? I look after the ranch while she does school and homework. She handles the changes on the full and new moons. We already worked this out."

"But you're not going to look after her *too* closely."

Seth's expression was deadly serious. Abel's shoulders tensed.

They studied each other from across the car. They might as well have been separated by a chasm.

"I'll look after her," Abel said finally.

"All right."

They shook hands.

Seth climbed out and went to catch his plane.

Rylie was sitting on the back step when Abel returned to the ranch. She twisted twine around the stems of dried leaves to form an autumn bouquet, and he stopped at the bottom of the hill to watch. She was absorbed in her arrangement and didn't seem to realize she was being watched.

She had changed since they returned from Gray Mountain. Not physically—she had the same almost-white hair, skinny legs, and heart-shaped face. But there was a new aura about her. Abel couldn't help thinking that she was haloed by a powerful energy. The Alpha spirit.

Abel was supposed to look after his brother's beautiful, sweet, *deadly* werewolf girlfriend for two years until she graduated high school—as long as he didn't get too close to her. What did that even mean?

"It's going to be a long goddamn two years," Abel muttered to himself, slamming the Chevelle's door.

Rylie looked up at the sound and smiled. She smiled to see *him*. It lit up her whole face.

Yeah. A really long two years.

And yet, somehow, twenty-one months, seven seasons, and forty-eight moons passed.

TWO

Departure

It was the night before a new moon, and Rylie was worrying.

She paced outside the door to Abel's bedroom, listening to him move inside as he packed for an overnight trip. Rylie already knew what he would take: an extra shirt, a pair of pants, and a handgun loaded with silver bullets.

He hadn't shot any werewolves in years, but it was better to have it. Just in case.

"Why don't we send someone else?" she whispered to the mirror at the end of the hall, rehearsing her speech. "Maybe Bekah could get this one? No, wait, she's got yoga in the morning..."

Dammit, Rylie just didn't want Abel to leave. Not the night before a moon. *Especially* not when she was still helping the new werewolf, Vanthe, get settled into life at the sanctuary.

June was late in the season for snow, but it wasn't unheard of. What if they closed the roads and he couldn't get back before the next evening's new moon?

She would have to handle almost two dozen werewolves.

Alone.

The door opened, startling Rylie from her thoughts. Abel loomed over her.

He was taller than Rylie. Of course, at six-and-a-half feet, he was taller than pretty much everyone. The sharp odor of silver and gun oils drifted from the backpack at his shoulder.

Abel didn't look surprised to see her waiting for him. "Hey, Rylie."

"You can't leave," she blurted, totally forgetting every single one of her not-so-carefully prepared arguments. She even forgot her authoritative "I am Alpha and you should do what I say" voice.

Abel's grin stretched the scars on his cheek. He barked a laugh and sauntered into the kitchen without responding.

She watched his retreating back, mouth hanging open.

He was pretty good at communicating without words—werewolves were big on that whole body language thing. And Abel's swagger spoke volumes.

They weren't polite volumes.

The Alpha wolf inside of her gave an offended growl.

Abel wasn't running, but his legs were so long that Rylie had to jog to catch up with him. By the time she reached the kitchen, the back screen was slamming shut with a rusty whine.

The newest werewolf, Vanthe, was helping Aunt Gwyn pull a tray of broiled meat out of an oven. "Food's almost ready," she said when she spotted Rylie. "Better warn the troops."

"They've been out in the fields all day. We'll have to ring the big bell," Rylie said, but she didn't grab the mallet. She squeezed between Gwyn's hip and the kitchen island.

"What's the rush?" Vanthe asked. He was a tall, lean man in his late twenties with dark skin and shockingly blond hair.

"Abel's going to pick up another wolf from the airport."

Gwyn threw a critical look over her shoulder as she turned off the second oven. They'd been forced to expand the kitchen in order to accommodate the ravenous appetites of twenty werewolves, and dinner took all three ovens to cook on most nights. "So...?"

"So tomorrow night's the new moon!"

"He's a big boy, Rylie," Gwyn said.

She also said something else, but Rylie didn't hear it, because she was rushing out the back door to catch Abel. It was one of the first really warm evenings of summer; the darkening sky was thick with the haze of heat, cicadas echoed over the hills, and a breeze sighed through the long grass.

Rylie found Abel throwing his backpack in the passenger's seat of the Chevelle. He had washed his car that morning, and it glimmered in the porch light like a steel blue jewel in the otherwise dusty ranch.

"Come to tie me to a chair so I can't leave?" Abel asked.

She ignored the taunt. "Let's send someone else to get this one. Like Levi—he's not doing anything."

"It's only a couple of hours away. Not a big deal." He slammed the door shut.

"But what if something happens?" Rylie pressed. "What if you can't get back in time?"

Abel rolled his eyes. "Then I'll lock myself in the hotel room for the change, and the Whyte family's going to get a huge cleaning bill. Like I said. Not exactly a big deal."

She bit her bottom lip, watching as he circled the tailgate. That wasn't what she meant. In fact, she hadn't even given consideration to Abel transforming without her presence.

He stopped to lean on the trunk of the Chevelle. Abel gave her an appraising look, and she stared back, chin lifted in challenge.

Abel had been mauled in a werewolf attack before they met, but every time he transformed, the scars healed a little more. The skin on his temple and chin was still twisted, but his eye and mouth were untouched now. He had actually managed to grow a complete goatee.

He still looked wholly terrifying to new people, which made him perfect for intimidating young werewolves into good behavior. But Rylie knew better than to be scared.

"Are you worrying about me?" he finally asked.

She dropped her gaze first. Some Alpha. "I just can't handle all the wolves without you," Rylie told her feet.

It had been almost two years since they officially opened the sanctuary and Rylie took charge of an endangered species. She had survived almost fifty moons as the head of her pack.

Fifty moons. Shouldn't that have been enough for her to feel confident in her ability to lead?

But the idea of getting through a moon without Abel at her back made her heart beat against her ribs like a mouse trying to escape a cage.

Abel pushed off the trunk of the car and stood over her. A hand touched her chin. Dull surprise jolted through her as she looked up at Abel.

Rylie expected him to tease her. He *always* teased her.

But his face was totally serious.

"I'll be back in time." Abel's deep voice vibrated with intensity. "I'm not going to leave you alone. I promise."

Her cheeks heated until she thought that she might catch fire.

It looked like he was thinking of saying something else. His golden eyes were fixed on hers, and his mouth opened. Rylie found herself staring at his lips. He was looking better and better now that the scars were healing.

But then he dropped his hand, and he was grinning again—that lopsided grin that looked so much like his brother's.

Abel climbed into the driver's seat of the Chevelle and rolled down the window. "You better have a bed ready in the barn when I get back tomorrow."

He gunned the engine, and she hugged her arms around herself as she watched him peel down the path toward the highway. The tail lights shrunk and faded into the sunset-lit hills.

Her heart was still beating hard, but not from fear.

Vanthe emerged from the kitchen holding the mallet. "Dinner's ready. Gwyn says to ring the bell to let everyone know."

She shook her head to clear it. "The bell is on the front step. You want to go around the other way."

He didn't move. "What's up with that guy?"

"Abel?"

"Yeah. He smelled like silver."

"He used to be a werewolf hunter," she said. "Old habits are hard to break, I guess. He still takes a gun with him when he picks up new guys. Like he did with you last week."

Vanthe's eyes widened. He had the same gold irises that all werewolves did. "How did a hunter end up your second-in-command?"

Because I bit him.

Rylie gave Vanthe a shaky smile instead of answering aloud. "You should probably go find the bell. Gwyn might not turn into an animal twice a month, but she's pretty scary when people don't do what she tells them."

He saluted her and loped around the building, vanishing into the shadows. As soon as he disappeared, Rylie sagged against the fence.

Just the thought of having to sit down to eat with the pack made her tired. Even Bekah and Levi treated her weird, and they had known her before the Alpha thing. Abel was the only one who made her feel normal anymore.

Up until the moment he touched her chin, anyway. Now she thought she might explode into a thousand pieces.

"What was *that*?" she whispered into the night, brushing her fingers over her jaw. She could still feel his skin on hers.

Loneliness. It had to be loneliness.

Only one more week until the semester ended. Then Seth would come home for the break between terms.

Summer couldn't come fast enough.

THREE

Mail

If there was one constant to life on a ranch—even a ranch filled with werewolves—it was the omnipresence of chores.

Rylie woke up to work before sunrise, and she could already feel the new moon approaching. It whispered to her from the dark sky beyond her window. She parted her curtains to gaze up at the smattering of stars fading into the velvety blue of false dawn.

The moon was only a sliver of fingernail over the hills.

I'm coming...

That whisper used to fill her with dread, but it no longer held any sway.

She closed the curtains and ignored it.

Hoping that she was the first to wake up, Rylie grabbed a pair of jeans and work boots off of her dresser and sneaked into the hallway.

The bathroom door was open.

"Success," she whispered. When was the last time she had gotten to shower without waiting in line?

Feet thudded down the hall. A shoulder bumped hers.

"Sorry! Emergency!" Bekah's honey-blond curls flashed past her, and the bathroom door slammed shut. The lock clicked.

The pipes in the walls rumbled as the shower blasted to life.

"Hey!" Rylie pounded her fist into the door, forgetting that everyone else was still asleep. "Showering is not an emergency! I was here first!"

Bekah started humming show tunes.

"I'm sending you back to California," Rylie growled, more to make herself feel better than anything else. The Riese twins, Bekah and Levi, split their year between the two sanctuaries. They would be going back soon anyway.

Grumbling to herself, Rylie hiked the jeans over her hips, stuffed her feet into boots, and went out to labor in the fields alone.

She usually shared the chores with Abel, so his absence quickly became hard to ignore. Feeding the chickens and checking the fence for holes wasn't nearly as much fun without someone to distract her.

By the time the sun rose, the temperature was already over seventy degrees, and she was sweating.

Rylie tried not to watch the highway for signs of the Chevelle, but when she finished making a lap around the outer layer of fencing, she found herself sitting on a post to watch for Abel anyway.

Only a few hours until the moon. Only a few hours until she had to be Alpha again.

Where was he?

A car approached, but it wasn't the Chevelle—it was the mail truck.

Her heart jumped.

Rylie ran to the mailbox, and she arrived just as the truck pulled away with a cloud of dust in its wake.

There was a lot of junk mail and hospital bills, but there was also a padded manila envelope with Rylie's name on it. Another letter was addressed to her, too. All the return address said was, "Seth."

The sight of his slanted handwriting made loneliness gnaw at her stomach. Despite his promises to visit between every semester, he had started doing summer and winter classes, too—they hadn't been together for longer than a weekend since spring break the year before.

Opening the envelope made his smells wash over her, bringing back memories of their time together.

Meeting at summer camp. Fighting off his werewolf-hunting mother. Working on the ranch together. Having to leave him so she could get control of her wolf and become Alpha.

Before she could read the letter, the big red pickup rolled down the hill. Gwyn stopped beside her.

"Where are you going?" Rylie asked, passing the bills through the open window.

"Thought I'd stay in the city tonight. Escape the furry…" Gwyn whirled her finger through the air, as if searching for a word. "You know."

"Are you worried about getting hurt?" she asked, frowning. It had never been a problem before.

Her aunt's eyes were warm. She reached down to brush the hair over Rylie's shoulder. "Not with you in charge, babe. I could just really use the vacation. I'll only be a few days."

Rylie made herself smile and nod, but worry knotted in her throat.

The only reason Gwyn ever went to the city was for treatments at the hospital. But the antiretroviral cocktails had been working great, especially since Rylie had been keeping a close eye to make sure her aunt took them.

Things weren't getting worse again… were they?

"Love you," Rylie said as Gwyn wiggled the gearshift.

Her aunt shot a knowing smile at her. "No wild parties while I'm gone. And if you're going to drink, don't touch the liquor on the top shelf. That's the good stuff and it shouldn't be wasted on teenagers."

"Gwyn!"

"See you soon," she said with a wink.

The truck groaned down the path.

Rylie waited until she reached the privacy of her bedroom to read Seth's letter. She curled up among the fluffy white pillows in bed with it, leaving the padded envelope on her desk.

Rylie,

That last picture of you almost killed me. You're so damn beautiful. Being away from you makes it hard to breathe.

My every waking hour is consumed with studying for finals, but I keep losing concentration to think about you. The way your hair falls over your eyes when you're sleeping. The taste of honey on your lips lingers. When I try to study for my anatomy lessons, I can only think about your body.

Stupid as it sounds, I'm counting the hours until the last final ends and I can join you at the ranch. As I write this, only one hundred forty-six hours remain—only.

I've got a surprise for you. It's going to be good. Promise.

See you soon.

With all my heart,

Seth

Unable to control her smile, she hugged the letter to her chest and closed her eyes.

Saturday. Just three days, and she could have the real thing.

Her gaze drifted to the other piece of mail with her name on it. She sniffed the padded envelope. It smelled faintly of gunpowder—one of Seth's distinctive odors. It must have been the surprise referenced at the end of his letter.

Rylie peeled the envelope open. A small box fell into her lap, along with a dried red rose and a slip of paper. Even though the flower's petals were dried into curls, its perfume lingered. Sweet musk drifted through the air.

She opened the note. There was only a single line inside: *I'm coming for you.*

She blinked and reread it, then read it a third time.

I'm coming for you.

Her smile faded a fraction.

What a weird message. Of course Seth was coming for her. He would be back next Saturday.

Feeling uneasy, Rylie opened the box—and almost dropped it.

There was a silver bullet inside.

FOUR

Missing Wolf

The breeze cooled as the sun dropped low to the horizon. The barn cast long shadows over the fields, and lights turned on inside. Dark figures moved on the other side of the frosted glass.

After they got rid of the herd, they had converted the barn into a dormitory for the sanctuary's werewolves. Rylie kept an eye on them from the back step of the ranch house.

She should have been down there to help them prepare mentally for the night's transformation.

But she didn't get up.

Rylie considered the box in her cupped hands. She hadn't opened it again, but she could smell the silver bullet through the wood. It made her queasy to have it close.

Who would have sent her such a thing? She didn't have any enemies—none that were still alive.

Laughter floated over the breeze from the barn. The younger wolves were joking and roughhousing, like they were at a sleepover.

Why should they be nervous? Rylie had helped them through a dozen painless changes.

And they hadn't gotten any death threats lately.

Lights appeared on the highway at the bottom of the hill. She had watched enough cars approach and pass that she didn't get excited.

But this one slowed as it approached the driveway.

Her heart skipped.

Abel.

The wolf pressed against the inside of her ribs, like an excited dog leaping at the return of its friend. She shoved her beast aside, jumped to her feet, and stuffed the box into her pocket—bullet and all.

The Chevelle pulled up to the tree at the bottom of the hill. Abel stepped out alone.

She jogged to the car. "You're late."

He grinned when he saw her. His gold eyes flashed, and his cheek dimpled. "It hasn't even been a whole day. You're so impatient."

Rylie wanted to hug him, but she stopped a few feet away and ducked her head. "Where's the new kid?" she asked, forcing her voice steady even though her stomach twitched like she had swallowed a jar of lightning bugs.

"Never showed." He lifted one shoulder in a shrug. "The flight was late, and he wasn't on it."

"Then what are we supposed to do?"

"Dunno. We can call the Whytes later and see what they say." He slung his backpack over his shoulder and started toward the house. He hesitated at her side. "I told you I would be back in time."

Rylie's inner wolf swelled at his proximity, urged on by the approach of the new moon and the sounds of her nearby pack. She found herself leaning forward, closing her eyes, and smelling his chest.

There was so much information in his scent—his journey to the city, the beef jerky he had eaten on the trip, all the people at the airport, the hotel room. It flooded Rylie's mind with color and borrowed memories.

When she opened her eyes, Abel was staring at her.

"Sorry," she said. She meant to step back, but she had been rooted to the spot. Rylie had no control over her legs.

Normally, Abel would have picked on her for that slip in humanity. He never missed an opportunity to harass her. But this time, he smelled her back.

He lowered his face to her neck and brushed his nose over the skin bared by her tank top. His breath breezed over her throat.

Rylie shut her eyes and clenched her hands tight, resisting the urge to touch him.

The wolf wanted to rub the side of her face against his. Mark him with her scent, and be marked.

Abel's eyes flicked up to her lips. His face hovered close enough that she could smell the minty flavor of his gum.

My pack, the wolf whispered.

Shut up, Rylie responded, giving her beast a hard, internal jab.

It took all of her strength to take one step back, but once she did, the second step was easier. She cleared her throat. Nudged a rock with the toe of her shoe.

Abel straightened and didn't remark on the moment of weirdness—which only made it weirder. He rubbed a thumb down a ridge of scar on his cheekbone. "Better get everyone together for the change."

She stayed by the Chevelle as he entered the house.

Somehow, the box with the bullet found its way into her hand again, and Rylie's fingers tightened around it. The corners bit into her palm. A painful reminder of Seth.

What was she thinking?

Bekah jogged past with a couple of other werewolves—Eldon and Simone, who came from Canada—and Rylie waved at them. They were still new enough to the change that they needed to work out energy before moonrise.

Thankfully, Abel's door was closed when Rylie retreated to her room.

She found a pen and paper and sat at her desk. She had a computer, but the internet in the countryside was really slow, and there was something romantic about seeing his handwriting. It reminded her of swapping notes at summer camp.

Contemplating the blank page, she twisted the pen's cap between her fingers.

Should she tell him about the bullet?

A door opened and closed somewhere else in the house. Abel flashed by the outside of her window and headed toward the barn.

She ducked her head and didn't look at him.

The silver bullet sat next to her lamp as she wrote.

Dear Seth,

Hard to believe the end of the school year is already here. Finals made the last couple of weeks fly past.

It's always kind of bittersweet when summer comes around: on one hand, I'm deliriously happy, because it means I get to see you; on the other hand, knowing that I'm leaving all my friends and teachers for a few months is sad, too.

Now there's an added dose of melancholy when I walk the halls of our high school. It's been empty without you for two years, but it was something we had shared together. Being there made it easy to retreat into thoughts of you and your arms tight around my body.

But once the bell rings on the last day, that's it. I'm never going back. A chapter of my life is ending and I don't think I'm ready for it.

There's so much I'm leaving behind. Memories of being friends with people like Tate—I still miss him, even if I still can't meet his eyes after what happened to his mom. Watching you at football games. Studying together in the library.

I worked so hard to finish high school. I had to make a lot of sacrifices.

I should be happy, right?

Rylie hesitated, pen hovering over the page. She bit her bottom lip.

She didn't want to worry him with the bullet yet—there was no way to know who had sent it anyway. But a million other things were on her mind, and she didn't know how to approach those, either. The werewolf that didn't show up at the airport. Gwyn's worrying secrecy.

And worst of all, The Abel Thing.

What could she say about that? "Hey Seth, I've been having funny feelings for your brother lately. My wolf wants to rub him. What do you think I should do about that?"

Yeah, right.

She sighed and propped her chin on her hand. Abel was gathering the rest of the werewolves at the bottom of the hill. They were knee-deep in long grass, and butterflies and bees flitted through the air around them.

Rylie had worked at his side enough that she could imagine the way the summer heat would make his sweat glisten on his shoulders, the smell of his perspiration, the pleasant baritone thrum of his voice.

As she watched, he stripped off his shirt and tossed it onto the rocks by the pond.

Her cheeks heated. She turned back to finish the letter.

I miss you. Come back soon. Please.
All my love,
Rylie

She folded the paper, stuck it in an envelope, and took it down to the mailbox.

FIVE

Changing

Twenty werewolves.

The number went up and down as months passed. The previous summer, there had been thirty at the sanctuary; over Christmas, it had been only a dozen. But twenty was what they had on the night of the new moon.

The werewolves were volunteers, not prisoners. They were strongly encouraged to spend every moon at the ranch, and many of them did. But they had jobs, families, friends—lives that they couldn't all leave.

Twenty werewolves meant a lot of families missing their daughters, fathers, and brothers.

There was nobody to miss Abel. He hadn't spent a single moon away from the sanctuary since they opened it.

Bekah and Levi had already stripped naked and waited by the pond, talking quietly about mundane things. A couple of others began to follow suit, but most people stayed dressed until their changing forms ripped through their clothing. It was hard to let go of human modesty.

Abel would have stripped too, but it embarrassed Rylie. Instead, he waited with her on the back porch of the ranch house wearing nothing but sweatpants.

Rylie surveyed her pack from the back porch of the ranch, hands gripping the wood railing.

Everyone was spread over the hill. Watching her. Waiting.

She drew in a breath and let it out slowly. From a few steps away, Abel watched her shoulders rise and fall under the straps of a white linen dress. The gown was laced together with loose threads that would fall apart when she shifted. It was only a shade paler than her skin in the starlight.

If the moon had taken form and walked on Earth, Abel was pretty sure it would have looked like Rylie.

"Five minutes," she said in a low voice.

Abel repeated it louder for the benefit of the other wolves. "Five minute warning!"

She twitched, as though the volume of his voice startled her.

Rylie glanced at him. Her eyelashes fluttered as she drew in a shuddering breath and bit her bottom lip. Abel found his gaze strangely fixed on the indentations her teeth left in her skin.

She returned her gaze to the pack below them, but she spoke directly to him. "Where do you want to change? Do you want to go down with them, or...?"

"I'll change with you. Always do, don't I?"

"I just thought..." Rylie trailed off. He watched her throat work as she swallowed.

He briefly considered going down the hill to change with the other wolves, but the idea of leaving Rylie alone made his hackles rise. She always walked among the pack in her human form. What if one of them attacked before she could change? Even an Alpha's throat could get ripped out.

"I'm not leaving your side," Abel said.

Rylie nodded, but didn't speak.

Five minutes passed too quickly in the still silence. They always did on the night of a change.

Movement rippled through the waiting wolves. A brown-haired girl named Pyper cried out.

It was time.

The energy shifted around Abel. His skin prickled, and the hair stood up on the back of his neck. "Rylie?"

She looked at him again. There was no human left in her eyes.

Rylie held out a hand. Abel took it.

Their interlocked fingers were in stark contrast to each other—his skin darker than the midnight sky, and hers paler than the moon. The calm, assuring aura of the Alpha swept over him.

He transformed quickly.

The bones in his face made muffled cracking noises as they extended into a muzzle. His knees reversed and unbalanced him, forcing him to the ground.

His fingernails fell out. Rylie hadn't released his hand—the sharp tips of his new claws pressed gently into the back of her hand. She had to let go once his fingers shortened into paws, but she sat at his side until he was done. Her hand stroked the ruff of fur that sprouted from his neck.

Only a few minutes later, he was done.

Gwyn had taken a photo of Rylie and Abel's wolf forms once, just so he could see what he looked like. She put the picture on the mantle like it was a family Christmas shot. He was the size of a small pony, with sleek midnight fur and luminous eyes.

He shook himself, and flecks of blood sprayed the patio.

"Are you okay?" Rylie asked. She was frowning and biting her lip. Damn, that drove him crazy. He bumped his nose into her hand to tell her that he was okay.

The sounds of other changing wolves filled the night. Rylie rose to her feet, and he followed her down the hill.

She remained human as she moved through the pack. When a werewolf cried out, she sat with them until the transformation ended, and Abel watched to make sure they wouldn't lash out at her. But none of them dared. Her power was too immense.

One by one, human flesh yielded to fur. Two legs became four.

Within twenty minutes, everyone had changed.

Their hairy bodies milled around Rylie, struggling to get as close to her as possible. She lifted her arms so that they could butt their noses into her ribs, the small of her back, her calves. They smelled her, licked her, bowed on their forelegs to show submission.

Abel remained at her side. Her fingers brushed his forehead.

"Go," Rylie said. "Run."

He threw his head back and loosed a howl. A small wolf the color of honey—Bekah—echoed his wail.

That was all the permission they needed. The werewolves scattered, jumping over rocks and tearing lines through the tall grass.

Rylie didn't change.

Abel tilted his head and whined.

"Not tonight," she said. "I don't want to be with the pack in this mood."

Abel pushed his head low to the ground, tail high in the air. Even though he didn't use words, his message was meant to be obvious: *Come play with us.*

Rylie laughed. "But Abel..." He darted at her heels and nipped lightly. She jumped. "Hey! Don't forget who's the Alpha here."

He rolled onto his side in a good patch of dirt and wriggled. More wolf-speak. This time: *I'm not listening to you.*

She rolled her eyes. "You're a disrespectful jerk."

Pyper zoomed past with Analizia and Levi hot on her tail. Rylie whirled to watch them run, and Abel couldn't resist—he lunged into Pyper's side, sending both of them rolling down the hill.

Levi pounced. The three of them were a tangled mess of legs and tails, and Abel had no idea who he was biting.

Rylie's laughter drifted toward the stars.

Abel would have done pretty much anything to evoke that noise from her.

"Okay," she said. "Fine. I'll be right there."

Rylie changed, and the pack ran as one.

Abel woke up covered in dew with someone pressed against him. He twisted around to see Rylie curled in the fetal position, her back against his. The sun hadn't quite risen yet. A line of sugar ants marched over her bare hip.

He sat up to look at her, and for once, he really *looked* at her. The long line of her ribs down to her waist, the swell of her hip, the delicate lines of her legs. The bottoms of her feet were dirty. Four parallel, silvery scars marked her chest. Feathery white-blond hair fanned through the grass.

They were laying in the grass near the pond, far from the barn and any other wolves. Abel wasn't sure how they had ended up alone. He couldn't remember his nights as a wolf. But he had the vague impression of a beautiful night and the wind in his face.

And Rylie. Always Rylie.

His brother's girlfriend.

But when was the last time that asshole spent longer than a weekend with her? Seth had sent her flowers for her eighteenth birthday. Flowers. That was it. He hadn't even been able to go to her graduation.

She was turning into a woman while he was away at medical school. How was Abel supposed to keep from noticing that? He wasn't selfless. And he definitely wasn't blind.

"By becoming a priest," he muttered, glancing at her bare hip again.

He brushed the ants off of her. Rylie gave a sigh and rolled onto her back without waking up.

Abel's fingertips lingered on her skin, so soft and smooth.

Bad idea.

He turned from her with a groan and rubbed a hand over his eyes. Coffee sounded good. Better than thinking those kinds of thoughts about Rylie.

Abel left her sleeping peacefully by the pond and went to make coffee.

As it turned out, Abel really sucked at not thinking about Rylie. And the faster Saturday approached, the harder it became.

He probably should have been excited for his idiot brother to come back. They always had fun when Seth was around. It meant getting to tussle in the dirt, race through the fields, and shooting cans in the back forty. Brother stuff.

It also meant that Rylie was going to spend every waking moment with Seth instead of Abel.

He watched her out of the corner of his eye while they ate dinner together the next night. The werewolves were enjoying an entire cow's worth of beef in the barn, but he sat on the stoop with Rylie, like the two of them always did. The setting sun turned her skin the same shade of gold as her hair.

"I've decided to take the year off," Rylie said. She cut her steak into a lot of tiny pieces and ate them one by one. "Before going to college, I mean. If I go to college at all."

"But you got a million acceptance letters."

She shrugged. "Seems weird to leave when you still need me here." Rylie glanced at him. "I mean, the werewolves need me. All of them. It's not like a year without school will atrophy my brain."

He pushed lightly on the side of her head. "It might. You could turn into a vegetable." She elbowed him.

"At least I would be safe here. Werewolves don't eat vegetables." Rylie's smile faded. "But they might eat my aunt if I'm not here to control them."

"You think I can't protect Gwyn?"

"That's not it. I know you would take care of her. I trust you." Her golden eyes zeroed in on him. "What do you think I should do?"

Their momentary scuffle had left them sitting a few inches closer on the step. They weren't touching, but electricity made the air between them vibrate.

He opened his mouth to tell her that she should go to college in the fall. It's what Seth would have said if he was there. It was the *selfless* thing.

But it wasn't what came out.

"I don't want you to go anywhere," Abel said.

The corner of her mouth lifted in the tiniest smile. "Me neither."

Inside, the phone rang.

They both moved, but Abel was faster. He launched to his feet and almost spilled the plate.

"I'll get it," he said.

He left Rylie on the step.

Bekah had reached the phone first. She paced through the hallway as she talked. Levi lounged on the couch with his head propped on one arm and a book on his lap.

Even though the call had been answered, Abel let the door fall shut behind him anyway.

Levi looked up from his book. "You remember that Rylie's dating Seth, right? And that they're totally, completely, head over heels for each other?"

"No. I've got amnesia and completely forgot the mushy bullshit that happens when they're together. Are you stupid?" Abel didn't bother trying to make it sound like he was joking.

"Just checking, because I saw you guys eating dinner out there. You looked pretty comfortable."

"Aren't you and your bitch sister supposed to be in California?"

"Dad told us that we're staying for an extra couple of weeks," Levi said, licking his thumb and turning a page. "He's worried about hunters around the sanctuary in California." His eyes flashed to Abel over his knees. "And if you call my sister a bitch again, I'm going to mess you up."

"Then you better mind your own damn business."

Bekah entered the living room and held the phone out. "Scott wants to talk to you, Abel."

He glared at Levi and took the phone into his bedroom.

When the Riese twins were in town, Abel had to share a room with Levi. *Everyone* shared their living space— only Rylie and Gwyn got to have private rooms. Levi decorated his half of the room with soccer posters. A bong stuck out of a shoe under his bed.

Abel had his guns hung on the opposite wall, just to help remind his roommate what would happen if Levi got into his private space.

"Abel?" Scott asked over the phone. He had a deep, pleasant voice that was probably really good for soothing patients. Scott Whyte was a therapist and witch of the Wiccan persuasion. He also owned both of the werewolf sanctuaries, east and west.

"Yes, sir?"

"I thought you would want to know that Isoba Briggs's family has filed a missing person report."

It took him a minute to remember why he recognized that name. "You mean, the werewolf kid who never showed up at the airport?"

"That's right. He's not at home and he's not in your hands. Which begs the question... where is he?"

Abel felt an all-too-familiar sense of looming dread. He ducked to peer out the window. Rylie was still on the step.

"I can go look for Isoba," Abel said.

"I've already asked Seth to make a detour before joining you at the ranch. He agreed. I want you to stay close to home—I've seen strange activity from hunters in the region, and I wouldn't be surprised to see it in yours, too."

"Union?"

"Yasir said it's not them, and I believe him," Scott said. "These appear to be freelancers. But a lot of creatures are turning up dead—mostly demons so far. I don't want any of them to be werewolves."

"Understood. We'll protect the pack." He hesitated. "So when will Seth be back?"

"When he finds Isoba."

Rylie wasn't going to be happy to hear that. Abel, however, suddenly felt light. "Thanks for keeping me informed, sir."

"You're welcome. Stay safe."

Scott hung up.

Abel watched as Rylie stood from the step and stretched her fingers high over her head. Her shirt lifted, baring a line of midriff over her belt.

It was a lot less than he saw on every new and full moon, but a strange feeling guttered through him anyway.

Abel *really* sucked at being selfless.

SIX

Dominance

Saturday arrived, but Seth didn't. Instead, he called Rylie's cell phone.

"I'm in North Harbor," he said.

That was all the way on the east coast. Her eyebrows knitted. "What? Why?"

"The missing werewolf—Isoba Briggs. Scott asked me to go looking for him, since I'm the only hunter he knows that isn't working for the Union. You know how I can sense werewolves and stuff."

"You were supposed to come home today," Rylie said, sitting on the edge of her bed. She almost missed.

"I know, but I'm the most capable of tracking Isoba down. I can't help it."

Her voice came out barely louder than a squeak. "You couldn't help it last winter, either. You haven't been back in a long time."

"Come on, Rylie. It's only until I find the werewolf. I'll be back soon." When she didn't reply, he went on in a lower voice, like he was trying to soothe her. "You know I would rather be with you."

She swallowed down her anger. The wolf stirred at the emotion, and she was dangerously close to growling. "Fine."

"I'll move as fast as I can."

"Okay."

"I can't wait to see you," he said, still in that deep voice that stirred feelings deep in Rylie's midsection. That was how he talked to her on their long nights alone in the fields together, or when they locked themselves in her room for days on end.

She sighed. "Miss you."

He apologized one more time. He sounded like he really meant it.

Then she hung up.

A day passed, and then two.

Gwyn came home from the city and wouldn't tell Rylie what she had been doing.

A few werewolves left. A couple of others came in. The days quickly turned into a week, and then the full moon came and went.

Still no Seth.

Rylie was frustrated by hanging around the ranch without him. It didn't help that the Riese twins hadn't gone back to California yet—Scott hadn't given them the all-clear, so they were still sharing the house and its lone bathroom.

And something had changed with Abel.

He hadn't been arguing with Levi as much. He was sticking closer to Rylie, too.

He also stared at her a lot.

Every time she turned around, he was watching her. Like when she was working on repairing a hole Pyper had ripped in the fence—he stayed on a nearby hill the whole time, like he expected her to run away. Or when she was cooking dinner for the other werewolves, he actually stuck around in the kitchen to help. He never helped with dinner.

Abel didn't take his eyes off of her. Not even once.

The werewolves threw a party in the barn a few days after the full moon. They played loud music, stomped their feet, clapped their hands, and danced. Occasional howls— the kind that came from drunken human mouths—broke the night.

Rylie didn't join them. She watched from the fields beyond the ring of light.

They had opened the barn door and turned on all of the lights, so she could see into the common area inside. Scott had given them several couches and a big TV, which was playing a horror movie. Bekah was dancing on the coffee table. Kiara piped music from her Mac Book through the big stereo. Rylie could smell the liquor from yards away.

Levi stumbled out of the barn.

"Rylie? Is that you?" he called, shielding his eyes to peer into the darkness. When Rylie didn't step forward, he lifted his nose and sniffed. "Why are you hiding?"

"I'm not hiding," she protested.

Levi followed the sound of her voice to the side of the barn, where she sat in the grass. He flopped beside her and propped his head up on his arms. He reeked of whiskey. "Seems you're having fun out here."

"I'm just enjoying the stars," she said, picking at her thumbnail.

"Why don't you ever spend time with the pack?"

Rylie frowned. "What are you talking about? I'm always with the pack, especially now that school's over. I have nothing else to do."

"Sure, you're always *around*, but you don't spend time with us. You're usually off with Abel."

"I'm not right now."

"That's because he's dancing with Bekah," Levi said.

Rylie's head snapped up, and she searched the barn until her eyes fell on Levi's sister. She had taken over the Mac Book and had found a cowboy hat somewhere. Abel was on the opposite side of the room—sitting on a leather couch to talk to Vanthe.

Her pounding heart slowed. "He is not."

"No, but I wanted to know what you would do if he was." His gaze was a little too sharp for someone who smelled very, very drunk. "Why do you care what he's doing?"

"Why do *you* care? Are you dating Abel? Are you jealous of him?" Rylie snapped. "No. You're not."

"I care what the Alpha is doing. And yeah, before you ask, it *is* my business. The Alpha's mating is *everyone's* business."

She had been prepared to storm away, but she froze. "Mating? What mating?"

Levi picked a piece of dry grass out of the earth and picked at his teeth. "Oh, Scott hasn't mentioned that yet? Whoops." The way he met her eyes full-on was werewolf body language. And it was just as disrespectful as anything Abel did. Even worse, it was a challenge to her dominance.

Her voice hardened. "Tell me what you're talking about. Right now."

Levi stood. He was only an inch or two taller than her, but he seemed to loom.

He flicked the grass to the ground. "You know, Alpha isn't something you're born into. Status as Alpha has to be earned. Or taken."

Blood rushed through her ears as the wolf grew inside of her.

Her fingernails itched. She looked down, and was surprised to see blood spotting on the edges—the way it did when she was on the verge of changing into a wolf. She clenched her fists to keep them from falling out.

"Are you saying you want to fight me?" she asked, and there was a growling edge to her voice.

Before Levi could respond, someone else spoke.

"Having fun out here?" The words were light, but the tone wasn't. Rylie smelled Abel on the breeze as he took position at her back.

Levi faltered, glancing between Rylie and Abel. Tension corded his neck with muscle. "We were just talking."

Abel stepped in front of Rylie, blocking her view of Levi with his broad back.

"Go talk with someone else," Abel growled.

Levi backed away slowly. "I was getting bored out here anyway."

Rylie watched until he was in the barn party again, and then she sank to the earth, hands gripping her temples.

Mating? Alpha challenges? Shouldn't she have known everything there was to know about werewolves three years after she was bitten?

"Was that punk threatening you?" Abel asked, hovering over her. "I'll take him down. I'll go and—"

"No," she interrupted. "I mean... yeah. He was threatening me. But you can't take him down. I think I have to do it." Rylie looked up at Abel. He looked angrier than she had seen him in a long time. "I'm the Alpha. I have to keep control."

Abel's lip peeled back to bare his teeth. "Help never hurts."

"Have you heard anything about..." She hesitated.

It seemed really, really awkward to ask her boyfriend's brother about the mating habits of werewolves.

"What?" Abel asked.

Rylie shook her head and checked her fingers. Only the nail on her thumb had come loose. It would grow back soon. "Nothing. Never mind. Forget about Levi. You were having fun—you should go back to the party."

"I should have been watching you." Resolve hardened his jaw. Her eyes followed the scars from his temple down to his neck, where they disappeared under the collar of his black tank top.

She faced the waxing moon, hugging her arms around herself. Rylie had to stop staring at him. "I miss Seth," she sighed.

Abel didn't respond.

"Is there any word on the missing wolf?" she asked.

"Not yet. And there's nothing we can do about Seth unless you want to go look for this Isoba kid yourself. So you should stop worrying about it. Come on, let's go party—they're playing good music."

"That's a great idea," Rylie said.

Abel started to walk back to the barn. "Awesome."

"No, not the party. Looking for Isoba. Let's go."

"Seriously?"

If the choice was between waiting at the ranch for Levi to challenge her, or leaving to be with her boyfriend... It was hardly a difficult decision.

"Seriously," Rylie said. "Let's do it."

SEVEN

Seaside

Rylie called Scott and made arrangements. By the time dinner rolled around the next evening, she was on a flight with Abel to North Harbor.

She hadn't flown since becoming a werewolf, and getting confined in a metal tube with a few hundred humans was overwhelming. Cigarette smoke. Body odor. Deodorant. Shampoo. Leather. Cotton. Dirty feet. She could barely distinguish one odor from the others.

Her hands gripped the armrests. Rylie took shallow breaths and tried not to smell anything until they landed.

Seth didn't answer his cell phone, so they headed straight for his hotel when they hit the ground.

North Harbor was a small town with cramped streets that stunk of fish. A gray haze hung over the air, and a storm brewed over the steely ocean. The damp breeze cooled her to the marrow. Fifty-five degrees in early July—there had to be some kind of law against that.

The back roads were too narrow for vehicles, so the cab dropped them off at the end of Main Street, less than a mile from the hotel.

Rylie stopped to look in a shop's window. They had cable-knit sweaters prominently displayed on the mannequins. Apparently, cold summers didn't surprise anyone but her.

"Hang on," she called to Abel, who had walked away without her. "I want to buy a sweater real quick."

He stopped and rolled his eyes. "We're a block away from the hotel."

"But it's cold."

Abel shucked his shirt so that he was wearing nothing but the tank top underneath. He draped it over her shoulders. It was warm and engulfed her in his smell.

To her surprise, he reached back to pull her hair out of the collar. His hand lingered on her shoulder.

After a second, he stepped back. Coughed into his fist.

"You can get a sweater later." Abel's voice sounded weird. "Let's go."

Scott Whyte always made sure they had first-class accommodations when they traveled, and the hotel he had put Seth up in was no exception. It was an old building that smelled like it had been recently remodeled—Rylie detected the aroma of paint and newly-quarried stone.

They went inside. The lobby had marble floors and a chandelier, and the man at the front desk gave them a skeptical look when they asked to call Seth's room.

"Are you expected?" he asked without reaching for the phone.

Abel leaned over the desk, using every inch of his six and a half feet to tower over the receptionist. "Yes."

The man shrunk back and dialed.

When Seth didn't answer, it took him two tries to hang the phone up again. "I don't think he's in his room."

Rylie frowned and stepped outside to call his cell phone again. No response.

"He's probably hunting," Abel said, appearing at her side.

"But I haven't heard from him in two days. What if he's hurt or something?"

She expected Abel to blow off the suggestion, but his brow drew low over his eyes. "I'm going to look around town. See if I can find Isoba's house. Stay here, at the hotel."

"But—"

He didn't give her a chance to argue. Abel strode away, leaving her alone with a chilly breeze and darkening skies.

She kicked a rock into a rosebush.

"Some Alpha I am," she muttered.

Rylie waited on a stone bench in the gardens, sheltered under the branches of a tree. She played games on her cell phone until she beat her score on Bejeweled Blitz for the third time, and then put it away to keep from killing the battery.

Still no Abel or Seth.

An older couple jogged into the hotel, casting worried looks at the sky. They didn't even give her a second glance under the tree.

Five minutes later, she understood why. Thunder rolled in the black clouds as wet circles began appearing on the cobblestone path. The hush of rain on leaves followed an instant later.

Within seconds, it was pouring.

Rylie was dry under the tree, but she couldn't leave unless she wanted to get soaked. She sat tight with her carry-on bag at her side and Abel's shirt hugged around her, more grateful than ever for its warmth.

A woman ducked under the tree with her, holding a newspaper over her head. "Nice day, huh?" she asked, shaking rain out of her jacket's lapels. Rylie shirked back as she got splashed.

"Yeah. It smells nice." The scent of wet asphalt and soil wasn't the only nice part about the rain—it also had a dampening effect on all the other confusing smells that had been bothering Rylie.

The woman gave her a weird look at that. Her silky black hair was chopped in a perfect A-line at her angular jaw. "I was being sarcastic." Her jacket gapped, and Rylie glimpsed a camisole and shorts. The newcomer was no more prepared for the weather than Rylie.

"Are you a guest at the hotel?" she asked.

"No. I'm just looking for someone who is." She folded the newspaper and glared at the sky. "I'm Pagan. What's your name, kid?"

"Rylie."

Pagan arched a thin eyebrow. "That's a man's name."

Annoyance made the wolf stir inside Rylie.

"Oh yeah? What kind of name is Pagan?"

"Heck if I know. You'd have to ask my parents that one." The woman stepped beside the bench, and her perfume wafted toward Rylie—a musky, flowery scent that almost made her gag. "Looks like the rain isn't letting up anytime soon. Man, the streets get totally dead when it pours, don't they? But that's good. Means there aren't any witnesses."

Witnesses?

Too late, Rylie smelled silver.

And then there was a gun in her face.

She ducked. A shot rang out.

Rylie hit the ground with her hands over her head, braced for the burning agony that followed getting hit by a silver bullet. Someone cried out, and it took her a moment to realize that it was Pagan—not her own voice.

The pain never came.

Pagan fled. Her feet flashed past Rylie's face.

Another gunshot rang out.

A hand jerked her to her feet, and she thought it was Abel for an instant, and she was relieved enough that she wanted to hug him tight. But he was too short to be Abel, and his hair was too long.

Rylie recognized his smell before his face.

Gunpowder. Leather. The musk of sweat.

"Seth," she whispered.

"Are you okay?" her boyfriend asked, grabbing her upper arms. Seth looked a little older than she remembered. He was growing into a more adult frame. His shoulders were broader, his arms were thicker, and his voice was maybe a fraction deeper. "Are you hurt? Did she—"

"I'm fine, she didn't hit me, nothing hurts."

"Thank *God*." He lifted her in his arms, squeezing a laugh out of her. "You're crazy, you shouldn't be here," Seth said, but he kissed her before she could reply.

It had been too long since she had seen him, been held by him, kissed his lips. Rylie could have vanished into his embrace. She wanted to roll herself in his smells and drown.

He set her on her feet, and she ran her hands over his face, tracing the familiar cut of his cheekbones and ears and forehead. His skin was damp, and his straightened hair was starting to frizz from the moisture.

"You're soaking wet," Rylie said, and then she kissed him again, just because he was there.

"Let's get inside," he mumbled into her mouth.

"I don't care about the rain."

His eyes danced with mirth as he pulled back and grabbed her hand. "I'm more worried about the hunter who just tried to kill you. I didn't land a fatal shot. She's still out there—alive."

"Oh," she said. "Yeah. That."

Seth's room was decorated as nicely as the hotel lobby. He had a four-poster bed with fluffy pillows, a fireplace, and Rylie was pretty sure that she glimpsed a Jacuzzi through the cracked bathroom door. Scott Whyte *really* didn't skimp when making travel reservations.

As soon as they crossed the threshold, Seth locked the door, peeked out the window, and shut the curtains. He left wet footprints in his wake.

"You're making a mess of everything," she said, knowing it was stupid to be worried about the mud when

Pagan was still out there. She felt strangely numb. It had been a long time since she had a gun pointed at her.

"Just making sure the room is secure." Seth cupped her face in his hands. "Are you sure you're okay?"

She nodded. "I'm just glad she didn't hit you."

"Didn't hit *me?*" He laughed. "God, I've missed you."

He stripped his shirt off over his head and used it to dry off his chest. The ability to speak completely fled from Rylie as she took in the sight of his broad shoulders and muscular arms. Seth had *definitely* been finding time for the university gym.

"Who was that woman?" Rylie asked when she remembered how to use the English language.

"I think she's a hunter or something. I've been tracking her for days." He kicked off his shoes. She realized that she was dripping on the carpet too, so she followed suit. Seth pushed her shirt off of her shoulders and gave it a funny look. "What is this?"

Rylie took Abel's shirt from his hand and dropped it on the pile of shoes. "You mean, a hunter like you? A kopis?"

"I don't know," he said. "I haven't been able to get close enough to get a good read on her. But I'm glad I was following her today."

His hands went to her jeans and popped the button open. "What are you doing?" she asked.

His eyes sparked. "Helping you dry off." He lifted the hem of her shirt, and she obediently raised her arms so that he could strip it off. It wasn't even wet. He lowered his lips to her neck. "I've missed you so much," he murmured.

Rylie had meant to call Abel and tell him that she found Seth. She also had meant to head out and help search for Isoba so they could go home as soon as possible.

But as soon as Seth touched her, all those thoughts were completely forgotten.

The rain poured outside, but they were safe and dry in his hotel room.

EIGHT

A Second Present

Abel picked up the smell of other werewolves a half a mile away from the hotel, and he followed it to a cluster of houses built on a cliff over the ocean. They looked like vacation rentals, and judging by the empty streets and dark windows, they were all unoccupied. It smelled like nobody had been inside of them for weeks.

Except for the one on the end. Someone had touched the front door. He detected the scent of skin oils on the handle, and the sour perfume of silver.

How many people walked around vacation rentals carrying silver?

Abel drew the gun at the small of his back and kept it aimed at the ground as he walked around the house looking for an open window. The back door was cracked.

He perked his ears up, listening for the slightest hint of motion. But the house was completely still.

Abel glanced at his phone to make sure there was no text message from Rylie before slipping inside.

The back hallway was empty, but as soon as he crossed the threshold, a new smell smacked him in the face—like copper pennies and slabs of pork. Blood and human flesh.

He led with his gun as he eased around the corner into the living room.

That was where he found the werewolf.

The body was spread-eagle in front of the fireplace. The bearskin rug underneath was ruined with blood. Seth wouldn't have been able to find it—he could only sense living werewolves, and this one was definitely dead. He'd probably been dead for days.

Abel wiped the blood off of the face of the corpse using a blanket from the couch. His features were sunken and pale, but it definitely looked like the picture he had seen of Isoba. He was starting to decompose.

"Damn," Abel swore under his breath.

He did a quick check for the source of the blood and found a bullet wound in his chest. Whoever killed him must have smeared it everywhere. There were red footprints on the carpet and a smear on the wall.

Abel followed the smear into the kitchen and found something written on the counter.

It was hard to read—finger-painting in werewolf blood wasn't exactly the most legible way to leave a message. He squinted at it but couldn't read past the first word: "this."

A silver bullet had been left on the counter, and a dried red rose. Abel pocketed them and took another look at the bloody message. When he finally made it out, a chill settled over him:

This is for you, Rylie. Sincerely, Cain.

The fireplace in Seth's hotel room crackled with merry flames. Rylie crouched in front of it, warming her chilly fingers as Seth talked on the phone.

"It's definitely a hunter," he said. He had called Scott Whyte after taking a shower with Rylie, and his hair was tied back with a bandana. It was also the only thing he was wearing. Orange firelight danced on his bare skin. "She was armed with silver bullets."

She listened carefully to pick up Scott's end of the conversation. "*Have you found Isoba yet?*"

"No, but Abel is looking."

"Let me know as soon as you find him. I'll book flights for all of you. We need to stay close to the sanctuaries and protect our packs. Look after Rylie."

"Yes, sir."

He set the phone down, and Rylie watched as he dressed. When had he become so confident, so self-assured? When had he become such an *adult*?

She found herself rising to her feet and rubbing her hands down his bare back, enjoying the feeling of his muscles under his skin as he zipped his jeans. He had a tattoo of the moon and a wolf's paw on his shoulder.

"I'm not going to get dressed very fast if you keep doing that," Seth said.

"I'm okay with that." Rylie pressed her face between his shoulder blades and took a deep breath. He smelled so familiar, so warm.

But not like pack.

She stepped back, disappointed, and he faced her. His smile faded when he saw her expression. "You okay?"

Levi's mention of Alpha wolves mating almost spilled off her tongue. But she bit it back and forced herself to smile. "I'm worried about Pagan."

Seth pulled her close and wrapped his arms around her.

"You're safe," he whispered into her hair. "I promise."

Rylie didn't like having to think of such dire things when she was finally with him again, after so long. She nestled her head under his chin. "I got your present."

"My letter?"

"No, the box and the flower," she said. "It was weird, but... sweet? I guess? I don't really understand it."

He took her by the shoulders and held her at arm's length, brow furrowed. "I didn't send you a box and a flower."

Her stomach flipped. "But you said you had a surprise for me."

"That wasn't it. What was in the box?"

"I brought it with me. Here..." Rylie opened her carry-on bag and pulled out the present she had received at the ranch. She handed it to him.

Seth opened it. His face darkened. "Was this all you got?"

So it wasn't from him. She felt like she could have thrown up. "There was also a note. It said..." She swallowed hard. "It said 'I'm coming for you.'"

The atmosphere in the hotel room was suddenly a lot less romantic. Seth held Rylie close, and she clung to his shirt, longing for a time that they could be together without the looming threat of mortal peril.

Abel met Seth in the hallway outside the hotel room. Abel tried not to feel annoyance when Seth slipped out and quietly closed the door behind him, like he was trying to keep his brother from seeing into the room.

"What did you find?" Seth asked, leading him a few feet down the hallway.

"Isoba's body, and a note written in blood. It said, 'This is for you, Rylie.' And it was signed by someone named Cain." Abel kept his tone level, but he didn't miss the Biblical implications of the name—Cain had killed Abel, after all.

Seth didn't miss it, either. "You think that's really the killer's name, or is that a direct threat?"

"No idea. But Isoba was shot with a silver bullet."

"There's way too much silver flying around today." Seth turned off the phone and clenched it in his fist. "A hunter tried to shoot Rylie outside the hotel today. And someone sent her a silver bullet at the ranch."

Abel felt his eyes widen. "When?"

"She said it was a couple of weeks ago."

And she hadn't told him? A low growl rose in his throat.

How the hell was he supposed to protect Rylie from hunters if she didn't tell him when she was in danger?

Seth blew a breath out of his lips. "I don't think she needs to know about the note from this Cain guy yet. It'll worry her too much. But we have to get her somewhere safe."

Abel nodded sharply. "The ranch isn't good enough. We should stay on the move. We should—"

"Rylie's not the only one we need to protect," his brother interrupted. "We should go home and fortify."

"And risk Rylie? They know where she lives."

"They haven't attacked the ranch yet—or Rylie." Seth glanced back at the hotel room. "Not until today, and I think that was an accident. Pagan didn't know she was going to stumble on Rylie here. She must have been looking for me. No—something else is going on."

Abel wanted to argue further, but the hotel room door opened, and Rylie's head poked out. She was wearing a bathrobe. Which meant that she had gotten undressed at some point.

Anger surged through Abel, sudden and powerful. He knew that Rylie and Seth had sex. Lots of it. Their bedrooms at the ranch shared a wall, after all, so it was hardly a revelation. But he couldn't shake the mental image of throttling his little brother.

"What's going on?" Rylie asked, glancing between them.

"We're going back to the ranch," Seth said, joining her at the door. "Get your bag together." She disappeared, and Seth tossed something to Abel. He caught it. It was the shirt he had given Rylie. "I think that's yours."

He closed the door and locked Abel out.

NINE

Surprise

The drive from the airport to the ranch was silent and tense. Rylie wasn't sure if she was imagining it or not, but Seth and Abel weren't looking at each other. They didn't speak—not even once—the entire time they were in the car.

Gwyn met them by the Chevelle. She hugged Rylie first, but she embraced Seth extra tightly, too.

"What's the word?" she asked.

Rylie didn't bother sugarcoating it. Not for someone like Gwyn. "We found Isoba dead. There are hunters after us, and we need to prepare for the worst."

Her aunt didn't even blink.

"Possible war, huh? I'll haul out the spare lumber in case we need to block the windows. Dinner is cooking. Check on it in five minutes, unless you want your meat burned."

She headed down to the shed, and Seth followed. "I'll help you."

Rylie suppressed a smile. If she had been the hunters, she would have thought twice about attacking anywhere that Aunt Gwyn was protecting.

After a moment, Abel and Rylie were alone aside from the bees and the summer heat. He stared at a fixed point on the horizon, expression unreadable.

"What are we going to do?" she asked.

"Don't get all worried. I'm sure Seth will look out for you." Abel vanished into the house.

"But who will take care of you?" she whispered.

Rylie was too wired to sleep after dinner. She kept thinking about the bullet she had gotten in the mail, Pagan attacking her under the tree, and Isoba—poor Isoba.

She decided to put her energy to good use and check for holes in the outer fence one more time. Their barbed wire helped contain the werewolves on full and new moons, but would it be enough to hold off an attack by hunters?

Hunters. Rylie shivered. It had been a long time since she had to fight for her life.

Indentations in the mud on the other side of the fence caught her eye, and she crouched to take a closer look. They looked like tire tracks—deep ones, like those a semi might leave behind. And there was also a set of footprints.

Rylie sniffed. The faint hint of perfume lingered around the mud. Even though it was starting to fade, the odor of flowers was cloying and sweet.

That was Pagan's perfume. She must have followed them—it smelled like she had been there just hours earlier.

Rylie straightened, half-expecting to come face-to-face with a gun. But the terrain was empty as far as she could see. The clear silver light of the summer moon showed her that.

A dark figure moved in the fields behind her.

Unease crept over Rylie, and she briefly considered running. But then the breeze carried Seth's smell to her.

She waited for him to join her. "What are you doing out here alone?" he asked, eyes scanning the fields around them.

"Look at this." Rylie pointed at the tracks. "I smell Pagan. She was here this afternoon."

"She's checking us out." Seth shook his head. "You shouldn't be out here."

"I couldn't sleep. I've been worrying."

He squeezed her hand. "Nothing is going to hurt you. I promise. I won't let it happen."

"But it's already July. You'll go back to school next month—and then what?" Rylie's voice trembled. She took a deep, steadying breath. "I mean... it's fine. But it's easy for you to tell me not to worry when it won't be your problem soon."

"Your safety is always my problem," Seth said, pressing her hand to his chest. "You fill my mind and heart. I'm not going anywhere until I know you're safe."

She wanted to say, *What about Abel?* But she kept her mouth closed.

"We should go inside," she said instead.

"Wait a second." He gave her a lopsided grin. "You never asked about the surprise I have for you."

She had completely forgotten about it. Mortal peril was pretty distracting. "Oh—what is it?"

"Well, I wanted to wait until we could go somewhere special or something, but since it sounds like things might be getting crazy soon..." He scrubbed a hand through his hair. "I've been thinking a lot lately. About our relationship."

Rylie hung her head. "Yeah. Me too."

"I want to be with you more, and I just worry we don't have enough time. You know? And with everything happening now—this Cain thing and missing werewolves and silver bullets..."

Cold fear washed over her. "You're not breaking up with me, are you?" she asked, cheeks heating and eyes blurring.

Seth's chuckle stopped her before she could start crying. His smile made her heart skip a beat. "Are you serious? I would never let you go, Rylie. I'd have to be stupid."

"Then what?"

Without letting go of her hand, he dropped to one knee.

He pulled a small box out of his pocket and opened it. A slender gold ring was nestled inside.

Rylie's heart gave up beating entirely. She couldn't breathe. She could barely even stand up straight.

His Adam's apple bobbed as he swallowed hard.

"Rylie... will you marry me?"

She searched for words and found none. But then motion on the hill caught her eye.

There was somebody watching Seth's proposal.

The night was bright and clear enough that, even at that distance, Rylie could see the stricken expression on Abel's face.

And she also saw when someone stepped up behind him and raised a gun.

Pagan.

"Abel!" she yelled, but it was too late.

The gun fired.

PART TWO

Blood Moon Harvest

ONE

Proposal

The longest journey was always the one going home. And it only seemed to take longer when Seth knew that his girlfriend was waiting for him... with his brother.

His years studying pre-med seemed to take torturous decades. But even slow time marched forward, and his endless, aching days at the university did pass.

July came, and Seth finally went home.

He stood in the middle of the Gresham Ranch house's living room, drinking in the sights, sounds, and smells he had been missing all semester.

Aunt Gwyn's furnishings were looking even more beat up than usual. After a few months of having werewolves play-fight, eat, and sleep on her couches, they were looking more like very sad piles of leather and wood than actual furniture.

A vase of blossoms decorated the mantel. Dried scales, taken from shedding rattlesnakes, were hung by the door. Everything smelled a little bit like wet dog, even though Seth knew Gwyn was anal about cleanliness.

But it was home. *Home.*

Rylie's jacket hung on a hook by the rattlesnake scales, nestled in Abel's duster. Seth tried not to look at them as he stacked a pile of lumber from the shed by the windows.

Preparing to fortify the ranch wasn't enough to dampen his relief at being home; where werewolves were concerned, the threat of impending danger was pretty homey, too.

Once he had everything set down, he pulled a hammer and nails out of the closet, set them on the coffee table, and considered the room's entry points.

The kitchen. The front windows. The hall. It wouldn't be too hard to secure, if things got ugly.

He was about to go looking for Rylie when he realized there was one entry point he hadn't considered: the fireplace. Seth kneeled and glanced up the chimney. It was probably too narrow for a human to squeeze inside, but he wasn't certain that they were dealing with humans. Better to board that up, too.

As he straightened, the pictures on the mantel caught his eye. There was a picture of two wolves among the school headshots of Bekah and Levi, and the Gresham family photos. One of the wolves was slender and gold; the other was a hulking black beast. Seth would have recognized Rylie and Abel anywhere. He had spent more than enough nights running with them as a human.

He picked up the picture of the two wolves. They were seated beside each other, shoulder-to-shoulder. They looked like yin and yang.

Seth's jaw clenched. He set the picture back down a little too hard.

He unpacked his suitcase in Rylie's bedroom. She always saved the bottom two drawers of her dresser for him, even though he never had enough to fill them, and their laundry would end up all mixed together by the end of the week anyway.

Seth put his guns in the safe under Rylie's bed, but left it unlocked. And then he pulled the last item out of his bag—a small jewelry box.

There was a gold ring inside, which he had bought at a shop in the town where he attended college. He hadn't been planning to buy a ring for Rylie that day. He just happened to be passing the window when it caught his eye.

Rylie wasn't the kind of girl who would be impressed by a diamond ring, but what he saw was something different, something special—a milky white rock that Seth had instantly recognized as a moonstone. It was bordered by clusters of tiny, sparkling diamonds. It looked like the full moon and the stars in the sky.

Perfect for Rylie.

Seth had found himself going into the shop, and a few minutes later, he had walked out with a lighter wallet and the ring in his pocket.

That had been over a month ago, and he had been thinking about the ring ever since. He spent a lot of time just opening the box to stare at it and contemplate what it meant.

He closed the box again, put it in his pocket, and went looking for Rylie.

Abel was sitting on the back patio, sharpening a hunting knife.

"How's it going?" Seth asked, pausing at his side.

His brother glanced at him. "Fine." That one word spoke volumes—resentful volumes.

"I put lumber by the front door. We should probably prepare to guard our rooms, too. Do you want me to put some by your bedroom window?"

Abel grunted.

"I can get Levi to do it if you're busy," Seth ventured.

"Yeah. Fine. That works."

Aunt Gwyneth stepped out the back door, brushing out one of her thick gray braids. "Have either of you seen Rylie since dinner?"

Adrenaline rushed through Seth. "No. Why?"

"She's not inside. I thought she might be with you boys."

Abel stood, clenching the knife. "I'll look for her."

But Seth was already backing down the hill. "I've got it. She probably just went for a walk. It's almost the new moon—she always gets restless about now."

He jogged into the night, stretching out his senses for the tickle at the back of his neck that would tell him werewolves were nearby. He could always feel plenty of them around the ranch, but Rylie's energy resonated with him in a different way. Seth wasn't sure if it was the Alpha thing or if he just loved her so much that he couldn't keep away.

Seth found her pale form by the highway. She climbed over the fence onto their property again when she saw him approach.

Every time he went away to college, he started to forget just how beautiful Rylie was. He always *knew* she was pretty—just thinking about her made him feel warm and possessive. But the reality of her beauty never failed to shock him.

She looked surprised to see him approach, but she extended her hands toward him anyway, and Seth caught her in an embrace.

"What are you doing out here alone?" he asked, scanning the fields without releasing her. Rylie fit under his arm perfectly.

She leaned her head on his chest. "Look at this." She pointed to tracks in the mud on the other side of the fence. "I smell Pagan. She was here this afternoon."

A surge of protectiveness rocked through Seth, so sudden and strong that it was hard to breathe. "She's checking us out. You shouldn't be out here."

"I couldn't sleep. I've been worrying."

"Nothing's going to hurt you," he said. "I promise. I won't let it happen."

She shuddered against his chest. "But it's already July. You'll go back to school next month—and then what? I mean... it's fine. But it's easy for you to tell me not to worry when it's not going to be your problem soon."

Seth pressed her hand against his heart and took a long look at her.

He hadn't told Rylie yet, but he wasn't going back to college that fall. He had rushed through the last few semesters with almost double the normal credit load. Between his crazy schedule and the summer and winter terms, he had already completed his undergraduate degree.

He was taking the year off before entering medical school, which gave him a lot of time to be with her. There would be plenty of time to explain that later, when she wasn't trembling with fear.

"Your safety is always my problem," he said firmly. "You fill my mind and heart. I'm not going anywhere until I know you're safe."

It didn't seem to soothe her at all. She remained tense. "We should go inside."

The hint of sadness in her voice was just too much for Seth to bear. He felt the weight of the ring box in his pocket.

He gave her a weak smile. "Wait a second. You never asked about the surprise I have for you."

She blinked. "Oh—what is it?"

"Well, I wanted to wait until we could go somewhere special or something, but since it sounds like things might be getting crazy soon..." Seth blew a breath out of his lips. "I've been thinking a lot lately. About our relationship."

She pulled away from him and hung her head. "Yeah. Me too."

"I want to be with you more, and I just worry we don't have enough time. You know?" he asked.

Rylie didn't seem to know. She gave him a blank look.

Was he speaking in a foreign language? Everything was coming out in a jumble. He was trying to tell her that he had already gotten through pre-med, just for her, but it got lost somewhere between his brain and lips.

Seth took a deep breath to try a different angle.

"And with everything happening now—this Cain thing and missing werewolves and silver bullets..."

She gave a little gasp. "You're not breaking up with me, are you?"

He had to laugh. "Are you serious? I would never let you go, Rylie. I'd have to be stupid."

"Then what?"

He braced himself, dropped to one knee, and pulled out the ring box.

He watched the emotions flash over Rylie's heart-shaped face. Confusion turned to surprise in a flash. Was that a good thing, or a bad thing?

Rylie's white-blond hair fluttered around her face in the midsummer breeze. Her golden eyes flashed. She bit her bottom lip.

God, she was so beautiful.

He swallowed hard. He had to ask now, before he lost his nerve.

"Rylie... will you marry me?"

Her mouth moved soundlessly.

Then her eyes flicked over his shoulder, and that shock turned to fear.

"Abel!" she cried. Not exactly the response he had been hoping for.

A shot whip-cracked through the air.

Seth had heard enough guns firing to recognize it instantly.

He twisted to see what had gone wrong. Abel stood on the hill. A woman was behind him, gun drawn—Pagan.

His brother put a hand to his side and tumbled to his knees.

He had been shot.

Seth's gun was drawn and aimed in an instant. He fired off one shot, and then another; Pagan fled down the hill, leaving Abel bleeding on the grass.

"Save him," Rylie said with a growl, her spine hunched.

"Wait—"

But she was already gone. With a cry, her human form erupted.

Blood sprayed. Blond hair puddled on the ground. Her clothes shredded, bones popped, and she fell to all fours. Within moments, the girl he had just asked to marry him was a sleek, golden wolf, almost more catlike than canine.

Rylie looked at him for a moment as if to say, *Don't let him die.*

And then she vanished into the night, chasing Pagan.

Two

Injured

Seth was fast, but not fast enough to keep up with a werewolf on the hunt. *Save him*, she had said. Of course she thought about Abel's safety first.

He ran up the hill to find his brother groaning and sweaty. His shirt was stained with blood.

It looked bad. Really bad.

He kept his tone light and teasing to hide his worry. "Were you spying on us?" Seth asked, lifting the hem to glance at the injury underneath. It was too dark to tell if the bullet had made it all the way through, but touching the area made his fingers sticky.

Abel glared at him, lips drawn back in a grimace. "Proposing marriage in some muddy field? God, you're such a tool." That was a good sign. If he was being insulting, he probably wasn't on the brink of death.

Seth crouched and pulled Abel's arm over his shoulders, helping him stand.

They limped to the house together. Every step ripped a sound of pain from Abel's throat, and by the time they reached the back door, he wasn't walking for himself at all. He stumbled on the threshold.

Seth dropped him on the kitchen floor.

"Jesus," Gwyn said, stepping in from the living room wearing her nightgown with a hammer in hand. Several of the werewolves from the barn were behind her, trying to see over her shoulder. "What happened?"

Seth barked out one word: "Hunter."

Rylie's aunt pointed at two of the wolves—Levi and Sora. "You two, come with me."

Then she stepped into the living room long enough to grab her shotgun and headed out the back door.

"Turn on the lights," Seth ordered, and Bekah hurried to obey.

The fluorescents flared on, and he inspected his brother's injuries. There was both an entry and an exit wound, and it was shallow. If Pagan had been using normal bullets, it wouldn't have fazed Abel.

But she had been using silver bullets.

The skin was inflamed and red. Blood puddled underneath him.

Everything Seth knew about safe handling of wounds didn't apply to werewolves—Abel didn't have any diseases to protect against, aside from the kind transferred by a bite, and Seth didn't have to worry about contaminating the injury. Werewolves were immune to infection.

All that left for him to do was remove the fragments of metal at any cost. The alloy hunters used was soft and tended to spread inside the body. Silver poisoning was an ugly thing to witness. If Abel didn't die, he would go crazy.

Seth had watched it happen to Rylie before. He didn't want to see it happen again.

"Sorry," he muttered, plunging his fingers into the wound. Abel shouted and arched his back. His fists flailed. He almost hit Seth. "Someone hold him!"

Bekah helped pin him down as Seth removed two large bullet fragments. She was strong, despite her size, but it took all of her weight to keep Abel's shoulders flat on the linoleum.

Seth dug out the biggest pieces of silver and dropped them on the counter. He wiped his hands on a dishrag.

Abel sagged, panting and weak. "You are a shitty doctor, bro."

"You're welcome," Seth said. He would have to explore the injury further, and quickly.

Rylie dragged Pagan into the kitchen. She almost wasn't recognizable as the attempted assassin Seth had been hunting in North Harbor. Her arm was a mangled mess of blood, and her pale face was covered in dirt. She sagged in the jaws of the werewolf like a rag doll.

"Holy crap. Is she alive?" Bekah asked, hovering nearby with her hands held out, as if she wanted to help Rylie but wasn't sure how.

Gwyn entered next, tracking muddy boot prints on the linoleum. "She's alive, but I think something's wrong with that woman," she said, nodding at Pagan. "Rylie took it easy on her. It's like her skin is tissue paper."

"Throw her in the cellar," Seth said. "Padlock the door. I'll look at her when I'm done with Abel."

Bekah threw Pagan over her shoulder and took her out the back door again.

Rylie's bones popped and crunched. The shift back from wolf was smoother, but it took a few minutes longer than her last transition.

Gwyn draped a blanket over her niece's bare body. "I'm going to make sure that Pagan doesn't wake up and hurt Bekah."

Rylie didn't respond. She only had eyes for Abel.

"Are you okay?" she asked, gripping one of his hands in both of hers. Her mouth was still stained with Pagan's blood. A streak ran from the corner of her lips to her right ear.

Abel responded by lifting a hand to Rylie's cheek. She closed her eyes and tilted her face into his palm.

Nauseating venom surged through Seth. He took Rylie's hand to distract her. "I need to finish extracting the silver," he said as calmly as he could manage. "Can you help me move Abel?"

She could have lifted the weight of three people at once if she wanted to, but Abel was tall and unwieldy. They had to work together to drag him down the hall to his bedroom.

He gave a low groan as he settled into the mattress.

Seth ducked into the bedroom he shared with Rylie to find tweezers and gauze. When he returned, she was kneeling beside Abel, and they spoke in low voices.

"Pagan won't be firing another gun anytime soon," Rylie said, eyes burning and cheeks flushed. Seth hadn't seen her that angry in a long time. "I ate her arm."

Abel didn't seem to care about the implications of a werewolf bite that didn't kill. He gave a faint smile. "That's my girl."

Seth sat down on the side of the bed, shoulder muscles tensed into knots. "This is going to hurt," he said, and without further warning, he began to operate on his brother.

Rylie couldn't watch Seth work on Abel. It made her nerves tie into knots. So instead, she got dressed and paced outside the cellar door.

It was almost an hour before Bekah and Gwyn came out again. They wrapped a chain around the handles and padlocked it.

"Is Pagan going to survive?" Rylie asked, gnawing on her thumbnail.

"I don't know," Gwyn said, checking the safety on Pagan's pistol and stuffing it in her belt. Her eyes roved over the darkened hills as she guided her niece toward the back porch. "She's bleeding a lot."

Guilt twisted in Rylie's stomach. "I was angry."

"You're a force to be reckoned with, babe. For now, that woman's not going anywhere. What did you call her? Pagan? What kind of name is that?"

"You would have to ask her parents," Rylie said, echoing what the assassin had told her the first time they met. The joke fell just as flat the second time.

Gwyn faced Bekah. "Start boarding the living room windows." She waited until the Riese girl went inside before speaking again. "Rylie, there's something not right about that woman down there. It's not just the severity of the injury. Her skin—I could see through it to her bones."

Rylie blinked. "What?"

"I know it sounds crazy, but... I don't think she's human."

"Then what is she?"

Gwyn shook her head. "Maybe a ghost."

THREE

Questioning

Seth spent the entire night locked in Abel's bedroom. "Pagan used some kind of bullet that encapsulated silver pellets. The wound *looks* superficial, but the damage is deep," he told Rylie when she checked on them at three in the morning. His eyes were rimmed with rings of exhaustion, and his brother was unconscious. "I keep finding more fragments buried in the muscle."

"Can you get it all?" she asked, twisting her hands together.

Seth's eyes were dark as he returned his attention to the injury. "I have to."

She slipped out of the room. He didn't acknowledge her exit—he was too absorbed in fixing his brother.

Vanthe was in the hallway outside, like he had been listening in on their conversation.

"What are you doing here?" Rylie asked.

He leaned around her to see into the bedroom. She shut the door before he could get a peek. "Is Abel going to be okay?"

"Yes," she said firmly, like saying it would make it true.

Anger sparked in Vanthe's golden eyes. "Who would have dared come into the sanctuary for an attack?"

"It doesn't matter. We've got the shooter locked up, and we're safe for now. I promise."

"Who was it?" he pressed, stepping closer.

Rylie squared her shoulders and lifted her chin, staring him in the eye. He was a new werewolf, so he probably didn't realize that she was asserting her dominance, but it should have triggered an instinctive reaction anyway.

It didn't. He looked too angry to notice that she was challenging him.

She was already on edge from being attacked. The sting of disrespect was enough to tip her over the edge. "Sit down," she growled through her teeth.

The weirdness of the command broke through Vanthe's temper. "Why?"

"Because if you don't, I might rip your throat out."

That got him moving. He dropped onto the chair against the wall.

As soon as he was shorter than Rylie, her heart stopped pounding quite so hard. It still took a few deep breaths before she could speak rationally.

"I'm an Alpha werewolf," she said in a tight voice that was about an octave deeper than normal. "Don't ever look me in the eye. Hunch your back when we're talking. And if you're going to argue with me, you better do it when your head is below mine. Otherwise, I could bite your head off—literally."

"Abel doesn't do any of that."

Her fading anger spiked again.

"You're not Abel," she snapped. "Show some respect."

Vanthe focused his gaze on her feet, and it looked like the effort was physically painful. "Fine. I can do that."

"Good." Rylie took one more deep breath and let it out. She tried not to be too obvious about checking her fingernails for blood. They were usually the first thing to go when she was on the brink of wolfing out, but all of them were secure.

"I'm just worried," Vanthe said, quieter than before.

It was normal for werewolves to seek their Alpha when they were scared—and she had snapped at him. The new guy. God, she was the worst Alpha ever.

She sighed. "I'm sorry."

"I'll get down to the barn."

He kept his shoulders hunched until he was out of sight.

She caught a glimpse of her reflection in the mirror. There was still blood on her mouth, and her eyes blazed with anger. She looked terrifying. No wonder Vanthe had been scared.

She took a blanket to the porch swing and wrapped herself in it, watching the hills lit by the moon's waning crescent. The muffled sounds of hammering rang out in the night as Gwyn and the pack locked down the ranch house.

Rylie glimpsed the occasional flash of Bekah and Levi running laps around the perimeter. She watched them for what felt like hours.

But she must have dozed off at some point, because she woke up with the light of sunrise warming her cheeks, and Seth's hand on her shoulder.

Rylie sat up with a jolt. The swing tilted at her motion. "What's going on? Are we under attack?"

"Not right now," Seth said, settling next to her.

"Abel?"

"He's going to be okay. I think I've got everything. I'll have to watch his symptoms for a few days to make sure he doesn't have silver poisoning, but he's stable for now."

She sagged against his arm. "Thank God."

They sat together for a few silent minutes, watching the ranch stir with the onset of day. Someone must have taken charge while Rylie was asleep. There were still werewolves running laps around the fence, but Bekah and Levi had been replaced by Trevin, Vanthe, and Analizia.

A few other people had already gotten down to chores, too. Raven was pulling weeds down the hill, and her sensitive ears and nose suggested that others were working in the back acres, somewhere out of sight. Nothing inspired proactivity in a bunch of lazy werewolves like an attack.

"Everything looks normal," Rylie said.

"Everything is, as far as I can tell. Pagan was alone." Seth's arm tightened around her. "But why?"

She leaned over to kiss his cheek. He hadn't shaved in a while, and his skin was coarse with stubble. "Let's find out."

Nobody had gone down to check on Pagan since Gwyn locked her in the cellar. Rylie had been secretly hoping she might have died—not just because she hurt Abel, but because that would mean they wouldn't have to deal with her turning into a werewolf.

But when they opened the chains on the door and descended down the dark steps, she found Pagan sitting in the corner, wrists tied behind her back, very alive and looking totally bored. She was in the same shorts and camisole that she had been wearing in North Harbor, although they were much bloodier than before.

There was no sign of the transparent skin that Gwyn had reported. But there was blood—lots of it. She didn't seem to have clotted at all, and the floor under her was drenched with sticky crimson fluid.

"How can I help you?" Pagan asked in a too-bright voice, like a cashier at a coffee shop. She looked totally unimpressed by the rifle Seth had propped against one shoulder.

"Why are you hunting us?" Rylie asked.

"I'm watching you for Cain." She twisted her arms in their bindings. Fresh blood flowed around the ropes, filling the air with the iron scent of blood until Rylie couldn't smell anything else. "He told me to reconnoiter, but to save your deaths until he could enjoy them properly. But it's hard to pass up the opportunity to kill when it arises."

Seth crouched in front of her, gun aimed safely at the wall. "Who's Cain?"

"He's your reckoning."

He turned the barrel so that it was pointed at her chest. She didn't even glance at it. "Tell me who Cain is."

"Oh, please." Pagan focused on Rylie over his shoulder. "Is he serious?"

"Deadly serious," Rylie said, hoping that it sounded threatening. She had never needed to question a prisoner before.

"Who are you? *What* are you?" Seth asked.

Pagan gave an exaggerated roll of her eyes. "You don't have the testicular fortitude required to get me to talk, little boy. I'm older than I look, and I could tell you things about my life that would give your grandkids nightmares."

"Maybe he's not going to do anything to you, but I could," Rylie said, baring her teeth.

"Be my guest. I still have another arm for you to eat."

Rylie didn't really know what to do when she got called on her bluff. She wasn't really going to bite Pagan again. Just the thought of trying to torture someone made her queasy.

Pagan saw the doubt in her eyes, and she laughed again.

"I can prevent you from bleeding to death from your injuries if you talk to us," Seth said.

"I can't bleed to death. Are you kidding? My God, this is the most fun I've ever had being captured." She kicked her feet up on a box of canned green beans. Pagan grinned. "I bet it's going to be even more fun when Cain frees me, and we kill every last one of you."

Seth stood. Stepped back beside Rylie. "Is he coming?"

"Oh yes." Pagan shifted on the floor to bare her wounded arm. Her hair fell over her neck. There was a tattoo on her neck of an apple dripping with black blood. "And your flooding fluids will taste so sweet."

As if to illustrate, she twisted her arm hard. The rope dug into her wrists. Fresh blood cascaded down her hands.

And she kept laughing.

"She's not human," Seth said after they had locked the cellar again and returned to the surface.

It was a warm, bright day, but Rylie felt cold all over. "If she's not human, than what is she? I couldn't smell her. There was way too much blood."

He gave a stiff shrug. He looked pale and tired. "Werewolves aren't the only dangerous thing out there. Some hunters kill other monsters." He cast a glare at the cellar door. "Like demons."

Rylie shivered and crossed herself. She hadn't been to church in a long time. She wasn't even sure she could walk on holy ground now that she had become one of the scary things that lurked in the night. But the gesture made her feel better.

"You mean we have a demon in my cellar?"

"Maybe." Seth glanced at the bright blue sky. "I guess we'll be able to tell in three days. If she doesn't transform on the new moon, she's definitely not human." He sighed and started unloading his rifle. "We need help on this, Rylie. I'm going to make some phone calls."

He dropped the rounds into his pocket and headed for the house.

Rylie bit her bottom lip, watching his retreating back. "Seth?"

He paused in the doorway. "What?"

"Last night... when you proposed..."

Seth seemed to know what she was thinking. He gave her a lopsided grin that lacked its usual brilliance. "The timing was bad for that. I don't need an answer now. Just... think about it. Okay?"

She wanted to tell him that she didn't need time. That she was totally ready to marry him, even though she was only eighteen, and they hadn't seen each other much lately.

But that wouldn't have been true, would it?

Remembering Abel's stricken expression when he saw Seth's proposal made her feel sick.

She took a deep breath to brace herself. "Have you ever heard of something about... mating? In relation to Alphas?" It was hard to make the words come out. She wanted to crawl into the cellar with Pagan and die.

Seth's eyebrows drew together. He stepped away from the door. "The only Alphas I've ever seen were in small family packs. One was married, and one was some guy with two kids. Mating wasn't an issue. But I didn't spend a lot of time studying the werewolves before killing them."

"Oh," she said.

He dropped the rifle to his side. "Why are you asking?"

"Levi mentioned it," Rylie said, her pulse speeding. Before she could think better of it, she went on to add, "And I've been feeling weird about Abel lately."

"Weird?" Seth echoed.

"Yeah. Like... drawn to him. Levi suggested it might be an Alpha thing."

Seth stared at her for a long time. She had no idea what his expression meant, but it made her feel about three inches tall.

"That would actually explain a lot," he said, and there was no anger in his voice.

"What do you mean?"

"I'm not blind, Rylie. I noticed you guys are acting... weird. Like you said." He shrugged one shoulder. "There's still a lot we don't know about werewolves. Nobody studied them other than my dad."

"How do we get more information?" she asked.

He smiled again. It was a little brighter than before— almost encouraging. "I'll see what I can find out."

Seth went inside, and the screen door groaned shut behind him.

FOUR

Reinforcements

A black SUV with government license plates arrived the next day. It had a bumper sticker that said "Union of Kopides and Aspides," and long antennas drooping over the hood. Both of those were normal for a Union transport. They were terrible at subtlety. The government markings, however, were new.

Seth was waiting for them at the gate to the ranch. The SUV stopped, and a man with shoulders nearly as wide as he was tall jumped out.

Yasir strode toward Seth. "Hey, kid," he greeted. They clasped hands. He had pleasantly rough palms, and his knuckles made it look like he punched brick walls for fun. Maybe he did. The Union had some pretty intense training regimens.

"Long time," Seth said, studying the commander. He had a few new scars and a gold tooth replacing one canine.

Yasir snorted. "Not long enough."

The last time they had seen each other, it had been in the aftermath of the Union hunters fighting against the werewolves on Gray Mountain. Yasir had made it pretty clear that he didn't want to have anything to do with werewolves anymore, regardless of what the Union's command center said.

"Thanks for coming to help us," Seth said.

Yasir crossed his arms. "Officially, Stripes and I are on leave. This isn't Union business. Understand?"

"Stripes came with you?"

"Yeah. He was bored. But we don't have any other support. Got it?"

"Got it," Seth said. He preferred not to have the rest of the Union getting involved anyway.

Yasir's eyes skimmed the ranch. "How many do you have?"

"Over twenty right now." Seth jerked his thumb at the barn. "Most of them are sleeping out there."

"And the demon?"

"In the cellar."

Yasir waved to the SUV, and Stripes jumped out. He had a black duffel bag slung over one shoulder that bulged at the seams. Jumper cables hung out of the open zipper. "I'll see what we can find out," Yasir said, pointing Stripes toward the house.

Seth grabbed his arm, stopping him before he could leave. "One more thing. You guys use my dad's research on werewolves all the time. Did you know there were chapters he didn't publish in his book?"

Yasir nodded. "There were missing chapters on Eleanor's body when we recovered it from Gray Mountain."

"Is there anything about werewolf mating habits in there?"

"There might be." Yasir looked wary. "Why? We don't have to worry about the pack breeding, do we?"

"We promised that the werewolves would die out, and we meant it."

The commander nodded. "I don't know what the extra research said, but I can put in a request to get a copy. It'll take a few days to pull it out of the archives, though. Would that help?"

It was even better than Seth had hoped for. "Yes. Thank you."

"Can we go now?" Stripes asked from a few yards up the hill, shaking his duffel bag. "I want to talk with the demon."

Seth nodded.

The men went up the hill and disappeared into the cellar with Pagan.

Rylie steered clear of Yasir and Stripes and kept her pack patrolling the sanctuary's perimeter to watch for attack. But there was no sign of any other hunters, much less anyone trying to save the captive in her cellar.

If nobody came for Pagan when she screamed like that, Rylie seriously doubted anyone was going to come for her at all.

Three days passed in a blink. The moon dwindled in the sky. It turned into the barest sliver, and then vanished on the last night.

Rylie sat with Abel as the sun set on the evening of the new moon. He had been sleeping for almost three days straight.

The room smelled like sweat and sickness—the odor of a silver-poisoned wolf. Seth had done two more passes in the wound and still hadn't found everything. No wonder Abel looked so miserable.

She touched his cheek. The skin was scorching. "Wake up, Abel." His eyes opened to slits, and she smiled. "Hey, lazy bones."

He grimaced. "Don't bother me. I feel like shit."

"Yeah, I bet you do. But it's the new moon tonight. Seth thinks that you have a shot at healing once you transform."

"Can I do it in bed?"

"Gwyn says that you have to buy new furniture and repaint the room if you do," Rylie said. "Let's save a few hundred dollars and go outside, okay? I'll help you."

He pushed her away and tried to get up on his own. He staggered.

"Floor's tilted," he said when she stepped in to grab his arm.

"No, you just suck at walking."

Rylie half-carried him outside to the waiting pack. Bekah was at the door, and she took his other arm as soon as they emerged. The rest of the pack was waiting in the field behind the barn.

"Where's Seth?" Abel asked.

"He and Gwyn are keeping an eye on Pagan in the cellar tonight," Rylie said. "Just in case."

He shot her a look. "In case of what, exactly?"

In case she started to transform.

Yasir and Stripes were in the cellar, too, and they had rifles loaded with silver bullets. Rylie had promised that there was no way the werewolf species was going to grow.

If Pagan began to change, they would shoot her.

She laid Abel on the grass, and everyone circled around them.

"Silver," Vanthe said, closing his eyes to taste the air. "There's silver in his blood."

A murmur spread through the pack. Pyper and Analizia actually drew back, like the silver might be contagious.

Rylie raised her voice so everyone could hear her. "Abel's been poisoned. When he changes, there's a pretty good chance he's going to be wild. Whatever happens, we have to keep him in the sanctuary. But don't get in a fight with Abel. Let me handle him."

"I can do that," someone piped up from behind her. She craned around to see who had spoken. It was Eldon, with his nervous laughter and habit of disappearing whenever chores needed to get done. Of *course* it was Eldon.

Rylie opened her mouth to snap at him, but the energy of the moon rippled over her before she could.

It was getting dark quickly. There was a patch over the hills where stars weren't emerging—blocked by the new moon. Her muscles warmed.

"Five minutes," she said. The pack spread out, but Rylie stayed on her knees beside Abel. She lowered her voice so only he could hear her speak. "There's one more thing you need to know. The Union is here."

"What?"

She shushed him, glancing around to make sure nobody was listening. The closest people were Bekah and Levi, and they were deep in conversation.

"Pagan said that Cain would come for her. Seth thought we needed help—and I agreed. When would be a better time to attack than when everyone in the sanctuary is a mindless animal?"

"When they don't have teeth and claws that can turn a hunter into French fries?" Abel groaned and pressed a hand to his injured side. "The bandages..."

His skin rippled, like something was moving under the surface.

It was time.

"Hang in there," she murmured, removing the gauze as his body began to distort.

The wound looked worse than it had on the night he received it. Parts of it had healed, but what remained looked like it was rotting. Even tiny bits of silver had a way of festering in a wolf's blood.

Abel caught her hand at his side. "Don't let me hurt you."

"What?"

"It's going to be bad tonight. I can feel it." And, as if on cue, he gritted his teeth, his back bowed, and his grip tightened until her bones ached. He took several deep breaths before speaking again. "If I'm going to be bad—don't come near me. Don't let me hurt you."

"You would never hurt me," she said, trying to focus her energy to calm his transformation. But it couldn't touch him. Not a silver-poisoned wolf.

There was a pop deep inside his body, muffled by muscle. Abel's cry split the night.

"I can't make it easier on you." Her eyes burned. "I'm so sorry."

Abel's body twisted with the transformation. It was hard to see what was happening to him in the dark, moonless night, but Rylie had been through it enough times to know what he was going through.

His teeth would loosen and fall out. His fingernails would follow. Then his hair.

His spine would grind against itself as new vertebrae grew, extending into a tail. And judging by the quiet popcorn sounds and Abel's piercing shriek, it was happening fast.

His knees would break—she could already hear the cracking—and switch sides.

Rylie tried to focus on sending her energy out to the pack at large, controlling the transformations of the twenty other wolves she *could* help, but it was hard when Abel was in so much pain and spraying blood on the grass.

He flipped onto his side, curled into a ball of half-human, half-wolf flesh that writhed and rolled.

His eyes caught hers. There was no man in them—only beast.

And it was hungry.

"Run," he whispered.

"No, Abel…"

His shoulders popped and slid into place as he climbed to his paws. Glistening claws dug into the soil.

Abel's scream shattered the night.

"Run!"

FIVE

Rescued

Seth sat on a box in the cellar with his rifle across his knees. The howling of the pack was muffled by several feet of earth and a heavy door, and he wondered which of them was Abel.

"They'll be all right," Gwyn said, patting his shoulder. "The pack's got Rylie. She's tougher than you think."

He found a smile somewhere inside of him, but it was weak and brief. "I think she's pretty damn strong, so that says a lot."

They were positioned at the front of the room, watching the door in case someone—or something—tried to enter. Yasir and Stripes sat in the back with Pagan, a battery, and jumper cables. There were marks on her papery skin where the Union men had shocked her.

She wasn't laughing anymore.

Pagan stared at her captors with fury in her black eyes, but her mouth was shut. She didn't talk back to them the way she talked back to Rylie.

Stripes stared at the ceiling, knuckles white on his gun. "Those noises." He shivered. "It's like that night on the mountain again."

Yasir checked his rifle's safety, and checked it again, like something could have possibly happened to it in the three seconds since his last inspection. "Don't think about it." He glanced at Pagan. "How do you feel?"

She sneered. "Like a car with a dead battery. What do you *think* I feel like?"

"That's not what I meant, and you know it."

"I already told you, I can't turn into a werewolf!" On the last word, her skin flickered like a dying light bulb. For an instant, her bones were visible underneath.

"Megaira," the commander said.

Seth blinked. "What?"

"I think she's a megaira. Maybe half-megaira, half-human. It's a demon that feeds on human aggression. That's why you can lock her in a cellar for three days without food and she doesn't die. But electrical current..." Yasir nudged the battery with the toe of his shoe. "It interrupts infernal energy."

Pagan rolled onto her side. Her hair fell over her face, but Seth could still see her white teeth when she smiled. "Give the boy a diploma. He figured it out."

"A demon?" Gwyn asked, eyebrows lifting toward her hairline. She tipped her hat back with a knuckle. "Say that again, because I'm thinking I heard you wrong."

"Creatures from Hell," Stripes muttered, shooting a sideways look at Pagan.

"There aren't many of them in this part of America," Yasir said, speaking over his companion. "They stick to major urban areas. Out here? Not enough humans, not enough food."

"You know, I don't believe in God," Gwyn said.

Yasir barked a mirthless laugh. "Neither do I."

The door rattled.

Seth stood up, putting the gun to his shoulder. Gwyn took position at his side.

The door rattled again.

"You are all in deep trouble," Pagan said.

Stripes kicked her. "Shut up!"

The door rattled a third time, and Seth heard the chains sliding against the handles. He raised his voice. "Whoever is there, I'm warning you—anyone who comes through that door tonight is getting shot."

"It's not one of your dogs out there," Pagan said. Her eyes glimmered darkly, and blood stained her teeth. "Cain's come for me."

The single light bulb popped, showering sparks on them.

Darkness filled the cellar, so black and complete that Seth couldn't see his own hands.

The door slammed open.

The air split with the sound of gunshots as four firearms were simultaneously discharged. Cloth shifted and metal clacked.

A grunt. A meaty slam, like a body hitting the floor.

Someone shouted—someone male. Stripes?

Seth spun, searching for something to shoot. He couldn't tell the difference between Gwyneth and Yasir, much less an intruder.

Another gunshot. Someone screamed.

"Lights—we need lights!" Gwyn shouted.

Seth fumbled, and his hand fell on a camping lantern on the shelf. It took three tries to flip the switch.

A brilliant LED glow flooded the cellar. Two other people were standing nearby—Gwyn and the commander.

And there was a body on the ground.

Seth kicked over the dark shape on the floor, and Stripes rolled onto his back. His eyes were empty.

Dead.

"Where's Pagan?" Gwyn asked.

Yasir was already running up the steps. Seth followed, gun hugged to his chest.

Even without a moon, it was so much brighter on the surface than it had been in the cellar. A dozen dark shapes tracked over the hills, each of them the size of a small pony. Werewolves.

And somewhere among them, Pagan and Cain.

Seth moved to chase. But before he made it three steps into the field, he realized something was wrong.

The werewolves were usually playful under Rylie's control, but they were scattered and wild that night. They chased each other through the hills with piercing howls.

The entire pack was out of control, which meant their Alpha was too focused on something else to notice them.

Abel must have been worse than Seth expected.

Was that his brother's dark form among the trees? Seth cupped his hands around his mouth. "Abel! Rylie!"

The wolf didn't react.

Seth prepared to shout again, but the smell of something burning stopped him. It was a cloying, powerful scent. If his human nose could pick it up, then something had to be burning hot.

He glanced at the ranch house. No hint of smoke.

"Seth!" Yasir yelled. He was on the opposite hill, and his silhouette was lit on the edges with a dancing red glow.

Swearing under his breath, Seth ran to his side.

The barn was on fire.

Flames leaped in the shattered windows, licking at the walls and turning them black. Sparks lit in the dry grass.

"Cain," Yasir said. "It must have been Cain." Seth pulled out his cell phone, starting to dial the emergency number, but Yasir grabbed his arm. "Wait! We can't have firefighters come to a ranch filled with werewolves."

He was right.

Seth groaned and scrubbed his hands over his hair. "Okay. There's a pump on the other side of the barn. I'll get the hose."

"I don't think we can stop this fire," Yasir said.

"No, but we can stop it from spreading. Come on. We have to move fast."

Seth abandoned the hunt for Pagan and rushed to save what little of the barn he could.

Rylie ran, and Abel chased.

She flew through the long grass, her feet thudded against the soil, and the nighttime wind blasted hair back from her face. Her chest heaved as her arms pumped. Her legs burned.

And behind her, the wolf was growling.

She could run for hours, if she had to—but Abel was faster. She could hear him gaining.

Rylie needed somewhere safe to transform so she could stand a chance against him. But he was snapping at her heels.

A wolf scurried past in the corner of her vision. He was dark brown with streaks of gold.

"Vanthe!" she yelled, and the word was whipped away on the wind. "Help!"

He wheeled around, looping wide through the hills. Rylie jumped behind a tree to put the trunk between her and the sleek black monster that was Abel.

The werewolves crashed together.

A yelp.

She glanced around the tree long enough to see that Abel had raked his long, silver claws down Vanthe's side. He wasn't slowed by the other wolf—not for long.

Rylie shut her eyes and began to change.

It was hard to focus with her heart beating a panicked tattoo against her ribs. She focused on fur and claws, and heat swept over her skin.

Too slow.

Another howl, and paws were pounding on the ground again. Abel rounded the tree.

"Oh no," Rylie whispered.

She turned to run again. But her legs were reversing, her bones were growing, and her coordination was shot.

Abel plowed into her back, knocking them both to the ground.

She threw up an arm to protect her face, even as it blossomed with fur. Abel's teeth clamped on her skin, snapping just inches from her face. Blood splattered onto her chest.

"No!" she cried. "Abel!"

He twisted his head back and forth, nearly wrenching the arm from its socket. It felt like her arm was being crushed under a car.

Her spine popped and twisted. Her muzzle grew, blurry in the bottom edge of her vision.

Rylie brought her mutating legs between them and shoved her feet into Abel's chest, launching him off of her body.

He flew into the air. Hit the tree with a yelp.

She flipped onto all fours and finished the change as quickly as she could. Rylie took a short inventory of her body—paws, tail, fur in all the right places—and faced Abel as he got to his feet.

Drool hung from his bottom jaw, which was half-scarred, just like his human face. But his sharp eyes focused on her.

She issued a growl, trying to warn him: *I am Alpha, Do not fight me.*

He stepped forward anyway.

There was no play-bowing or impudent wriggling in the dirt. Abel was completely serious and completely out of his mind. There was no man in him. Only beast and raw instinct.

A real werewolf.

"Abel! Rylie!"

A human voice echoing over the hills—*Seth's* voice.

Rylie's head snapped up, and she searched the horizon for her boyfriend. He was by the ranch house. What was he doing out of the cellar? Did that mean Pagan had changed?

She didn't have long to consider the implications. Abel heard Seth's voice too, and he growled.

Sibling rivalry could get awfully ugly when one of them was a monster.

Rylie snapped at his side, drawing his attention back to her.

He struck. Her vision blurred and doubled, and they rolled down the hill together. Rylie twisted her head around, searching for any part of Abel to bite, trying to restrain him.

His teeth snapped on the ruff of fur at her neck. Her paws. Her muzzle.

The pressure of his jaws on her limbs drew forth the mind of Rylie's wolf. She surrendered to it, letting instinct carry her away.

The wolf was a calming force—raw logic and cold anger.

And it could fight.

They bounced over rocks and slid to the shore of the pond. She flipped him over and bit his muzzle. The taste of blood flooded her tongue.

Her teeth ripped into his shoulder, pushing through the fur to tear at the vulnerable skin underneath.

He seized her back leg. She broke free, but only for an instant. Abel dived for another attack. She lowered her head and slammed it into his side.

The force of the impact threw him into the pond. Water slopped over the rocks.

He thrashed, growling and howling.

By the time he emerged from the pond, fur dripping with crimson-stained water, Rylie had the higher ground. But even with blood streaming down his face and flank, his eyes burned. Challenging her.

Abel jumped, and he slammed her into the rocks. His weight pressed against her shoulders. Forced her chest to the ground.

Jaws clamped tight on the back of her neck.

A sense of peace spread through Rylie—an acknowledgment of dominance. She sagged underneath him.

He growled and shook her, but it was gentler than before.

Someone was calling her name. Humans were somewhere on the other side of the property, searching for Rylie and Abel.

The wolf didn't care. She didn't acknowledge them. She didn't even notice when smoke rose over the hills.

Abel was dominant—Alpha. And she was at his mercy.

SIX

Abandon Ship

Rylie woke up at the furthest edge of the sanctuary, in the back corner where a barbed wire fence protected the farms beyond from an onslaught of werewolves.

And she was bleeding.

She rolled onto her back with a groan. Everywhere hurt. Her back, her legs, her head—it had been a *long* time since she had a headache.

There was no accompanying rush of healing fever. Just pain.

She sat up to look at herself in the blue light of dawn. Her body was a mess of scrapes and tears. How was that even possible?

Weirdly, the ache was kind of... good. Rylie had the kind of heavy, satiated feeling she enjoyed after devouring a deer or cow as a wolf. But there were no prey animals on the ranch, and she obviously hadn't escaped. It made no sense.

Someone else groaned.

Rylie twisted to find Abel laying a few feet away. He looked a lot like she did—naked and bleeding. But he hadn't woken up yet.

"Oh my God," she said, crawling to his side.

Abel had healed the silver injury. There was a neat scar on his side where he had been shot. But his shoulder was torn open, and the skin was ragged all the way down his chest. A ring of puncture marks on his arms formed the shape of teeth.

Wounds inflicted by the Alpha didn't heal as quickly as those delivered by another wolf. Which meant that Rylie must have ripped him open the night before.

She squeezed her eyes shut and struggled to remember what had happened, but nothing came to mind. Rylie had the impression of body clashing against body, a struggle in the grass, the rush of adrenaline—but that was all she could bring to mind.

A fight between them would have explained what happened to Abel. But what had happened to *her*?

Abel roused enough to walk on his own, and they staggered toward the house together. Climbing up and down the swelling hills was much harder on two tired legs than four.

When they crested the hill by the pond, Rylie saw the barn. She gasped.

The skeletal remains of a building stood where the barn should have been. Ribs of iron jutted from the earth, and broken red wood was scattered everywhere, like something had exploded. The surrounding grass was scorched and wet.

Her mind tried to make sense of the debris. Was that the TV? Had those been beds?

It didn't matter. Everything was destroyed.

Seth was still wetting down charred embers with Gwyn and Yasir's help, but he dropped the hose when he saw them.

"Rylie!"

He scrambled to the top of the hill, and she sagged in his arms. He was covered in ash.

"What happened?" she asked, clutching at his shirt. His hands cupped her elbows to keep her on her feet.

"Pagan escaped," Seth said, addressing Abel as well. "Cain came for her. They burned the barn.

Even after seeing it for herself, hearing the words from Seth made Rylie feel like she had been punched in the chest.

They had spent months converting the barn into a living space for the pack. She spent so many long hours picking out furniture for the bedrooms, laying carpet, getting into paint fights with Seth—and it was gone. All gone.

"Survivors?" Abel asked.

"Stripes was killed, but the pack is fine." Seth hugged Rylie tightly. "I was so worried about you. You vanished."

"I'm fine," she said with a wince. The pressure hurt her scrapes.

Seth only just seemed to realize that she was wounded. His eyes widened into huge circles. "Why aren't you healing?"

"I don't know," Rylie said. "I really don't know."

When the last of the fire was put out and dirt was spread on the coals, everyone moved inside. A lot of the pack was crying and angry, but if Aunt Gwyn was shaken, she showed no sign of it. She immediately bustled off to prepare coffee, which was her idea of being comforting.

Seth sat with Rylie on a few inches of couch and hugged her chilled body to him. She was strangely quiet, but he couldn't exactly talk about her feelings when the living room was packed tight with werewolves.

The front door opened, and Yasir stepped in. He caught Seth's eye over the crowd.

"Can I talk to you?" Yasir asked.

Seth gave Rylie's shoulders one last squeeze, and then joined the commander outside. There was a light breeze and just enough clouds to keep it from getting hot. It would have been a beautiful day, if not for the destroyed barn."

"What's wrong?" Seth asked.

"You mean, aside from the obvious? It's Stripes." Yasir jerked his thumb down the road. "I found something while moving his body. Come look."

The dead Union hunter was stretched out on a tarp in the back of the SUV.

Stripes's throat had been torn out. It was fast and messy, but Seth had been dealing with so many cadavers in school that he only saw the anatomy of it—the mangled carotid, the digastric muscle, the glisten of his cervical vertebrae. If Pagan had gone a few centimeters further, she might have decapitated him.

"A megaira can do this?" Seth asked.

Yasir shook his head. "That's the thing—they can't. You saw her. No teeth or claws." He pulled on a latex glove and parted the skin to show Seth where muscle had been torn away. "This damage looks like it was caused by an animal."

"You mean Cain is a werewolf?"

"If that was Cain rescuing Pagan last night—yes, maybe." But he was still very tense. That obviously wasn't his only news.

He pulled Stripes's shirt down, baring his left pectoral. The skin was rubbery without the flow of blood underneath.

Stripes had a tattoo of a bleeding apple.

"Look familiar?" the commander asked.

"That's the same tattoo Pagan had on her neck."

"Exactly." Yasir covered the mark, mouth twisting with distaste. "We've had some hunters jumping ship from the Union. I thought it was normal defection, but what if they're leaving to join Cain?"

"But if Pagan and Stripes were on the same side, then why would he have helped you interrogate her?"

"I can only guess. Punishment for getting herself caught? But someone wasn't happy with Stripes, and it wasn't Pagan." Yasir waved a hand at the destroyed throat. "We should prepare ourselves for the possibility that a member of the pack may also be a follower of Cain."

Seth's head was spinning. A traitor inside the pack? "Nobody was missing this morning."

"We didn't see who attacked last night. It could be anyone." The commander wrapped Stripes's body in the tarp, removed the glove, and disposed of it in a biohazard bag. "I need to tell Union HQ what's happening. There's no way to hide Stripes's death from them, and they'll want to conduct their own investigation. So that means at least one unit out here." Yasir shrugged. "Sorry."

Seth blew a breath out of his lips.

"Okay. Do what you have to do."

Rylie spent the next month doing two big things: recovering and avoiding.

The first one was the easy part, relatively speaking. The barn was a total loss, and healing from her wounds was mostly a matter of time.

She healed slowly—it took two weeks for her bruises to vanish. Much longer than usual.

The avoiding thing was a lot trickier.

Yasir brought the rest of his unit to investigate the fire. They brought two of the Union's RVs, which gave the displaced werewolves somewhere to sleep, but it still wasn't enough room. Rylie began spending her nights outside in a sleeping bag.

It was also hard to sleep when men who had tried to kill her two years ago were patrolling her home.

"This is a good thing," Seth told her one morning when the unit was jogging in formation along the highway. "They can protect us better than I can alone."

"But do they want to protect us?" Rylie asked.

He said yes, but he didn't sound very convincing.

The Union wasn't the only thing Rylie was avoiding. She was also avoiding talking about marriage—although Seth only tried to bring it up once or twice after the first night—and avoiding Abel.

And *everyone* was avoiding the obvious truth that was staring them in the face: it was time to abandon the sanctuary.

Scott Whyte flew out to help them file the insurance reports. He had gained weight in the last couple of years; he used to look like Sean Connery, but the rugged jaw had since gotten a few layers of fat over it. He looked more like Santa Claus than an aging James Bond.

"Nothing in the barn can be recovered," he told Rylie and Gwyn. "I can arrange to have it bulldozed and rebuilt. But this location isn't safe now. Cain has made it clear that he's not afraid of attacking the ranch. We need to move everyone to the California sanctuary."

Gwyn nodded. "There happens to be somewhere I can stay in the city."

"You're not coming to California with us?" Rylie asked.

"I don't belong with a bunch of werewolves, babe. I have friends in the city." Gwyn paused. "A girlfriend, actually."

"What?" All of her other concerns immediately vanished at Gwyn's confession. "You're dating again, and you didn't tell me?"

That would definitely explain all of her aunt's mysterious disappearances, but Rylie didn't have time to interrogate her for detail.

Scott stepped in.

"I should probably warn you now—Seth isn't going to California either, Rylie," he said, putting a heavy hand on her shoulder. He wore a thick gold thumb ring etched with pentagrams. "Not at first. I need his help finding Cain."

"But he's supposed to be going back to college in a couple of weeks."

Scott's bushy eyebrows joined together. "He graduated in the spring. He's not starting medical school until next year."

Shock washed over her, and Rylie shielded her eyes from the sun to watch Seth training with the other hunters on the opposite hill. They were all wearing black Union sweatpants and practicing fight moves. Seth was better than everyone but Yasir—he had grown up hunting werewolves, and even a couple years of college couldn't soften those hard edges.

He had graduated. He was taking a whole year off of school. She felt a little dizzy at the realization.

Why hadn't he told her?

Seven

A Promise

"I didn't know that you already graduated," Rylie told Seth that night. They were curled up together in a sleeping bag to watch the stars. Even with the autumn chill, it was far better than sharing a bedroom—and she definitely wasn't cold while wrapped around her boyfriend.

It was almost the full moon again, and it sparkled on the water of the brook. They had chosen to camp in a valley where nobody could see them, and it was quiet, private, and absolutely beautiful.

Seth traced a line on her shoulder. "After everything that happened, I didn't want to make you worry about it. I don't want to pressure you."

"How would that pressure me?"

He propped his head up on his hand. "I took the year off so that we would have time to get married." Seth laughed at her expression of shock. "See? But I can wait. I really don't want you to worry about it."

She snuggled deeper into his shoulder, breathing in all of his warm, distinctive smells. Even when they were naked with their legs tangled together, he still smelled like leather.

"But instead of taking a year to plan a wedding, you're taking a year to hunt down homicidal maniacs," Rylie said.

He shrugged. "At least I'm being productive."

"I don't think I deserve you."

Seth flung an arm toward their pile of clothing, which rested on a towel so it wouldn't get too damp with dew. When he rolled back, he was holding the ring box again.

"When I bought this for you... Well, I wouldn't have gotten it if there was a single doubt in my mind, Rylie." He took the ring out. Her heart made a funny flop as he held it toward her. "I want you to wear it. Not as an engagement ring—not yet. But I got it for *you*, and it shouldn't sit in a box."

He slipped it over her right ring finger—not her left.

"I love it," she said, tilting her hand to study it. The moonstone sparkled with starlight.

"Think of it as a promise. When you're ready..." Seth touched her left ring finger, tracing a line around the place the engagement ring should have sat. "Just tell me. I'll be back for you as soon as I can."

"Do you know where you're going yet?"

He sighed. "Yeah. There's this house about three hundred miles away—near Akron. Scott thinks there might be information there."

"Why? What's special about that house?"

"It's where Abel and I grew up before our dad was killed by werewolves." He squeezed her hand a little too tight. "The connection between Cain, Abel, and Seth is too big to ignore. In the Bible, they were all brothers. The sons of Adam. Scott thinks that means that Eleanor is related in some way."

"But she's dead," Rylie said. "I pulled her off the cliff on Gray Mountain and watched her die." Seth only nodded. She considered the lines of worry on his face. "I want to come. Let me hunt Cain with you."

"Rylie..."

She could already hear the argument in his voice, so she cut him off. "I'm not exactly vulnerable. I can change between human and wolf whenever I want now. I heal fast, my sense of smell is amazing, and I can fight. We can get him together."

"But what about the pack?" Seth asked.

"They can survive without me for a few weeks," she said. "They'll have Abel, and he usually controls them during the moons anyway. I just make it hurt less."

Seth's mouth turned down at the corners. "What's up with you and Abel lately?"

Rylie had no idea what to tell him.

She had been doing a pretty good job of avoiding Abel most of the time. They had barely spoken for over a month. She was too busy dealing with the sanctuary, and he was too busy dealing with the wolves.

But something had changed on the night of the fire. Something huge. When she woke up on the new and full moons, she was always curled up with Abel—and she had the feeling that they had spent all evening together.

"Nothing's going on," she said, but the words rang false, even to her.

Seth kissed her. It was sweet and lingering, and Rylie wished they could have kissed forever. No werewolves, no killers, no worries.

But it ended eventually, like it always did.

He rolled his weight so it was on top of hers. "I love you, Rylie. The thought of taking you hunting scares me. But if it's what you want..."

"I want to be with you," Rylie said firmly.

They kissed in the cold night, alone except for the nearly-full moon.

The ranch bustled with activity as the pack prepared to leave the next day. While the wolves loaded moving trucks, Rylie packed up enough clothing for a week and put them in the Chevelle with Seth's bag.

Abel's belongings were still in the trunk from the last time he used the car. She stared at his backpack and felt pained, but she wasn't sure why.

She wandered down to the moving trucks and watched from a few yards away. Abel, Bekah, and Vanthe were doing the bulk of the work under Gwyn's supervision.

Rylie thumbed the moonstone ring as she studied Abel. He was talking to Vanthe and laughing over something. He looked so different when he smiled. More like his brother.

He caught her staring and hesitated halfway into the truck with another box.

Something had *definitely* changed between them.

"Hey, Rylie!" Bekah called, waving a hand over her head. "Come help us!"

"Sorry, I'm busy," she yelled back.

And then she retreated to the house like the big coward she was.

Rylie poured a cup of Gwyn's extra foul black coffee, sat at the kitchen island, and stared at the steam swirling off of the surface.

One more moon before she parted ways with the pack. Another morning waking up with Abel instead of Seth.

"I'm not changing tonight," she whispered into her mug. "I'm going to stay human this time."

The front door opened and shut. Abel clomped into the kitchen, wearing heavy work boots that sounded like a sledgehammer blow on every step. "Where's your box?" he asked, wiping dirt off his hands onto his jeans.

It was the first time they had spoken directly to each other in weeks. She longed to press herself against him and drink in all of his smells, but she stayed firmly planted on the barstool.

"My box?"

"The stuff you're taking to California," he said.

"I'm not going to California. I'm going to help Seth hunt Cain."

Abel stared at her. She sipped her coffee.

After a moment, he left the kitchen without saying a single word.

Rylie didn't spend the last full moon outside with the pack. She remained inside the house instead.

She stared in challenge at the moon through the window. She could feel its silvery rays prickling in her skin and making her gums itch, but she pushed it away.

You don't own me.

Outside, the pack transformed one by one. Rylie exerted her control over them from a distance, suppressing their pain and making everyone shift smoothly.

Howls broke the night, echoing around the house.

She thought she heard Abel's lonely cry rising above the rest.

Seth was helping the Union patrol the perimeter, which left her alone in the house all night. But she couldn't get comfortable enough to sleep through the long hours. Her muscles hurt like she had the flu. Her stomach cramped. Her fingertips ached.

But she didn't change.

The sun rose. The pack changed back.

And everyone prepared to leave the sanctuary.

EIGHT

Battlefield

They left in waves. First, Bekah and Levi went to the airport with Scott, and then half of the pack departed with a Union escort. By the time night came around again, everyone that remained was preparing to leave. They loaded the RV outside, leaving the house silent.

But Abel was in his bedroom, door closed. He hadn't come out all day.

Rylie paced in front of his door. She kept replaying the moment that Seth kneeled in front of her with the ring, and the stunned look on Abel's face before Pagan fired and all hell broke loose. And she thought about how he looked when she told him that she was leaving.

She raised her hand to knock, and then dropped it. She paced down the hall. Bit her thumbnail. Paced back to his door.

What was she going to do after she knocked? She didn't have a plan. She had no clue what to say.

Rylie didn't really want to apologize for leaving anyway. She wanted to apologize for being in love with his brother.

She stared at his door like her gaze could make it catch fire.

Before she could come to a decision, it opened.

Abel stood on the other side. He was shirtless, and his shoulders glistened. It looked like he had been pummeling his punching bag again.

He looked at her. She looked at him.

Are you okay?

That was what she meant to say. But that wasn't what she *wanted* to say.

She wanted to ask him if it was okay to leave with Seth. Like she needed his permission.

There was a disconnect somewhere between her brain and her mouth, and instead, all she could say was: "I'm sorry."

Abel responded by grabbing her shoulders, dragging her into the room, and slamming the door shut.

He shoved her into the wall, and her back hit hard enough to dent plaster. His hands captured her face. She clung to his shoulders, unable to trust her ability to stand, but the burning brand of his fingers held her suspended.

And then they were kissing.

His mouth crashed over hers. He tasted like blood and meat, and it was so deliciously *animal* that her wolf rose to meet him.

Abel's hands were everywhere—on her shoulders, lifting her hips, spreading her thighs. He pushed himself between her knees and all she could do was hang on as he crushed her to the wall with his chest and hips.

Her wolf should have been angry that he would manhandle her. That he would be so presumptuous as to take charge.

But it was *happy*.

It was Abel who shoved himself back, stumbling away from Rylie and leaving her suddenly cold.

She almost fell over, but caught herself on the end of Levi's bed. Abel glared at her from across the room, breathing as hard as if he had just been running.

The reality of what she had done sank in.

She had kissed Abel.

And the worst part of it was that it didn't feel particularly new or strange. It felt like something they had done a thousand times.

And her wolf loved it.

"Oh my God," Rylie whispered, her hand flying to her bruised lips.

Abel strode toward her again, and she braced herself, as if expecting to get hit. But he only pounded a fist into the wall by her head. The already-weakened plaster cracked again, and she jumped at the sound.

"God*dammit*, Rylie," he hissed.

Her legs were jelly and every inch of her skin was hot, and she couldn't seem to catch her breath. She also couldn't seem to raise her voice above a squeak. "I'm sorry," she said again, and she felt twice as stupid the second time.

"You're sorry?" He gave a bitter laugh. "*You're* sorry?" His arms were braced on the wall at either side of her shoulders, trapping her underneath him. "I'm the one who can't stop thinking about his brother's girlfriend." He bent forward, like he might kiss her again, but he stopped an inch away. "Where were you last night?"

She swallowed hard. "I stayed in the house."

"Why?"

"Because..." It was so hard to breathe when he was looking at her like that. He was close enough that if she licked her lips, she might just lick him, too. "Because I don't know what we've been doing when we're wolves. Kissing you feels... familiar."

"Familiar," he echoed.

She didn't know how to elaborate beyond that, so she just nodded.

Abel's eyes raked over her face, like he could violate her with his gaze alone. "I want you so damn bad," he said, biting out every word. "When I look at you—it's like I'm an alcoholic, and you're the last bottle of whiskey on Earth." The heat in his voice weakened her knees.

"But—"

He cut her off. "Why did you come here?"

"I don't know," Rylie said, her trembling fingers running over the broad planes of his chest. She couldn't seem to stop touching him. "I guess... because I want you, too. And I don't know *why*."

He seized her arms. "You don't know why you want me? You don't think it's because of this?"

Abel's second kiss was shorter, but no gentler. He pulled her against him with an iron grip. He consumed her like a forest fire, savage and merciless. And when he dropped her, she desperately regretted it.

It took all of her strength to push the wolf away, forcing it deep inside of her.

She clenched her fists. "I don't love you," Rylie said. "I love Seth."

Abel grabbed her chin, forcing her to look up at him. "You can keep telling yourself that, but it doesn't change anything."

"I'm leaving with him."

"But you'll be back for me," he said.

"No." Her protest was weak.

But wasn't that true? How could she stay away from her pack?

How could she stay away from her Alpha?

The thought rose to the surface, totally unbidden, and she couldn't shake it once it crossed her mind. Abel wasn't Alpha. *She* was Alpha.

"I'm sorry," Rylie said one last time, stepping away from him. "I shouldn't have come here. Take care of the pack."

And then she ran out of his room, away from Abel, away from the heat of his lips on hers.

But she couldn't escape the memory of his kiss.

NINE

Lost Chapters

Rylie was already sitting in the passenger's seat of the Chevelle when Seth joined her. She had her knees hugged to her chest as she stared out the window.

Yasir met him at the car, carrying a binder under one arm. "You need to let us know if you find Cain before we do," the commander said.

Seth nodded reluctantly. He didn't want to call the Union in for anything he didn't have to, but it was hard to deny their usefulness. "You'll be the first to hear about it."

Yasir handed him an earpiece—the same one worn by every member of the Union. "The button on the side goes directly to me. Don't lose it." He hesitated, and then also handed the binder to Seth. "It took a while to requisition, but I finally got a complete copy of your father's book from Union HQ. This is all we have. I hope it has the answers you want."

"Thank you."

They clasped each other's forearms, and with a short nod, Yasir left to escort the rest of the pack to California.

Seth climbed into the Chevelle, set the binder in the back seat, and started the engine.

"Ready to go?" he asked Rylie.

She nodded silently.

Rylie was unusually quiet on the long drive out of town. Seth waited an hour before trying to strike up a conversation, but she only responded by shaking her head or nodding. And when he asked if she wanted to take a break, she just shrugged.

Seth pulled into a gas station parking lot to buy a soda. He hesitated before getting out. "Is something wrong, Rylie?"

She glanced at him. Ducked her head. "No."

Rylie was a horrible liar. The truth was written all over her face: she was freaking out about something, and it was killing her.

Seth glanced down at her right hand. The moonstone glimmered on her finger.

"Do you want anything to eat?" he asked.

She shrugged again.

Seth left her in the car while he bought a soda for himself and a green tea for Rylie.

When he returned, she was still staring out the window without acknowledging him. Her arms were folded tightly across her chest and her cheeks were pink.

Seth kept driving.

Another two hours passed. Two long, boring hours with nothing to do but stare at the asphalt.

The air was cool with autumn's chill. Most of the trees were caught between summer and fall, with half of their leaves a dull shade of green, and the other half shimmering gold. The trees became more dense as they moved north, and then turned sparse again as they passed through a city. Nothing waited on the other side but plains.

"Let's trade," Rylie said at the next rest stop. She hadn't touched her tea.

While she drove, Seth read the binder that Yasir had given him. He flipped through the pages one by one.

He had been drilled on werewolf hunting procedure using that manual a thousand times, and Seth knew the rules by memory.

Be careful when verifying a suspected werewolf. Double-check all of your sources.

Look for a history of crime, mental illness, and especially domestic violence. Werewolves are unstable and struggle to integrate into society.

Make sure that the werewolf is who you think they are before killing them.

Don't kill them when they don't have four legs and fur.

That was pretty much it. As far as hunting and killing tactics went, anything had been considered fair game by his parents.

There was nothing new in that part of the book. He flipped through the familiar chapters—the section on skinning, the section on removing teeth to keep track of the kills, the part about different species—and found a chapter that he didn't recognize.

Pack behavior.

He read a few lines into it, skimming for words like "Alpha" and "mating."

What he found made his blood run cold.

"What are you reading?" Rylie asked, breaking the silence.

He closed the cover. "Nothing interesting." It was late afternoon; they must have traveled a pretty good distance while he was distracted, because he didn't recognize any of the landmarks anymore. The long shadows of trees stretched across the road. "Where are we?"

"Nowhere right now. We'll get to Aguilar in about an hour," she said. "I'm getting tired. Where do you want to stop for the night?"

"Aguilar works."

Seth zipped the binder up in his bag, and they finished the drive in silence.

The motel in Aguilar wasn't much to look at. It definitely wasn't up to Scott Whyte's standards of cleanliness—just looking at the yellow curtains and tarnished brass numbers on the doors probably would have made him break out in hives.

But they hadn't made advance arrangements, and there were no five star hotels in the middle of nowhere. So Rylie waited in the car while Seth went in to book the room.

They were in room number six, which was almost at the end. They parked in front of it and took their bags inside.

All they had by way of furniture was a TV stand, a side table, and one big bed. The comforter was probably even older than the curtains. But the TV was new, and there were streaks on the mirror, which meant someone had tried to clean the room at some point. Maybe even that week.

Rylie looked at Seth, and he looked at her.

I kissed your brother.

"I'm going to take a shower," she said, grabbing a towel out of the closet and ducking into the bathroom.

When Rylie had gone to school in the city, some of her guy friends liked to play the field. Nick had bragged constantly about making out with different girls.

It was no big deal, he had said. As long as we didn't have sex, it wasn't even cheating.

But that word stuck inside her brain like a thorn.

Cheater.

She washed using the tiny bottle of shampoo that smelled like jasmine. It made her hair feel weird and crunchy, but it was the first time she had showered in months without Bekah banging on the bathroom door, so she tried to enjoy it.

That word hung over her like Pagan's foul perfume.

Cheater.

She was going to have to tell Seth. She couldn't keep quiet anymore.

After a few minutes, she gave up trying to enjoy herself. She got dressed, combed out her hair, and rejoined Seth.

He was sitting on the bed, still fully clothed except for his shoes, and watching the news while he oiled his gun. He smiled when she came out. It only made her feel guiltier.

"Good shower?" he asked.

She nodded mutely and sat beside him. The mattress springs creaked under her weight.

There was nothing interesting on the news. They were going on about all the disasters that had been happening in the west, from Oregon down into Nevada and Arizona, and Rylie was so sick of hearing about earthquakes and fires that she tuned it out.

But that left nothing for her to think about except Abel's bruising kisses, and how much her body ached to do it again, and her resolution to tell Seth what had happened.

Her boyfriend set down his gun.

"Okay, Rylie. What's eating at you?"

She threw her legs over the side of the bed and turned her back so that she wouldn't have to see his expression.

Deep breaths.

"I kissed Abel," she said, twisting the moonstone ring on her hand.

"You kissed..." He trailed off, like he couldn't quite understand the words.

She bit her bottom lip and nodded.

He was quiet for so long that she had to look over her shoulder to see his reaction. But his face was blank as he stared at the wall. There was no way to tell what was going on in his head.

The news program switched to commercials. A used car ad blasted through the room. Something about big deals and low interest rate and no payments for a few months.

Seth didn't move.

She couldn't stand his silence. "What are you thinking about?"

"You kissed my brother," he said. He sounded numb. "What do you think I'm thinking about?"

Rylie smothered her face in her hands. "I'm sorry. I don't know what happened. I'd been trying to avoid him, but like I told you, I've been feeling so—so *weird* about him—and when I realized I was leaving, and he was—"

He stood up abruptly, pushing his chair back. "Stop."

Seth didn't sound numb anymore. He sounded angry.

She shut her mouth. *Here it comes.*

He strode to the bed, and she tensed. But he only unzipped his suitcase.

"I shouldn't be surprised." He pulled out the binder he had been reading in the car while she drove. "That's what this said would happen."

Seth tossed the binder on the bed. It slid across the old bedspread to her, so that she could read what was printed on the cover at an angle. *Hunting the Once-Human Beast.*

She reached out to touch it, and then decided she didn't want to. "Is that...?"

"Yeah. It's my dad's book. He did more research into them than he originally published, including an entire chapter on Alphas. My mom had a copy of his rough draft on Gray Mountain. I've been reading it."

"What does it say?"

Seth gave her a long look. His gaze was almost pitying. "In traditional pack structure, there are two Alphas—a male and a female. It's a matriarchal structure. The female who runs the pack chooses her Alpha by mating with him."

Rylie's stomach dropped out. She wavered.

"Oh."

"It's supposed to be for the good of the pack. She picks the strongest man and... well, you know." He shrugged. "Alphas are a weird thing with werewolves anyway. They only start popping up when the pack is in duress. You were chosen because werewolves were about to go extinct anyway, so your job includes the... expectation... that you'll help repopulate the species."

She clenched her fists so hard that her fingernails bit into her palms. "I won't bite anyone. I'm not turning anyone else into a monster."

"That's the thing." He blew a breath out of his lips. Stared at his feet. "My dad's research said that werewolves can be born, too."

"What?"

He held up his hands and took a step back, like her shock was a physical force that had shoved him. "There were no references cited on his research. There's no way to verify that it's true."

Rylie let the words sink into her.

Werewolves can be born.

She crossed her arms over her stomach. "So... if I had a baby, it would be a werewolf?" Her cheeks heated, and her vision blurred. "So you and me... we can't ever...?"

He sank onto the bed at her side.

"We don't know that yet." Seth pulled Rylie against his chest and buried his face in her hair. His breath was hot down the back of her neck.

So her wolf's attraction was worse than she expected. It wasn't just something wildly out of her control—it was a drive to breed a species of monsters.

Rylie thought she was going to throw up.

"I'm not doing that," she said. "I would never."

He rubbed small circles over her back. "I know." His chest rose and fell under her cheek. "You don't have any control over what's happening between you and Abel. This is a werewolf thing. The wolf choosing Abel as her mate isn't your fault any more than the wolf killing all those people years ago."

Tears burned paths down her cheeks.

"But it *is* me," Rylie said. "I kissed Abel."

"Because the wolf took control of you. Hey, look at me." He took her by the arms and fixed a serious gaze on her. "You are not the wolf. The wolf is not you. I love *you*, Rylie Gresham. We're stronger than this. And I'm not giving you up to some ridiculous werewolf mythology without a fight."

She hung her head, unable to meet his eyes. "I love you, Seth."

"Do you?"

"Yes," she said. "You know that. I've loved you since the first time I saw you at camp. That won't ever change."

"Then that's all that matters," he said. "We'll get through this together. Okay?"

She nodded and leaned against his shoulder. He held her tightly and didn't let go all night.

TEN

An Answer

The drive wasn't as tense the next morning. They kept the windows rolled down, even though the air was cold. It felt good whipping around Rylie's face.

They arrived at Seth's old house by late afternoon.

It was at the end of a long, empty road that had no name, and it was so isolated that Rylie thought it might have once been a hunting cabin. Yellowing trees crowded around it on every side. Her feet crunched on leaves as she got out of the Chevelle.

"Is it abandoned?" she asked.

Seth took his rifle out of the car and slung the strap over his shoulder. "You tell me."

Rylie tilted her nose to the air and sniffed. All she smelled was rotting leaves, squirrels, and the droppings of deer that had passed by the previous week. "Humans haven't been here in a while."

"Good."

The front door wasn't locked. Seth pushed it open, and the hinges gave a protesting whine.

The curtains were drawn, so the living room was dark. Half of the furniture was missing—there was still a coffee table and couch, but judging by the discoloration on the walls, shelves and paintings had been removed.

Aside from the dust, it looked like a family easily could have lived there just the week before. There were even photos over the fireplace.

Rylie stepped in behind Seth, taking another short sniff. Old smells lingered in the air—smells she couldn't place. Animals, maybe.

"So this is where you grew up," she said, trailing her fingertips over the mantel. Her skin came up covered in a thick layer of dust and dirt.

She brushed the glass over a photo clean. There were two smiling faces underneath—little boys with broad grins, big eyes, and coarse black curls that stuck out in every direction. They were hugged by a man with blue eyes and brown hair. He had the same lopsided smile that Seth did, and Abel's lips. It had to be their dad.

Her heart fell looking at the picture.

"What was your father like?" she asked, picking up the frame to rub off more dust.

Seth stuck his hands in his pockets and glared at the house. Even if he looked happy in the photo as a child, he didn't seem happy to be there now.

"I don't remember him very well, but I know he was driven. He was pretty funny, I guess. He laughed a lot." He scrubbed a hand over his stubble. "He yelled a lot, too. Mostly at my mom. But Eleanor gave as good as she got."

"I believe that." Rylie showed Seth the photo.

His eyes raked down the image. "That was a few weeks before Dad died." Seth opened his mouth, like he was going to say something else about it, but then his jaw clapped shut.

He took the picture from her and set it on the mantel again.

Seth moved into the kitchen, leaving Rylie alone.

A chill settled over her as she stood in the middle of the ghost of Seth's childhood. The dusty furniture, the dirty photos, the dark room—it suddenly had the feeling of a mausoleum.

She cracked a window to let in the breeze. Light splashed over the room. The sun warmed her face. "I don't think Cain has been here," she called into the kitchen.

No response.

She opened another window to let in more light, but it didn't help much. Everything looked more miserable with better lighting, from the cobwebs hanging from the ceiling to the tattered rug in the hall.

There was a notebook on a table next to the couch. She opened it to the first page.

Seth had been practicing his handwriting. His name was written on it in a dozen different sizes, with the occasional backwards letter. Seth and Abel had been kept out of school for most of their childhoods. He'd had to teach himself to read and write.

She closed the notebook again.

A breeze fluttered through the curtains, and the faint smell of flowers reached her. It smelled like roses.

Had there been any roses outside?

"Weird," Rylie muttered, following the faint smell of flowers outside.

It was the wrong time of year for anything to be blossoming. The only thing growing in the flower beds were weeds and grass.

Rylie circled around the back.

There was that flower smell again. It caught her nose, and she turned to look for the source in the trees.

And then she heard it—the crunch of feet on fallen leaves.

Rylie turned too late.

Something whistled through the air and connected with the back of her skull. Stars flashed in her periphery. Her vision faded at the edges.

She hit the ground. Dirt impacted her cheek and nose.

Her head swam, and Pagan's shuffling footsteps sounded distorted, as though she heard it through rippling water.

Rylie was stunned, but the wolf wasn't.

Move.

She rolled onto her side. An instant later, a silver knife whistled through the air and plunged into the dirt where she had been laying.

Pagan jerked it free of the ground.

Rylie turned inward, focusing on her wolf. *Help me!*

Something buried deep in the wolf's instincts recognized Pagan's black irises, the pale skin, the sour smell.

The demon swung the knife again. The wolf lifted Rylie's forearm to protect her face, and Pagan's wrist struck her on the elbow.

Rylie lifted her feet, planted them in Pagan's stomach, and kicked.

Her attacker soared through the air. Struck the tree with a cry. Dry leaves showered around them.

Rylie rolled onto all fours, and her hands were bloody. It wasn't an injury—her fingernails had fallen out when she wasn't paying attention. They had already been replaced by fresh, glistening claws.

Pagan lunged for her, and Rylie swiped. Her claws raked through the air.

The demon leaped out of the way just in time.

But the wolf anticipated that, just as it anticipated that she would attack again from the left. Her eyes and the tension in her muscles gave her away.

Rylie drove her elbow into Pagan and threw her to the ground.

The demon didn't attempt another attack. Her eyes focused on something in the distance.

"Cain! Help!" Pagan shouted.

Cain?

Rylie turned. But before she could see who was attacking, something struck the back of her skull, in the same tender spot that Pagan had beaten earlier.

She blacked out before she hit the ground.

Seth wandered through the house alone, gazing at everything his family had left behind.

The front bedroom had belonged to Abel, and there were no toys in it—even as a child, he had been more interested in knives and handguns. His bed had plain sheets. The walls were bare.

How many hours had the brothers spent in that room, making up stories and wrestling on the floor? He couldn't begin to count them.

The next bedroom had belonged to Seth. It was barely bigger than a closet, but it had been his kingdom. The only place he was safe when his parents argued.

He didn't open the door to look inside.

Seth went to his mom's bedroom and stood in the doorway.

Once, Eleanor had thrown him over that chair in the corner and whipped him when he made a mistake.

Then there was the time she punched a hole in the wall when she was aiming for his head. It used to be hidden by a desk, but that piece of furniture was gone now. The hole remained.

Her straightening iron was on the table under the window—he didn't even want to remember what she had done with that.

Yet those were still the friendliest features of the room.

Eleanor had been obsessed with what she called The Process: a methodical way of identifying werewolves so that she could kill them as soon as they changed. But she had gotten The Process from his dad. And he had been the master of it.

Their bedroom walls were covered in corkboard, and every inch was layered in maps, handwritten notes, news articles, and receipts. It seemed his dad had been hunting an entire pack of werewolves the last time he had been in the house—probably the pack that eventually killed him.

It used to make him so angry to think about what the werewolves had done to his dad. To his family.

But now he saw the names and pictures of suspected werewolves in the pack, and it made him angry in an entirely different way. Each face belonged to a human, not a monster. A brother, a mother, a girlfriend, a son. Family.

No wonder they had killed his dad. He had been killing everyone they loved.

Something green and square under the bed caught his eye. Seth dropped to his knees and pulled it out. It was a metal case with a padlock, and a label affixed to the lid that said, "Eleanor."

His mother had threatened him every time he approached the lockbox as a child, like it was filled with dangerous explosives. But there was no way she had been worrying about his safety. That wasn't her style.

She must have been hiding something from him.

Seth found a hammer in his dad's toolbox and broke the lock open.

He lifted the lid, and the smell of a hundred memories swept over him. Some herbs, her favorite lotion, mothballs. There was a switchblade in the box, a locket with some hair in it, and a diary.

He remembered his mom writing in a journal frequently when he was young. Her entries had served to catalog their most recent kills; she hadn't considered them private or tried to lock them away. What made that diary different?

He sat with his back against the wall to read it.

The dates on the entries were old—well before he was born. Seth skimmed the early entries. She had grown up in the city, and it talked a lot about her time working at a diner. She wrote a lot about one particular customer. A handsome, unnamed man. Was that where she had met Seth's dad?

Aden. She called him Aden.

Seth read on in sick fascination as a teenage Eleanor wrote about her developing relationship with Aden. They started dating. Then they started sleeping together. She shared way too much information about that—he skipped those parts.

And then she wrote about discovering that Aden was a werewolf.

Seth stared at his mom's handwriting.

His mother had dated a werewolf before she married a werewolf hunter?

He realized that the house was awfully quiet. Rylie hadn't followed him back into the bedrooms, and it had been several minutes since he heard from her.

"Rylie?" he called.

No response.

He got to his feet and took the diary with him as he searched the house. The kitchen and living room stood empty.

Seth stepped out the back door. "Rylie?" he called. "I think I've found something."

The air was still and silent in the clearing behind his dad's house. Leaves drifted from the skeletal branches overhead.

He checked around the side of the house, but the Chevelle was where they parked it, and none of their bags were missing.

Where could Rylie have gone?

A soft, feminine voice called to him from the woods. "Seth?"

"Rylie?" he responded, following the sounds into the trees.

Someone was standing in the shadows behind an oak, but it wasn't his girlfriend. It was a tall, muscular woman shrouded in filmy black material. Her curls hung loose around her shoulders.

The skin on her leg was ragged below the knee, baring ankle bone. It didn't seem to hurt. In fact, she smiled.

Eleanor reached out a hand with fleshless fingertips to beckon to Seth.

"Hello, son."

PART THREE

Moon of the Terrible

ONE

The Challenger

Abel was pretty sure that Levi had a death wish.

The guy was obnoxious on his best days, but the day that the pack moved into the California sanctuary was definitely not his best day. In fact, it might as well have been the worst since Abel came to know Levi—and he had seen some pretty terrible days.

It started first thing in the morning.

"Whoa, where are you going?" Levi asked, grabbing Abel's shoulder when he moved to carry his bag into the west wing of the sanctuary.

Abel glared at the hand on his arm and swallowed back a growl. Scott was talking to a girl with a pixie cut at the end of the hall. He seriously disapproved of pack members fighting, and Abel tried not to piss off the man in charge.

"I'm going to my room," Abel said.

Levi stepped in front of him. "That's not your bedroom."

Abel looked at the door in the hallway. They all looked the same: heavy iron painted to a friendly shade of white. But his bedroom in particular was at the end of the hall. There was no mistaking it for another.

"This is always my bedroom when I stay here," Abel said. "And you better get that hand off of me if you want to keep it."

Levi straightened his spine. He wasn't nearly tall enough to intimidate Abel, but that didn't mean he wouldn't try. "I rearranged the rooms."

Abel ignored him and shoved the door open.

His bed was covered in an unfamiliar comforter. Posters of soccer players were plastered on every inch of wall, and those were familiar—Abel had tolerated having them in his shared bedroom at the other sanctuary for months, too.

"I needed a room close to my dad's office," Levi said. "You're in the east wing now." The smug, petulant voice was almost enough to make Abel clock him.

"On whose authority?"

Levi glared. "Mine."

Abel jabbed a finger at the adjacent bedroom. "That's Rylie's room. Remember Rylie? The Alpha? That's where she stays, and I'm supposed to be next to her. Did you move her, too?"

"The Alpha's room is intact, but you're not the Alpha. I can move you around all I want." He mimicked Abel's threatening tone. "Now you better get out of *my* room if you want to have any room at all."

Abel pulled his fist back to punch that look off of Levi's face.

Scott's voice cut through the hall. "Hey!" He stepped away from the girl to join them and Abel dropped his hand. He clenched his fist so hard that the knuckles popped. "Is there a problem?"

"Nope," Levi said.

He smiled and shut his door.

The day didn't improve after that.

There was an organization chart posted in the kitchen. Abel took a look over the heads of the werewolves clustering around it.

He had been moved to the smallest bedroom in the back corner of the east wing. The window faced the brick wall bordering the property. The bedrooms hadn't been renovated as recently as those on the west wing, either; the paint was a dull shade of seventies yellow, and there were weird stains on the carpet.

He tracked down Scott, who was helping move Eldon and his wife into their bedroom. *They* were in the west wing.

"I'm not sleeping out there," Abel said.

Scott didn't even look at him. "We'll talk about this later. The Union's trying to find a place for their generator. Can you go help them?"

He gritted his teeth and obeyed.

But Levi had already beaten him to the Union's RVs.

"What are you doing here, Abel?" Levi asked, stepping away from Yasir and the generator.

Abel counted to ten before replying. Seth was always encouraging him to do that when he was about to lose his temper, but it only seemed to make him angrier. "I'm helping the Union."

"I've got it under control. We don't need you. Why don't you go pine over your brother's girlfriend some more?"

Levi marched away before Abel could think of a response.

Yeah. Levi *definitely* had a death wish.

It only got worse over the course of the night. The kid was everywhere: in the kitchen helping Stephanie Whyte prepare dinner; in the dining room when the pack gathered to eat; and on the lawn when everybody moved outside to listen to Yasir explain their defensive strategies.

But Scott was there, too. Which meant that Abel couldn't respond the way he *really* wanted.

God, he missed the ranch.

He found himself wandering through the back fields of the sanctuary, alone in the cold night. The quiet was heavy. His only companion as he walked was the sound of his feet on the grass, and the occasional rustle of dried leaves.

Abel had never been at the Whyte sanctuary without Rylie before. Now he had only been there for twelve hours, and he already didn't like it.

The walk didn't improve anything. Not his mood or his situation.

He angled his path to head back to the house, hoping that he could sneak into the east wing without running into Levi again.

No such luck.

The pack was still talking outside when Abel returned. Levi spotted him and jogged across the grass to catch him, nose pink with cold. "I need you to take the early morning watch. We're going to work with the Union on defense, and rotate people around the walls to watch for hunters. You start at two in the morning."

It was already approaching midnight. Abel wouldn't even be able to sleep before his shift.

He lowered his voice to a growl that the rest of the pack wouldn't be able to hear. "What do you think you're doing? Rearranging rooms? Coordinating with the Union? Ordering the pack around? Ordering *me* around?" The last one was easily Levi's worst crime.

"I'm taking charge of my pack. Is that a problem?"

Abel laughed disbelievingly. "Your pack? *Your* pack?"

"Do you see anyone else here that can make that claim?" Levi asked, spreading his hands wide.

"Just because Rylie isn't here—"

"The position is always up for grabs. It belongs to whoever can take it." Levi turned to leave. "Have fun with the two o'clock shift. Howl if you get shot again."

Abel fisted Levi's shirt and almost jerked him off of his feet.

"Levi!" Scott called from the door.

Reluctantly, Abel dropped him. Levi smoothed his hands down his sweater instead of leaving immediately. "It takes more than being a bully to be Alpha," he said. "You've got to be a *leader*. Whether or not Rylie is here, she's no leader. And neither are you."

He turned on his heel and went inside.

Abel's mood was blacker than the night of a new moon. His nerves thrummed with tension, and he was pretty sure he would bite anyone that tried to mess with him on the way back to his new bedroom. Fortunately, there was only one other occupied bedroom in the east wing. The lights were on when Abel approached.

He spotted the room's inhabitant as she headed out the door with a towel under her arm and toothbrush in hand. It was the girl with the pixie cut that Scott had been talking to earlier.

She smiled brightly when she saw him. "Hi there! Are you in exile, too?" Abel only gave her a sideways look. She waved toward the west wing with her toothbrush. "All of the other rooms are filled, so Levi moved me out here. I think he doesn't like me because I accidentally trashed his computer." She stuck out her free hand. "I'm Crystal." She pronounced it with an emphasis on the second syllable.

Abel didn't take her hand. His flat response only seemed to make her smile brighter.

"You must be Abel. I've heard about you." She shrugged one shoulder. "Anyone who doesn't get along with Levi is cool with me. The enemy of my enemy... right? And now we're practically roommates. We can be friends."

"I don't need any friends."

The only friend he cared about was running across the country with his brother. Not a cheerful thought. He turned to leave Crystal, but footsteps pounded up the hallway.

Bekah appeared, out of breath and pale. "Oh, thank God you're here, Abel."

It was never a good sign when Bekah panicked. That could have meant anything—from "someone didn't rinse off their dishes" to "Scott had a heart attack and died." Either one would have her in a fit for days. "What's up?"

She grimaced. "Seth and Rylie are missing."

TWO

Elopement

"What do you mean, missing?" Abel asked.

He stood in the center of Scott Whyte's office, which was pretty much what he expected the office of a high priest to look like—pentagrams, brass tools, and old books everywhere. But he was barely aware of the weird gadgets on the shelves. He didn't even care that Levi was watching silently from the chairs by the bookshelf.

"Seth and Rylie haven't contacted us since yesterday," Bekah said as she paced by the door. "Seth had specific instructions to contact me every eight hours so that we would know immediately if something has gone wrong."

Abel crossed his arms. "And it's been twenty-four hours."

"Well… only eighteen. But he's missed two check-ins!"

Scott sat behind his desk, fingers steepled in front of his face. He was a big guy, but even his girth was dwarfed by his executive leather chair. The contents of his desk had changed recently—he had more animal skulls and grisgris and fewer herbs. "Worrying, but I'm not sure that's worth panic."

"Yeah," Abel said. "You don't think they're just somewhere without any reception? They were driving out to the big freakin' empty. There's no cell towers on the north end of the state."

"But I gave him a satellite phone like this one." Bekah pulled a phone out of her pocket. It was bulkier and uglier than most cell phones.

Scott's eyes widened. "Is that…?"

She gave a sheepish smile. "Yeah. This one is Levi's. I gave Seth mine. If he was okay, he should be able to reach me from the top of the Andes. Seth is responsible—he would never miss a call."

"Give it another eight hours," Abel said.

"They could be in serious trouble!"

Scott opened his mouth to respond, but the phone rang first. Seth's name popped up on the screen.

"See?" Abel said, trying to hide his relief. "God, Bekah. You're like some preteen girl. 'Oh no, I haven't heard from my boyfriend in eighteen hours, I think we're breaking up.' Give me a break."

Bekah shot him a look, and Scott held his hand out for the phone. She passed it over. "Seth. What's going on?"

The responding voice was tinny and quiet, but Abel's sensitive ears picked it up anyway. "Scott? Hi. Sorry I didn't call you earlier."

"You had us worried. What's going on?"

"I just got distracted."

A long pause. Scott frowned and turned his chair to face the window. A few pack members were playing football outside, enjoying the cool California night. "And...? What have you found?"

"Nothing. But I wanted to tell you goodbye," Seth said. "Rylie and I aren't coming back."

"*What?*" Abel asked, stalking around the chair. He reached for the phone, but Scott held up a hand to stop him.

"I don't understand, Seth," Scott said in a measured, psychiatrist kind of voice.

"We're getting married. We're going to move away and start our family. We don't want to be involved with the pack anymore." Another long pause. "I hope you can respect our wishes."

"But—"

"Tell Abel that I love him," Seth said.

And then he hung up.

Scott stared at the phone in his hand as Seth's name blinked and vanished from the screen.

"Nice," Levi said. "Good leadership skills." Bekah slapped his arm.

"Something is wrong," Abel said, ignoring the twins.

Scott turned his chair around again. "Rylie and Seth are both adults now. They're entitled to make their own decisions."

Abel shook his head. "No. You don't get it. *Something is wrong.*"

"I can see why you think that Rylie getting married is wrong, but that doesn't mean you have to freak out about it," Levi said.

He gritted his teeth. "I know my brother. I know when something's off. Seth never, *ever* says that he loves me." *And Rylie wouldn't run off to get married without warning.*

"Well." Scott pushed his chair back and stood. "It's a lot to think about. Maybe we should—"

"Get a search party together," Abel said. "We can track them down."

"I don't think they want to be found," Bekah said. She had a dreamy look in her eyes.

"Fine. I'll go alone." Abel turned to leave the office.

"Stop right there," Scott said sharply. "We need you here. You're an integral part of the pack." When that didn't stop Abel, he went on to add, "I understand you're angry and dismayed—I would be too, but it's late. Why don't you at least think about it for the night?"

He stopped with one hand on the doorknob. His knuckles were pale from gripping it too hard.

Think about it for the night? When for all he knew, Rylie could be getting married the next morning?

Abel flung the door open and left.

Many miles away, Seth turned off the satellite phone, and a gray-skinned hand snatched it out of his fingers before he could react.

Eleanor pocketed the device and stepped back. "Good boy. Did it sound like they believed you?"

"Probably," Seth said dully.

She laughed. She seriously *laughed*.

Seth tugged on his wrist experimentally. His captors had left one arm free so that he could use the phone, but his other was shackled. The chain looped through a hook on the wall and connected to Rylie's wrist on the other end. She was still unconscious and didn't stir at the motion.

The cell was better than being stuck in the crawlspace beneath a mobile home, which was what Eleanor had done one of the last times she held Seth captive. It was a broad, dusty room, like someone had dug into the dirt with a shovel. Roots jutted out of the crumbling walls. But there was a solid base of rock behind him, reinforced with cement bricks, and that was what Seth and Rylie had been tethered to.

It was almost laughable to think that his mother had captured him often enough to compare the quality of the lodgings. Almost.

"Well," Seth said. "This is fun."

Eleanor gave a thin-lipped smile. "We've been overdue for a family reunion." Her ankle was ragged, baring the bone underneath, but there was no blood. It didn't look like she was in any pain, either. The skin was dusty and dry.

"Are you a…?"

He wanted to ask her, *Are you a zombie?* But the words wouldn't seem to come out. It felt ridiculous to say it. And yet there she was, standing in front of him as angry and alive as she had ever been.

"Am I dead?" Eleanor prompted. Her hand smoothed down his cheek, and the skin was cool and spongy. The exposed bone of her fingertips scraped his chin. "What do you think, son?"

"Yes."

"Well, you're right. I'm dead." She straightened and spun with her arms out, like she was enjoying the sunshine in summer. "I'm dead!" Her voice echoed off of the cell.

So she wasn't just dead. She was probably crazy, too.

"How?" Seth asked.

"Consider it a temporary loan," Eleanor said. "There are ways to reanimate the dead, but it doesn't last long. It's... flawed." She parted the filmy dress over her stomach. There was a hole where her intestines should have been, and he could see all the way through to her spine. "But giving an old body new life? That's much more difficult. It requires a much more powerful sacrifice." She turned her black eyes on Rylie. "Like a werewolf."

Seth didn't even think before reacting. He leaned forward, straining against the chains.

"Don't touch her!"

"I can't believe you came out of my womb." Her hand trailed down her stomach, and for a horrifying moment, he thought that she was about to show him the aforementioned organ. But then she let the cloth fall closed again. "You and that waste of breath known as Abel."

There it was again—that all-too-familiar feeling of rejection, and being hated by his own mother, and the nauseating sense of defeat. He had thought he was done with that.

"Abel is twice the man you ever would have let him become," he said.

Eleanor sniffed. It whistled down her dry nasal cavity like wind through an abandoned house. "I don't need either of you now. I have a son. A *better* son."

The dread sank even deeper in Seth's gut.

"Cain," he said.

She nodded with a triumphant smile. "Cain."

"You had a son with Aden, didn't you? The werewolf?"

Her smile slipped. "How did you know about that?"

"I read your diary," Seth said.

Eleanor paced, and her feet left tracks in the dust. "Did you see the part where he started screwing another woman? Or the part where I tortured him with silver and ripped out his cheating heart?"

"I didn't read that far," Seth said. But he was not even a little bit surprised.

"He thought that he could love me and leave me." She gave a short sniff. "I guess he was right, in the end. But he left me a present first." She ran her hand over her hollow stomach again.

"So I have another brother."

"A better brother. A loyal brother. A brother who learned that I died, and harnessed the forces of Hell to bring me back. Not an idiot boy who ran off to college and is planning to marry a werewolf," Eleanor said.

The shock must have shown on his face, because she laughed riotously at him.

"Yes, I know! Cain is watching. Cain is *always* watching. You would be shocked at how much I know." Eleanor shoved her face close to his. "Cain is with the pack, even now. Before anyone realizes that he's there..."

She snapped her bony fingers. Seth jumped at the sharp sound of it.

"What are you going to do?" he asked, voice hoarse.

"First, Cain is going to kill the entire pack. Then he's going to come back, and he's going to kill your girlfriend to give me life." Eleanor smoothed her hand down Seth's cheek again. It was only then that he noticed the mark on the inside of her wrist: the tattoo of a bleeding apple. "As for you? We'll have to see."

A raspy, rattling cough rose out of her chest, and she hacked into her hand. Black fluid splattered on her fingers.

She backed away, stumbling a little.

Pagan must have been listening, because she immediately opened the door to the cell. She was wearing a hip holster weighed down by a handgun, like a cowgirl in black leather about to meet another shooter at high noon.

"Can I have fun with them?" Pagan asked, giving Eleanor a hand up the stairs. She wasn't too steady on her destroyed ankle.

All of Eleanor's mirth was suddenly gone. "Maybe later. I'm feeling a bit under the weather now."

The demon supported Eleanor under the elbow as she passed through the door.

"See you soon," Pagan said.

She blew a kiss at Seth and shut the door with a very solid *clang*.

THREE

Versus

Getting married. **Abel glared his** fury at the grassy fields, which were dotted with Union tents. It felt like he had swallowed a jagged boulder.

"Whatever," he muttered, stalking to one end of the patio, and then the other. "Forget them. Who cares? It's not like I wanted to be best man or something. Screw weddings."

So maybe they were eloping. He wouldn't put anything past Seth after that moronic proposal in some stupid cow field.

Abel never would have proposed in a field.

He growled at the train of his own thoughts. "What am I thinking? Shut *up*." Marriage was never an option for him in the first place.

But that didn't mean he wanted Rylie to marry Seth, either.

Levi strolled out of the kitchen, his hands stuffed in his pockets. "Talking to yourself is a sign of schizophrenia. You're at the age where that starts kicking in. Maybe you should talk to my dad about it."

Abel fumed in silence. His muscles vibrated with tension.

Don't hit him. Don't hit him.

But Levi kept talking.

"If Rylie bailed, I guess there *is* plenty of room for a new Alpha now. And I thought I was going to have to fight for it."

Don't hit him...

"You know what I'm going to do as soon as I become Alpha?"

"No, but I bet you're going to tell me," Abel said through clenched teeth.

Levi strolled over to him at the edge of the patio. His golden eyes were gleaming. "I'm going to get rid of you. That's what I'm going to do. You're like a poison in the pack. And I'm going to excise that poison."

Abel's fists clenched.

He glanced in the kitchen. Empty. He looked out at the grassy property. Also empty. Everyone was inside their tents for the moment.

No witnesses.

He hauled back and punched Levi across the face.

After wanting to do it for hours—actually, for months—all of the energy captive in his muscles was unleashed in a single blow. Levi was flung backwards off of the porch. He sprawled on the grass.

Abel stalked toward the other man, grabbed his shirt, and lifted him off of the ground.

"I am sick of listening to you talk," he growled, preparing to throw Levi.

There was commotion in the house. A door opening.

"Wait! Stop!" Bekah shouted.

Levi used the distraction to pull the silver pentacle out of his shirt. It was enchanted to keep from hurting him, and let him transform between moons. But Abel had no protection from it.

Levi rammed the silver pentacle into his face. Abel roared and dropped him, twisting away from the burn.

The sting of silver was even more sickening when he was still recovering from the recent gunshot wound. It made his ears ring and his eyes blur.

A fist appeared in his vision the instant before it struck.

Levi punched Abel in the face, and when he staggered, Levi struck him again in the gut. He doubled over as all of the breath rushed out of him.

He used his momentum to pile-drive into Levi, sending them both to the ground.

"Stop it!" Bekah cried.

It was more of a wrestle than an actual boxing match, but Levi fought dirty, jabbing his fingers into Abel's face and biting down on whatever limbs he could reach. He was full of jabbing elbows and clawed fingers.

The fight made Abel's wolf side wake up. He growled as he fought back, snapping his teeth and fighting to stay on top.

Levi's hands closed on his throat and squeezed.

He was already short on breath. Black fuzz crossed Abel's vision.

It took all of his strength to flip Levi onto his back, pin him down with his knees, and rip the hands off of his neck. Abel roared as he punched one more time—the *last* time.

He snapped Levi's head to the side so hard that something snapped.

Blood trickled out of Levi's nose and down his lip.

He didn't try to fight back. His eyes were dazed and unfocused.

Abel's wolf was satisfied.

"What did you *do?*" Bekah shrieked, grabbing his arm and pulling him off of Levi.

"He started it," Abel said.

"Oh my God!"

She dropped beside her twin brother and shook him. "Levi? Can you hear me? Are you okay?"

Abel glowered at Levi's semi-conscious form. "You don't have what it takes to be Alpha, asshole. Think about that next time you pick a fight with someone who's twice your size and twice as mean."

"You didn't have to do that," Bekah said. There were tears in her eyes.

"I know where I'm not wanted," Abel said. "When Levi stops seeing stars, tell him he can have what he wants. I'm gone. I'm not sticking around wherever he is."

"Where are you going?" she called after him as he strode into the kitchen.

"I'm going to find Rylie," Abel said. "And I'm going to bring the *real* Alpha back to take care of her pack."

Abel randomly selected a set of car keys from the drawer in the kitchen and then headed out to the vehicles parked on the lawn.

A group of people was already waiting for him: Trevin, one of the werewolves from the Gresham sanctuary, the girl with the pixie cut, and Vanthe. "Took you long enough," Trevin said.

Abel frowned. "What are you guys doing here?"

"We heard that Seth and Rylie are in trouble, and that you're going to go save them. Trevin and I thought you might want some backup." Vanthe puffed up his chest, as if to show off how impressive his stature could be. He was pretty tall, but he wasn't very muscular.

Well, it *was* going to be a long drive. Company wouldn't hurt. And it would go a lot faster if they could take shifts behind the wheel.

"Whatever," Abel said, pressing the "unlock" button on the keychain dongle. The headlights on one of the vans flashed. "What about you? What do you want?" He addressed the girl with the pixie cut directly. What was her name? Crystal? She already had a backpack on one shoulder.

"Levi's already made it pretty clear that I'm not wanted here," she said with a shrug. "Us east wingers have to stick together, right?"

"No," Abel said.

She smiled brightly. "So where are we going?"

"Hunting." He popped the trunk on the van and threw his bag inside. "There's a good chance we're going to come across bad guys. People will die."

It didn't faze Vanthe at all, but Crystal missed a step as she approached the van.

After a moment, she threw her bag in, too.

"Sounds like my kind of party," she said, just a little less brightly than before. "Let's go!"

FOUR

Pagan Poetry

Being held captive was pretty boring, so Seth was glad that Rylie reached consciousness shortly after Eleanor left. She groaned and winced as she sat up, but as soon as she heard the rattle of chains, her eyes flew open.

"Pagan!" she cried, as if suddenly remembering what had happened to her. She pulled against her bindings hard enough to jerk Seth to the side.

"Whoa, hang on!"

Her eyes traveled up the chain to where it connected with him. "Seth? What's going on? Where are we?"

He sighed, tugging on his shackle to give him a little slack. "We're in a basement or something. I don't know. We've been kidnapped."

"Kidnapped? Seriously?"

"Yeah."

She bumped her head back against the wall and stared at the dirt ceiling. She looked exasperated more than worried. "How long have we been down here? Scott's going to notice when we don't check in and send someone to find us, right?"

"Actually... they forced me to call Scott and tell him that we were eloping."

"Like, marriage elopement?" Rylie smothered her face with a hand. "Oh God. Abel." She wiped her hand down her face. There was still no worry in her eyes, and it made Seth love her just a little bit more. "You know, I bet none of my friends from high school have ever been kidnapped. But this is, like, the third time you've been taken."

"I know." Seth grinned. "At least I have really attractive company this time."

She rolled her eyes, but crawled along the wall to his side. "I don't feel well. I think I'm going to barf."

Seth rubbed a hand over her shoulders. "They must have hit you pretty hard. I'm sorry. It takes a lot to knock out an Alpha werewolf."

Rylie wiggled under his arm and pressed herself to his side. He squeezed her tight.

"Who is 'they,' anyway?" she asked. She started twisting the links between her hands, muscles straining as she fought to break them. The metal was too thick, even for a werewolf.

"Cain and all of his... I guess you'd call them followers," Seth said. "I only know about two of them—Pagan and Stripes, who's dead now—but I think there are probably more."

"Wait a second. You met Cain? Who is it? What does he look like?"

"It's kind of a long story," he said. "I haven't *met* Cain yet. But I know who he is." Rylie gazed up at him, and her big, golden eyes were so imploring. He sighed. "I guess I have another brother. A half-brother. My mom dated a werewolf before she married my dad."

"So Cain is a werewolf," Rylie said.

"Yeah. I guess so. But it's not just that—it seems like Cain is some kind of... a necromancer?"

Her brow knitted. "What's that?"

Here it comes. He took a deep breath. "It's a kind of witch. A really rare kind of witch. They can bring people back from the dead."

Seth didn't have to say anything else. Rylie's face darkened like a storm blocking the sun. The worry that had been absent earlier appeared, along with fear—and anger.

"Eleanor," she said. The words rippled out of her, already sounding inhuman and guttural.

"Wait! Don't shift!"

She peeled back her lips to bare her teeth. Her gums were dotted with crimson. Rylie grunted, and squeezed her eyes shut. "But I can break these chains if I change—and we can get out of here."

"That's what they want you to do. They want to sacrifice a werewolf. You have to stay human," Seth said.

Her eyes popped open. "Sacrifice?"

"Eleanor's a zombie or something. She thinks that sacrificing a werewolf will give her life again."

Rylie's lip dropped over her teeth again. "But I'm helpless if I can't change," she said.

"Not helpless," Seth said, taking her hand. She gripped it so hard that his bones creaked. "I'm here. I'm not going to let anybody hurt you."

She smiled weakly, licking away the blood that had emerged from her loosening gums. "I don't know if you noticed, but we're chained together. If I can't break these shackles, then neither can you. You're as helpless against Eleanor, Cain, and Pagan as I am."

The door at the top of the stairs squealed open, and Pagan stepped in. Her arm was still bandaged from Rylie's attack, but she looked otherwise unharmed.

"Did I hear the dulcet tones of my name being taken in vain?" she asked, shutting the door behind her. She wore a black bustier and boots that had six inch heels and laces all the way up to her knees. "Please, tell me what you're discussing. I love girl talk."

"I was just talking about how we're going to break free and escape in a few minutes," Seth said. He lifted his wrist. "Want to help me by opening the shackle?"

Pagan grinned. "Just like how you helped me escape your cellar by having a couple of Union guys torture me with a car battery?"

"You shot my brother."

She rolled her eyes. "Yeah, but he didn't die or anything."

"And neither did you," Seth said.

"That was your mistake." Pagan drew a silver knife from behind her back. "So here we are! Eleanor wants to torture you two, but she's not feeling her best. So she asked me to see what I could do about getting our wolfy friend here to Hulk out. Cain's busy, so we have a few days before he gets back. We can take our time. Fun, right?"

"I could just kill you," Rylie suggested, her voice gravelly.

"No, no, don't change yet. I haven't even gotten started yet."

Pagan drew a few more silver weapons from various places on her body—knives out of her boots, a stiletto from her bustier, silver pins from her hair. Seth was impressed that she could hide that much in such a tight outfit.

"Don't get angry," he whispered to Rylie. "She feeds on anger and aggression. It'll only make her stronger. Just… stay calm."

It was like telling a tornado to chill out. Rylie was a ball of tension and fury under his arm.

Pagan hummed happily as she laid everything out. She had a dozen silver objects—enough to poison an entire pack of werewolves.

She cooed over each of the knives, like they were something cute. "Oh my, this will do nicely. I bet I could get you to transform if I forced this one down your throat."

"What do I do?" Rylie asked Seth, barely moving her lips.

"Nothing. We can't do anything."

"That's the spirit," Pagan said.

But just because they couldn't fight didn't mean that Seth had to wait for the demon to torture them, either. He took a deep breath to settle his nerves. "What do you know about Eleanor and Cain?"

She crouched just out of Rylie's reach, resting her elbows on her knees. "I know that they pay my bills and keep me well-fed. Plus, they're going to let me torture you guys, which is—you know, total Christmas bonus here."

Pagan shrugged. "Money and blood. What else can a girl ask for?"

"Love," Rylie said.

Pagan rolled her eyes. "Please."

"Okay. If we can't appeal to your human side, maybe I can try your common sense," Seth said. "Eleanor used to be married to a kopis. A hunter. He specialized in werewolves, but they killed a couple of demons, too. If Eleanor comes back, she'll probably go back to her old ways."

"I don't know if you've noticed, kid, but I'm kind of hard to kill," Pagan said.

"So you want to ally yourself with someone who doesn't care about you? At all?"

"I'm a demon. It's how we roll. But please, do keep trying to talk me out of doing terrible things with your adorable hero talk—it's sweet. And while you do that, I'm going to get busy encouraging the wolf to come out and play with me."

Pagan trailed her fingers over the pins and knives, like she was trying to decide which one she wanted to use first.

Rylie growled, eyes blazing with anger as her nostrils flared. "Touch me, and I'll bite you. I don't need a wolf's mouth to rip your face off."

"No... we aren't going to use those on you yet, blondie," Pagan said. "I think I have a funner idea of how to get you to change."

She grabbed Seth's hand, clenched one of his fingers in her fist, and snapped the bone.

FIVE

Rest Stop

Abel hadn't bothered to spend time getting to know the other werewolves at the sanctuary. Going on an impromptu road trip with three of them changed that—but not in a good way.

Crystal insisted on taking a break at every rest stop they passed so that she could use the bathroom. Trevin liked to sing along with the radio—and not very well. And Vanthe always drove like he was trying to escape the law. Which they would be soon, if Abel let him continue driving about twenty over the speed limit.

It was the perfect storm of annoying behavior. If he had to listen to Trevin's off-key rendition of one more pop song, Abel was going to dig his eardrums out with a spork.

By the time they stopped at a gas station in Utah, Abel started entertaining fantasies of abandoning the other werewolves. How fast could he load up the tank, jump behind the wheel, and drive away? He eyeballed the rising numbers on the pump.

Unfortunately, Crystal came out before he had even finished filling the tank. It had started to snow, but like most werewolves, she didn't seem to care. She was wearing cutoff shorts, a midriff shirt, and drinking from a soda cup that rattled with ice.

"You drinking another one of those?" he asked. It was already her third one that day. No wonder they kept having to stop for the bathroom.

"I can't sleep in the van, and I'm tired," she said. "The caffeine helps."

Abel grunted. The pump clicked—tank full. He jiggled the nozzle and returned it to the hook.

"Where are the guys?" he asked.

Crystal shrugged. "Buying nachos or something. So what's with you and the Alpha?"

The speedy change in subjects almost gave him whiplash. "What?"

"Rylie," Crystal said. "You've got to be pretty good friends, if you're willing to drop everything and drive cross-country to find her."

He narrowed his eyes at her.

Friends? Did friends slam each other into walls and share the hottest kiss Abel had ever experienced? Did friends lay awake at night, thinking about what Rylie was doing in the room beside his, and wondering how she would react if he knocked on her door? Did it hurt like hell when *friends* were running off to marry other people—like his brother?

Resisting the urge to tell Crystal where she could shove her questions, Abel stuck to saying, "Yeah. We're friends."

He threw open the driver's side door and got inside. Crystal got in the passenger's seat.

"Alpha," she said. "That's pretty epic."

He turned on the van and pulled it into a parking space beside the station. And then he turned up the radio to try to drown out Crystal.

She didn't seem to notice or care. "So... are you dating her?"

Abel's hands tightened on the steering wheel. There were a lot of ways he could describe their relationship. *Weird. Frustrating. Complicated.* But dating? "No."

She sighed. "Good."

The satisfaction in her voice made him give her a second look. Crystal was angled in the seat so that she could face him, long legs extended under the dashboard as she twirled a lock of short hair around her pinkie finger.

"What did you say?" he asked.

She giggled. "Sorry. That's weird, isn't it? That's definitely weird. Can I try again?"

His brow dropped low over his eyes. "Try what?"

"I was just wondering if you're single. That's all." And then she giggled again, and he realized that it was a nervous sound.

Abel's eyes skimmed up her legs to her flat stomach, the low neckline of her shirt, and the mounds of her breasts. It had been a *long* time since he had been acquainted with those parts of a woman.

When he finally reached her eyes, he knew that she had seen him looking. She didn't look like she minded. Not at all.

"To be honest, I didn't really come on the trip because Vanthe mentioned that something was wrong with our Alpha," Crystal said.

Yeah. He was starting to get that impression.

For a minute, he was tempted by the offer she made by jutting her chest forward and leaning on his armrest—*really* tempted. All those mornings waking up naked beside Rylie weren't easy on a man. And he had been on edge ever since that last night at the Gresham ranch.

Crystal was hot. No denying that.

But the longer he gazed at the swell of her hip and her fingers tracing a circle on her thigh, the more he thought about a girl with pale skin, and skinny legs, and a smile that was as unique and beautiful as an eclipse.

Abel didn't have enough time to formulate a response. The back door slid open, and Trevin climbed inside.

"Burrito?" he asked, shoving a wad of aluminum foil that smelled like beans and eggs between the seats by Abel's face.

Abel curled his lip. "No."

Vanthe got in behind Trevin and closed the door. "How much further?" he asked.

After more than a day on the road, Abel hadn't thought even once about what was waiting for him on the end of it: his childhood home. But they were drawing close enough that he couldn't avoid it anymore.

He reluctantly opened the map and took a look. "I think we'll be there in about four hours. Depends on how many times we stop after this."

"Great," Crystal said, sliding back to sit in her chair properly and buckling her seatbelt. She never took her eyes off of Abel. "I can't wait."

He didn't think she was talking about reaching the end of the line.

SIX

Bite of the Wolf

Rylie and Seth had been dating for three years, and she thought she knew everything about her boyfriend by that point.

She knew that he talked in his sleep. She knew that he liked chocolate ice cream better than vanilla, especially when mixed with nuts. She even knew the name of the second grade teacher he had for two weeks before Eleanor moved him out of town again.

But she hadn't known that he could withstand having every bone in his left hand broken without screaming.

Guess she learned something new every day.

Pagan heaved a sigh as she turned Seth's purpled, swollen arm in her hands, looking for a place that she hadn't damaged yet. Each of the joints was turned the wrong way. His skin was mottled with purple bruises.

Seth hadn't made a single noise. Not since he told Rylie, "Don't watch."

She tried to do as he told her—it would only be worse if she got mad and gave Pagan what she wanted. So Rylie had only peeked twice. She regretted both times.

He remained silent as Pagan pinched his shattered thumb. "Well, this is no fun," she said, dropping his arm. "You're not getting angry at all."

Seth breathed hard through his nose. His skin was ashen gray, almost the same color as Eleanor's. "My mom trained me to withstand torture," he said without a hint of emotion. "You can thank her for it."

Pagan snorted. "Great."

She slammed her fist into Seth's face, knocking his head into the wall.

Rylie wasn't expecting it, and the shock made her wolf instantly take control. "Stop it!"

"That's a little better," Pagan said. "That's more of the animal I want to see. I think we're warmed up now—don't you?"

Rylie strained on the end of the chain, her hand swiping uselessly through the air.

She roared her frustrations.

"Rylie!" Seth shouted, jerking on the chain that connected them. "Calm down!"

"Well, don't do *that*. Things are just getting good!" Pagan said.

The door at the top of the stairs opened. A brunette man wearing a black polo shirt gestured. "I need you, Pagan," he said.

Rylie was surprised enough to see someone new that she immediately stopped fighting. She sniffed the air. The man wasn't a werewolf—so not Cain.

"Hold onto that thought, blondie," Pagan said. "I'll be back in a few minutes."

She went upstairs, and the door shut behind her.

Only then did Seth groan.

Rylie sat at his side, careful not to touch his arm. "That was amazing," she whispered. "How did you do that?"

He cradled his hand against his chest. "You kidding? That was no worse than sitting through my anatomy finals."

It was probably meant to make her laugh, but the wolf didn't think it was funny. Seth's pheromones smelled sick and heavy—like wounded prey. She found herself staring at his broken fingers.

Her stomach growled. When was the last time she had eaten?

"Are you okay?" Seth asked, stirring her out of her reverie. She slumped against the wall.

"Yeah. I just... I don't know how to get out of this without changing."

"What if I picked the locks on our shackles?"

Seth held up two of the silver pins that Pagan had laid out with her other weapons. Somehow, he must have slipped it away from her stash while she was torturing him.

Rylie's relief was instant, dizzying—and brief. "But your fingers are broken."

"I'll walk you through it," he said. She pulled her sleeve over her hand and let him drop the pins into her palm.

Footsteps beat against the floor over their head. It sounded like Cain's people were pacing.

Rylie's heart sped as she peered closely at the lock.

"What do I do?" she asked.

He described the process to her—pushing each of the tumblers into place with the first pin, and then using the leverage of the second pin to turn the lock.

Rylie tried. She really did. But she couldn't even imagine the inside of the lock based on his descriptions, and she wasn't nimble enough with her shirt over her hand. Especially not when the wolf felt like it was still circling inside of her skull.

She slipped and burned her fingers on the silver. The pins dropped to the floor. Her eyes burned. "I can't do it. I can't, Seth."

He rested his unbroken fingers on top of hers. "There's one other thing we can try. It's crazy, but we're running low on options."

"What?"

"Bite me," Seth said.

Rylie stared at him. "*What?*"

"You heard what I said. Bite me."

The implications of his order dawned on her, and with it came a creeping feeling of dread.

She shook her head fervently. "No, Seth!"

"Look, think of it this way," he said. "If you can infect me, all my wounds will heal within hours. Best case scenario, I heal my hand, pick these locks, and I can worry about the werewolf thing after we escape. Worst case scenario…" He gripped her hand tightly in his. "Cain wants a werewolf for his ritual? He can have a werewolf. But he can't have you."

She pushed him away. "No. I'm not going to do it. I would rather change and take my chances against all of them with my teeth."

"If Abel can handle being a werewolf, so can I," he said.

Rylie gave a disbelieving laugh. "That's not what this is about, is it? Like, some new phase of your stupid competition with your brother? Who can be the bigger, badder wolf? No! It's not worth it, Seth!"

"This is about survival, and keeping you safe. I can't protect you if I don't heal this hand," he said, getting onto his knees in front of her as the chains rattled. "I'm sorry."

And then Seth slapped her.

Rylie's hand flew to the heated spot on her cheek where he had struck. She sucked in a hard gasp. "Hey!"

"Bite me," he said, and he hit her again on the opposite cheek.

Anger built inside of her, making the werewolf stir.

Was he insane? Suicidal?

"Be careful," she whispered, scooting back into the corner until she hit the wall and had nowhere else to go. "You're making me mad. The wolf—"

Seth's lips were stretched into a grimace, as if he was the one getting hit. "I know."

His third blow was a close-fisted strike. Pain exploded in Rylie's jaw. She sprawled on all fours.

"I'm not going to bite you," she said, but her voice was deeper than usual, and her teeth were aching.

One of her canines dropped out of her mouth.

"Don't transform," Seth warned her.

She tried to say, "Then stop hitting me!" But all that came out was a low whine. The bones in her face ached.

He shoved his wounded arm into her mouth.

The wolf *bit*.

Rylie shoved him back, but it was too late. The taste of blood had flooded her tongue, coppery and tangy and sickeningly delicious.

"No," she whispered.

She tried to wipe the blood off of her tongue—tried to take back what she had done. But it was too late. It didn't take much to spread lycanthropy.

Her mingled fear and horror was strong enough to drive away the wolf, leaving Rylie feeling emotionally raw and exposed.

She had bitten Seth.

He leaned against the wall with a groan, eyes squeezed shut. His forehead shone with sweat. "Now we just have to wait," he panted, cradling his bleeding arm.

Rylie gave up fighting it. She collapsed in the corner and began to sob.

SEVEN

Bloodhounds

When they were less than an hour from the house, Crystal insisted on making one more pit stop. Just an hour away, and she couldn't hold it.

"Women," Abel muttered, leaning on the hood of the van while he waited. Trevin had gone inside for another burrito, but Vanthe stuck around to keep him company.

"No kidding," Vanthe agreed. He pulled off his knitted cap, rubbed the coarse blond hair on his head, and then tugged it back on. "I heard Scott and Levi talking before we left. They said that Seth was going to your old house."

"Yeah. But my family's not there."

"Where are they? I mean, I know that Seth's your brother, but what about your mom? Dad?"

Abel stuffed his hands under his armpits to keep them warm, even though he hadn't really been cold a moment before. "They're both dead. Killed by werewolves."

Vanthe clicked his tongue against the back of his teeth. "That's rough."

Abel thought back on the day his mother died. Eleanor had stabbed him with a knife before she went down. She used his transformation into werewolf as her excuse for attacking, but Abel felt like she had been stabbing him in smaller, less-literal ways for years.

Constantly showing preference to Seth, her precious baby. Ignoring him. Being condescending and outright hateful.

And yet, until she fell from the cliff, some part of him had still hoped that they could be a family again someday. A very small part.

"I guess," he said, even though it had been too long since Vanthe spoke.

The other werewolf lifted an eyebrow. "You guess?"

Abel shrugged. He kicked a pile of snow. "Things were tough between us. We had problems, but… she was my mom." He gave a stiff shrug. "You know?"

"Yeah. I know."

They shared a long moment of understanding silence.

Trevin and Crystal came back out. She attracted stares in her micro-shorts and midriff in the falling snow. She grinned at Abel. He didn't smile back.

"All right," he said. "Let's go."

Abel's childhood home looked exactly the way he remembered it: run down, crappy, and miserable. He could smell Rylie and Seth as soon as he stepped out of the van, and he could also smell that they hadn't been there in days. It was enough to make him want to get back behind the wheel and leave immediately.

"What is this place?" Crystal asked, coming to stand beside him. He could feel the heat radiating off of her exposed skin.

He glared at the windows, the curtains, the dead garden, the surrounding trees. Everything was covered in an inch of snow. It reminded him of the time that Seth and Abel had built a snowman in the yard—and how Eleanor had told them they were morons for wasting the afternoon like that.

"Nowhere important," he said.

The snowfall would have muted the freshest trails, and he was suddenly a lot less optimistic about finding anything at the house. But Vanthe and Trevin circled around the back anyway, noses lifted to the air.

"I smell gunpowder and leather," Crystal said. "Who is that?"

Abel drifted behind her, making no effort to sniff around. "My brother."

Her nose wrinkled. "And I smell... perfume?"

That was weird. Rylie didn't wear perfume anymore.

Abel took a deep breath in.

Crystal was right. The smell of perfume drifted through the air, thick and flowery. "Guess a woman must have been here recently," he said with a frown.

"Hey!" Trevin called from the back of the house. "I think I found something!"

He was kneeling on a patch of snowy ground when Abel sprinted to his side. He was still eating the gigantic burrito from their last pit stop, and one of his cheeks bulged with a mouthful of beans and tortilla.

"What are you talking about?" Abel asked. He didn't see anything weird.

Trevin used his ungloved fingers to scoop up a handful of snow and expose the ground underneath. The soil was stained with dried blood.

Abel felt like the ground had vanished beneath his feet.

Was that Rylie's blood? Or an enemy's?

He muttered a curse and bent low to smell the earth. "Good find," he told Trevin. "Where's Vanthe?"

The other werewolf took another big bite of burrito and jerked his head toward the trees. "He ran off into the forest."

"Why?" Crystal asked.

"Maybe he needed to pee. I don't know." Trevin held his food toward her. "Hungry?"

She wrinkled her nose. "No."

Abel ignored them as he cleared away more snow to inspect the blood. It was a small splatter, so it must not have come from a very big injury. Trevin's nose was good for picking it up under all of the moisture.

But he did smell more of that sticky-sweet perfume.

"You picking that up?" Abel asked Trevin as he swallowed the last of his burrito and wadded the aluminum foil.

Both Trevin and Crystal sniffed.

"That perfume," she said.

It smelled familiar, but Abel couldn't place the odor—it was too faint to get a good read. He got to his feet and started following it.

"Stay with the van," he yelled over his shoulder. "I'll be back soon."

Abel left the other werewolves behind. As soon as he disappeared into the trees, he drew the handguns he had in the shoulder rig under his jacket. They felt satisfyingly solid in his hands.

The smell of perfume grew stronger as he delved deeper into the forest. The ground sloped toward a river.

An old cabin squatted on the opposite shore. It was backed up against a cliff, and surrounded by split-rail fencing that looked so old that Abel thought it might crumble at a touch. Icicles hung from the edges of the roof.

As far as Abel could see, it could have been just about any cabin in the woods. Maybe it belonged to hunters—normal hunters, of the "let's kill ducks and deer" persuasion.

Except that he smelled more blood.

And Rylie.

It was the faintest trace of her lemony scent, but it stirred his wolf in a way that no other smell could.

Was that his mate's blood? Had she been hurt?

He slid down the embankment and crouched on the bank of the river to get a closer look.

A man stepped around the side of the house. He wore a black jacket, black slacks, black shoes. Was he a Union hunter? A flare of red, the scent of tobacco—he was smoking a cigarette.

Someone called out. The man turned.

Pagan approached from the forest, armed with silver knives and a dainty pistol. The angular cut of her hair swayed every time she stepped over the snow.

They exchanged words, but Abel saw their lips moving, he didn't hear anything they said. His head was filled with white noise. His heart pounded in anticipation.

Pagan stepped through the front door of the cabin, disappearing into its shadowy depths. The man in black paced around the other side of the house.

His back was turned. He was alone.

Abel slipped around the boulders, stepped through a shallow portion of river, and crept up behind the man.

The smell of Rylie was stronger on the other bank, and now he could smell his brother, too. Stress and pain hormones poured out of a tiny window near the base of the cabin. There must have been a basement.

His quarry stopped, dropping his cigarette and kicking snow over the embers.

Abel jumped.

He hit the man from behind and wrapped his arms around him in a bear hug. Abel clapped a hand over his mouth.

The guard gave a muffled shout of surprise as he tried to twist free. Weak little human—Abel barely felt him struggle.

Abel smothered him with one huge hand, using his other arm to drag the man to the ground. The kicking grew weaker. His beating fists slowed. After a slow count of twenty, he wasn't moving at all, but Abel kept his hand in place for a few more seconds—just to make sure.

When he dropped the guard, Abel wasn't sure if he was alive or not. It didn't really matter.

Rylie was close. He could *feel* her.

He dragged the body behind the house and listened at one of the windows, trying to detect motion within. He heard quiet footsteps. Smelled a strange, musty odor that reminded him of cemeteries. There were three, maybe four, distinct people within the cabin.

He checked the ammunition in his guns—each had twelve rounds in the magazine, and one in the chamber. Twenty-six silver bullets. Two idiots that needed to be rescued. One Abel.

"Hang in there, Rylie," he muttered, creeping toward the front door.

And then he kicked it open.

EIGHT

The White Knight

After a few hours of waiting for something to happen, Rylie came to two conclusions: First, that boredom was just as effective a form of torture as breaking bones, and second, that there was no way in heck she was going to let Seth get sacrificed.

Her boyfriend slept against the wall, curled around his hand and breathing shallowly. Rylie wasn't sure exactly how much time had passed, but his bones were still broken. Did that mean he wasn't going to become a werewolf, or just that he wasn't going to heal until the moon?

Either way, he was unconscious from the pain, and he couldn't pick their locks. They were still trapped.

And they were running out of options.

Rylie tried to pick the lock again while Seth slept, but it was just as impossible on her second try. She also tried to squeeze her hand out of the iron ring, but it was snug against her skin. Transforming wouldn't help—the wolf's leg was too thick.

What did that leave? Tearing the wall down? Chewing her arm off?

A new man entered the room, carrying a bucket under his arm. He looked like the other guy Rylie had seen—muscular, frowning, and dangerous.

He emptied the bucket that Pagan had left behind for effluence into the one he was carrying. His mouth twisted as he poured.

It was hard to tell under the smell of the buckets—which was an odor that the wolf found interesting more than disgusting—but she thought she could smell metal on him. Iron, like the shackles.

Keys?

Seth had his side of the chain pulled tight as he slept. The Union guy was just out of arm's reach. But if she could get him to step over just two feet...

"Hey," Rylie said.

Her captor didn't respond.

"Can you wait a second?" she asked. "I have to pee, and I don't want it sitting in the bucket."

That got his attention. He looked disgusted. "You couldn't have done that *before* I came down? I'm not watching you take a piss."

"Well, it's not like I knew you were coming. Please? It smells awful."

He rolled his eyes, picked up the bucket, and stepped over to drop it at her side.

She moved fast.

Rylie's hand lashed out. She caught his pant leg and jerked him off of his feet. He shouted as he fell—hopefully not loud enough for Pagan to pick up on it.

Before she could think too much about it, Rylie slammed his head into the wall.

His eyes blanked. He went limp.

"Sorry," she whispered, feeling nauseous.

Rylie patted him down as footsteps creaked on the floorboards overhead.

There was something hard in the man's left pocket—a cell phone, and a pair of keys.

The basement door opened. Rylie was still fumbling with her shackle when Pagan stepped onto the landing. "Crap," Rylie breathed, jamming the key into the lock.

The demon shot down the stairs in a flash and appeared at Rylie's side.

The shackle fell off of her wrist, leaving a raw ring on her skin. "Hey!" Pagan shouted as Rylie rolled under her arms, just barely dodging her swiping grip.

She darted for the stairs.

A hand clamped on her ankle, and she lost balance. Rylie slammed face-first into the steps with a shriek.

She kicked Pagan in the face. "Get off of me!"

The first blow wasn't enough to make her let go, but the second was—especially since Rylie's heel caught her in the jaw and snapped her head back.

Pagan stumbled, and Rylie scrambled into the cabin above the basement.

The building only had one room: a kitchen, den, and sleeping area all rolled into one. An ancient freezer stood against one wall beside a beaten sofa. A TV stood under the window. Everything smelled of age and dust—and Eleanor.

But there was nobody else in sight. Rylie bolted for the front door, hoping to draw Pagan outside.

The demon was too fast.

Pagan got to the door first and blocked it with her body. She drew the gun and pressed it to Rylie's temple.

"Think your super-healing can fix a bullet in the brain, Alpha?" she asked.

Rylie never got a chance to respond.

The front door exploded behind Pagan. Fragments of wood scattered over the floor, and the handle bounced near Rylie's foot.

"Freeze," growled a familiar, masculine voice that made Rylie's heart stop beating.

Abel stood on the other side of the broken door, covered in dust and wearing anger like a cloak of vengeance. He held two handguns, each of them the size of small cannons.

Pagan didn't listen to him. She swung her gun around to aim at Rylie again.

Abel shot first.

His bullets smacked into the wall. Pagan was a blur as she leaped behind the table. The demon shoved the couch, hard enough to knock it into his legs and unbalance him.

Abel shot two more times—and with werewolf reflexes, his aim never dropped from the demon, even as she darted toward them for a final attack.

Those bullets took her straight in the chest. She stopped with a cry as though running into a wall.

But she didn't fall.

Her black eyes glimmered as she stared down at her chest. A smile grew on her lips. "Delicious," she said.

Rylie recalled what Seth had told her about megaira—that they fed on aggression, and it could make them heal anything. Abel was like a turkey dinner for the demon.

But Rylie wasn't driven by aggression. It was fear that made her jump onto Pagan's back before she could return fire at Abel.

The gun flew from her hand and skittered across the floor. Pagan didn't even blink. She drew another knife and swung.

Rylie ducked and caught her wrist, twisting it to the side at the last moment.

She struggled to wrestle the dagger out of Pagan's grip, but the demon's fingers were locked tight around the handle. There were no bones in her hand to break—she felt weirdly slippery, like she was made of oil barely contained in a thin film of flesh.

They ran into the freezer, and the force of the blow knocked it onto its side. The cabin shook with the force of it. The floor cracked.

Rylie scurried over the top, trying to put it between her and Pagan as she swiped the blade through the air again.

She tripped over the cord and fell.

Pagan grinned as she chopped at the nearest limb she could reach—Rylie's leg. But Rylie jerked her foot away just before it hit.

The knife sank into the power cord.

Something popped, and Pagan screamed. Sparks flared.

All the lights went out.

Rylie's eyes took a moment to adjust. Pagan's hand was still locked on the knife, eyes wide and mouth hanging open. Her skin was completely transparent. Her bones glowed underneath.

Abel stepped up behind her, put the gun to the back of her head, and fired.

Pagan didn't heal that one.

The demon slumped to the floor and fell on Rylie's legs. She gave a little cry of shock and clapped her hands over her mouth.

Abel hauled Rylie to her feet, gripping her shoulders in his massive hands.

She was still dazed, in shock—everything had happened too fast for her to process it.

Her shaking hands lifted to his face.

He felt so solid, so wonderfully *real*.

"You came for me," Rylie said. "Seth told you that we were getting married, and you came for me anyway."

"Are you stupid? Of course I came for you. You're my pack." His eyes glowed in the dim light. "I know when something is wrong."

"But… that one night…" She couldn't seem to get the words out. She swallowed hard.

"When we kissed," he prompted. He stared at her lips when he said it, as if he was thinking of a repeat performance, and she flushed with heat.

"Yeah. After… *that*… I thought you weren't going to want to have anything to do with me."

His fingers tightened painfully. It was a good kind of pain. Like being wrapped tight in armor. "You're not getting rid of me that easily."

"Whore," said an all-too-familiar voice. "Isn't perverting one of my sons enough for you?"

Abel crushed Rylie to his chest as he turned, like he could protect her with the sheer mass of his body.

Eleanor stood in the open doorway.

She wasn't looking good. Her skin had lost a lot of its rich, dark tone and become a rubbery shade of gray. Her lips were shriveled, her hands looked like the branches of trees in winter, and—were those bones sticking out of her fingertips?

Abel froze in shock.

"Mom?"

"Beast," she spat, advancing on them. One of her legs dragged behind her. "Idiot. Failure."

Rylie broke free of his grip and stood in front of Abel. It was a ridiculous attempt to shield him—he was a foot taller and twice as broad, and no physical barrier could spare him from the sting of the insults.

"Shut up," Rylie said.

Eleanor's black eyes glimmered. "Useless slut."

Rylie lunged.

In life, Eleanor had been fast enough to match any hunter, or any werewolf—but in death, her dusty muscles were slow. Rylie drove into Eleanor's gut. There was nothing there to stop her. Rylie's shoulder sank into her dress and hit bone.

They both crashed to the floor.

Death might have taken strength from Eleanor, but it seemed to have also taken away her ability to feel pain. She recovered from the shock instantly, seconds before Rylie.

Her brittle fingers closed around Rylie's throat and squeezed.

She was strong—so impossibly strong.

But Abel's fury was stronger.

He roared something incoherent and filled with pain, and his hands clamped down on Eleanor's arms like shackles. He ripped her free of Rylie's throat, wrenched his mother to her feet, and lifted her in the air. Dirty, bony feet kicked near Rylie's face.

Abel shook her. "Never again!"

"Let me go!" Eleanor shrieked, beating against him. "You stupid, hideous—"

Whatever else she had to say about Abel, Rylie never heard it. He carried her from the cabin and into the woods. Their yells echoed and multiplied, bouncing off the trees and filling the valley by the river.

Rylie scrambled to her feet and chased them outside.

Abel and Eleanor grappled by the river. He held her over the rushing water, fury blackening his features.

"Wait!" Rylie cried.

She could barely understand Abel through his responding growl. "I'm going to rip her head off."

"But then we might never know who Cain is!"

He shook his mother hard. She clawed at his forearms with her bony fingertips. "Who is Cain? Where can we find him?"

Eleanor spat in his face. There was no saliva in her mouth—black fluid splattered over her lips.

Rylie hung a few steps away from them, torn between letting Abel get the revenge he had deserved for years and trying to spare the only person that she knew had answers.

She was so distracted by the confrontation that she almost didn't hear it when someone approached from the forest.

"Abel!" barked a sharp voice.

Rylie turned.

The newest werewolf at the sanctuary, Vanthe, had sneaked up behind them. And he was holding someone by the throat—Seth.

Vanthe's arm was covered in shaggy fur, claws dug into the tender skin beneath Seth's jaw, and his eyes glowed silver. Not gold. *Silver.*

"Let Mom go," he said.

"No way," Rylie exclaimed. "That's not possible."

"Surprised?" Vanthe asked. She tried to make the mental adjustment—he was Cain, not Vanthe. And as soon as she thought the words, she started to see the similarity.

His skin wasn't as dark as Seth and Abel's, and his hair was a very rough, very curly blond. His werewolf dad must have been white. But he did share features with Eleanor: the curve of his lips, the shape of the eyebrows.

How hadn't she seen it earlier?

Abel was still holding Eleanor off of her feet, but his anger had turned to shock. He was speechless.

"I'm not *surprised*," Rylie said, which was true—she would have had to be thinking clearly to be surprised, and it felt like her ability to process rational thought had evaporated. "I really mean that it's not possible. Pagan called your name before she kidnapped me. You couldn't have been here and traveling to California at the same time."

He smirked, like the incongruity amused him. "I have a few tricks up my sleeve."

"Like necromancy?" Seth asked, and the claws tightened around his throat.

Instead of answering, Cain focused on Abel. "I told you to put her down."

For a moment, Rylie thought that Abel was going to ignore him—or that he would drop Eleanor in the water. Would he really sacrifice Seth like that? *Could* he?

"Abel," she whispered, heart pounding.

His eyes flicked to her. Pain crossed his features.

Slowly, he turned around and set his mother on the snow. She staggered to Cain's side. "Son," she said warmly, placing a hand on his shoulder. Her gaze chilled when she turned it on Seth. "My *only* son."

"Now drop Seth," Abel said.

"Fine," Cain said. "He's not the one that I want anyway.

He didn't drop Seth—he *threw* him.

Abel's reaction time was good. He just barely caught him before he slipped into the river.

But it meant that neither of them were close enough to Rylie to keep Cain from grabbing her.

His hand clamped tightly on her arm, and he jerked her into his grip. She felt the silver pinch of claws on her throat and gasped.

"You killed my mother," he hissed into her ear, tightening his hand as he took a deep sniff of the side of her face.

The claws bit into her jugular, and Rylie knew that there was nothing she could do. She couldn't change in time. Abel and Seth were running, but they wouldn't be fast enough.

She was about to have her throat ripped out.

But Cain froze as blood trickled down her neck. "Wait," he said, taking another smell of her. He turned his burning gaze on his brothers. "Wait!"

They froze.

"What are you doing?" Eleanor asked.

Cain released Rylie's throat and shoved her. She stumbled over the ground and spilled onto her side. Abel stepped over her, hiding her behind their protective wall of bodies.

But Eleanor and Cain didn't try to attack.

"What happens right here, right now—it doesn't really matter," Cain said, hooking his arm around his mother's shoulders. "I have men in the Union. As soon as I left, they will have seized the sanctuary. They've killed the impure so we can start over."

"The impure?" Seth asked. He was still pale and wavering on his feet.

"Those who were bitten instead of born. It's time for a change." Cain's eyes glowed silver. "And that change begins with you, Rylie. Congratulations."

With that confusing proclamation, he hugged Eleanor tight and ran from the woods.

He vanished in an instant.

NINE

Talking in Code

Trevin and Crystal were still waiting by the van when Rylie reached the top of the hill. Abel lagged a few feet behind, carrying Seth.

As soon as he set his brother down, he rounded on Trevin. "Show me your arms and chest," Abel ordered Trevin, eyes burning with fury. "Take off your shirt!"

"Whoa there," Trevin said, holding up his hands in a gesture of peace. "Did we miss something?"

"Vanthe is Cain," Rylie said.

Both of the werewolves looked genuinely shocked. And they smelled genuine, too—although Rylie didn't think that meant anything. She hadn't smelled Cain's lies either.

Trevin took off his sweater and showed them his skin. He didn't even blink when Abel checked his legs, too. There was no tattoo of a bleeding apple in sight.

Crystal was barely dressed, so she had nowhere to hide a tattoo. Rylie checked anyway.

They were both clean.

"We have to get back to California," Rylie said.

They called the Whyte sanctuary at the first gas station they reached, but nobody answered. "It doesn't necessarily mean anything," Trevin said when they set out again. Seth was unconscious again from the pain of his hand, so Trevin was driving as quickly as he could to the nearest hospital. "Maybe they're just busy."

"Fifty werewolves, a coven of witches, and the Union are all too busy to pick up a phone?" Rylie asked.

Even Crystal didn't laugh at that.

Seth was showing signs of shock, so the doctors checked him into the hospital for a few hours of observation. Rylie borrowed a phone and called the sanctuary again—still no response.

Which left Rylie nothing to do but talk to Abel.

She found him standing outside in the snow with that girl werewolf, Crystal. Rylie hung back under the hospital awning to watch them talk.

Crystal was leaning toward Abel and giggling, like he was saying the funniest things ever. She poured flirty pheromones into the air. But even without Rylie's sense of smell, she would have been able to tell that Crystal wanted him—and *bad*.

Rylie swallowed back a growl as her inner wolf surged.

Don't get jealous, she told herself.

Easier said than done.

Crystal pressed herself against Abel's side, and before Rylie could think about what she was doing, she strode across the parking lot.

"Hi," she said, interrupting them.

Crystal hugged his arm tighter. "Oh, Rylie! I didn't hear you coming!"

She gritted her teeth together. "Yeah, I bet you didn't."

Abel's glower shifted into a hint of a smile, like he thought her reaction was funny. "What do you want?" he asked.

"You," Rylie said. Crystal looked surprised, and Rylie realized what she had said. Her cheeks heated. "I mean, I want to talk to you. Pack stuff."

Abel glanced down at Crystal. "Catch you later?"

The girl disengaged. "Okay. Sounds good." Her cheeks dimpled when she smiled.

Rylie glared at Crystal as she walked away.

"Want to walk?" Abel asked.

She nodded, and they set out. They walked together in the silent, snowy night, shoulder-to-shoulder. There wasn't much town to walk through—the hospital was on the outer edges of the city, and they were soon on an empty highway.

Abel stopped and sat on the fence, one knee propped up on the railing.

"Why did they let me go?" Rylie asked.

He didn't look angry anymore. Instead, he looked worried. "I don't know. A new beginning. What's that even supposed to mean?"

Rylie had no answers. It wasn't like she had ever thought to prepare herself for "what to do when your zombie in-laws rise from the dead and attack."

"What do we do if he was right? If we get back to the California sanctuary, and everyone is..." Rylie bit her bottom lip. She didn't need to say what they were both thinking.

Abel's brow dropped low over his eyes. "We'll find Cain and kill him." The words fell flat in the night. Rylie shivered. "Don't worry about it. Not yet. We don't know that anything is wrong."

That didn't make her feel any better. She bit her bottom lip and ducked her head. "I think we need to talk about everything that's been going on. Not the Cain thing. The... other stuff."

Abel lifted his eyebrows. "Yeah. I think we do." He hooked a finger in the waistband of her jeans and dragged her to stand between his knees. He grabbed her hips, dug his fingers into her lower back, and leaned toward her neck.

She pushed his hands off. "Not like that."

He gave her a look that was way too innocent to be genuine. He had instantly flipped from his gloom to something a lot more... intent. "Like what?"

"Just because we kissed once doesn't mean we have a..." She flapped her hands in the air. "Relationship. I'm already in a relationship."

Abel didn't seem to be listening. He stood over her, so impossibly tall and broad that he filled her vision. She could barely breathe.

She went on, even though it was really hard to keep track of her train of thought.

"Werewolf packs have two Alphas. A man and a woman. I think that our wolves are just... drawn to each other. But that doesn't mean..."

Abel's hand pressed into the small of her back, tugging her chest against his.

Wait, what had she been saying?

"I shouldn't have kissed you," Rylie rushed out. "I'm not going to pretend there isn't something between us. There is." In fact, there were two flimsy layers of clothing between them. And the wolf would have liked it if there was a lot less. "What's happening is some werewolf *thing*. Seth and I have something else."

"A tedious relationship that's hung around two years too long?" he asked, tracing his thumb over her bottom lip. How was she supposed to talk when he was doing that?

"Love," Rylie said. "And a history. He's given up everything for me."

"But Seth doesn't need you like I do." He caught her hand and brought it to his face, pressing her palm against his scars. It always surprised her how much softer the ridges were than they looked. "I *need* you, Rylie. Just like I need air. And just like you need me."

He bent down, and she knew with sudden surety that he was about to kiss her—and that she wanted to be kissed.

"Don't," she said faintly. He didn't stop, and his lips brushed over hers. So she shoved him harder. "I said, *don't*!"

He sprawled on the snow.

She was shocked to see him fall—she hadn't meant to hurt him. But Abel didn't seem bothered. He only propped himself on his elbows so he could stare at her.

"You need a werewolf mate," he said.

She took a deep breath. "Maybe I do. But... I bit Seth."

"You did *what?*"

She lifted her chin in defiance. "He forced me to."

Abel stared at some invisible object in the distance— maybe the horrible memories of the first time he had been bitten. "Why the hell would he have done that?"

"He was trying to protect me. And I think... I think he *wants* to be changed."

"What an idiot," Abel said.

Rylie didn't exactly disagree on that point. "We'll know if he's going to change tomorrow. On the next moon."

Abel stood, anger clouding his features. But there was something else there, too—something that looked a lot like pain. "So maybe you don't need me after all," he said in a low voice, almost too quiet for her to hear. "But nobody needs *me*."

"Abel..."

But he had already walked back up the highway, leaving Rylie alone in the snow.

The Gresham ranch was a short detour on the way back to California, and the moon was approaching quickly. Seth had been held at the hospital for too long—they were out of travel time.

So they returned to the abandoned sanctuary for what might be Seth's first night as a werewolf.

Nobody came out to greet Rylie, Seth, and Abel on arrival. The house's windows were dark, the burned husk of the barn was a black mark on the fields, and it was eerily quiet.

"Looks... nice," Crystal said in a falsely upbeat voice.

"Shut up," Trevin responded.

She gasped.

"Let's just get inside," Rylie said. "I feel too exposed out here, and moonrise is coming in a few hours."

Hot prickles rolled down Seth's spine.

Moonrise.

It came all too quickly. Seth lingered outside to watch the sunset, his hand in a cast and stomach knotted with nerves. After witnessing so many werewolves changing, he wasn't sure what to expect. He still felt normal.

Shouldn't he have been feverish? Restless? Hungry?

Trevin and Crystal ran into the fields before they had even shifted—in opposite directions. So when the kitchen door behind Seth opened again, he expected it to be Rylie. But the silhouetted figure was about a foot too tall, much too broad, and way too masculine.

It was Abel.

"What are you doing out here?" Seth asked.

Abel came to stand beside him. "I'm here to get you through your first change."

"I thought Rylie was going to help me."

"You got me through my first six moons. I'm going to get you through yours." He bared his teeth in an unpleasant grin. "I'm being sentimental, so shut up and appreciate it, numbskull."

"But you're going to change into a wolf, too," Seth said. "You won't be very helpful when you're licking your own nuts and chasing your tail."

Abel jerked his thumb at the house. "Rylie's watching from inside. She'll be using her magical powers to monitor our changes tonight."

"She's staying human again?"

"Guess so. She said she's been feeling crappy—like she has the flu or something. She didn't want to run around in the snow."

Seth frowned. The flu? Rylie never got sick. He didn't think werewolves *could* get sick. Was she avoiding him?

Or was she avoiding Abel?

After a long moment of silence, Abel asked, "How do you feel?"

"I'm okay, but that doesn't mean anything, does it? The shift is completely mental on the first moon," Seth said. "I don't even know if Rylie can control me. You might want to tie me down if it looks like I'm losing it."

"I'll just punch your lights out if it looks like you're going to change."

Seth rolled his eyes. "This is so much better than having my girlfriend with me."

"You're welcome."

"Thanks, by the way," Seth said, keeping his voice carefully casual. "For coming to rescue us. You probably saved our lives."

His brother shrugged it off. "Whatever. I knew something was wrong when you said that you loved me."

Seth's smile slipped off of his face. "Yeah?"

"Yeah. I knew you were talking in code."

Seth hung his head and kicked his foot in a clump of snow.

Actually, he had just been thinking about how much he had been fighting with Abel—especially since Rylie had come between them. And he figured that there was a pretty good chance of Eleanor killing him.

He didn't want to die without his brother knowing the truth: that he really did love him.

Seth laughed and raked a hand through his hair. "Good thing you caught onto the code."

"I'm not an idiot," Abel said. He blew a breath of fog into the cold air. "Who am I kidding? I'm a huge goddamn idiot."

"I don't know about *idiot*, but you did kiss my girlfriend. That's not cool, man."

"Look," Abel said. "It's probably hard for you to understand with your meaty doctor brain, but—God, you're going to make me say it, aren't you?" He folded his arms. Unfolded them. Stared at the ground. "What I... *feel*... for Rylie... is nothing that I've ever felt before. But she wants you. Not me. And now I'm *feeling* really gay, so can we drop the subject?"

A smile slowly grew on Seth's face. "And Abel's heart grew three sizes that day."

"Screw you, dork wad."

"No, it's cute. Really cute."

"Shut up." Abel shoved Seth a little too hard. "You guys will make great Alphas together. Just the perfect fucking prince and princess of wolves." He stripped off his shirt and unbuckled his pants. "You don't need me. Not tonight. Not ever."

"Wait," Seth said, but his brother only turned away and loped into the night.

Seth stayed outside, waiting for his change. Younger werewolves changed later—sometimes not until midnight. But midnight came and went, and he still felt fine. Cold, but fine.

He went inside and listened to the wolves howl until he fell asleep on the couch.

Seth woke up after sunrise totally human.

TEN

An Answer

Rylie didn't expect to be able to sleep the night of the moon—not when she couldn't reach the California sanctuary, Cain and Eleanor were still out there, and there was a chance that her boyfriend was about to become her mate in a literal way.

But she did sleep, and she woke up with the sun creeping over the horizon. She felt just as tired as she had been before sleeping.

And nauseous.

Rylie rolled over in bed and threw up on the floor.

She groaned. Her mouth tasted horrible.

Where did that come from?

Rylie staggered into the hallway. Seth was on the couch, human and asleep. She sneaked a towel out of the linen closet and wiped up her bedroom floor.

He was still sleeping when she threw the towel in the laundry and got into the shower.

Rylie stood under the hot water feeling dizzy and tired. She had to lean against the wall to stay standing. As if getting kidnapped by her zombie in-laws wasn't enough misery on its own, she had to go and catch a bug, too.

"Bad timing," she muttered to the showerhead, like it cared.

Rylie popped open the shampoo bottle, and the smell of flowers wafted through the bathroom. It reminded her of Pagan. Her stomach clenched.

She closed the bottle and breathed shallowly, trying to suppress the nausea.

When the surge subsided, she toweled off, wrapped herself in her robe, and slipped back into her bedroom. The couch was empty—Seth must have finally woken up. The house smelled like cooking bacon. That didn't help her nausea at all.

Even though it was cold, Rylie threw open her window to try to air out the room.

A piece of paper fluttered to the ground.

She bent down to pick it up, and for an instant, she thought it was going to be another gift from Cain—another threat. But the handwriting was too blocky and uneven.

It was from Abel. All it said was, *Gone to hunt Cain.*

Abel was gone?

She sat down on the edge of her bed, feeling even sicker than ever.

Rylie showed Seth the note at breakfast, while Crystal and Trevin devoured a cow's worth of steak. All he said was, "Okay." Like it wasn't a big deal. Like Rylie didn't feel like an important part of her life had just been amputated.

They got back on the road an hour later—even though Rylie felt like she was on the verge of throwing up again, and the smell of the car's oils weren't helping.

Nobody talked as they beelined for California.

They stopped in town to fill up the gas tank, and Rylie took the chance to pace the parking lot, hands hooked together behind her head. She was feeling a little better than before—still exhausted, but not as queasy.

Maybe she wasn't sick after all. Maybe it was just stress.

But then she walked around the back of the gas station, and it came over her all at once.

Rylie threw up all over the ground.

She groaned and wiped her mouth clean on the back of her hand. A feeling of dread crept over Rylie as she stared at the puddle of vomit.

Werewolves *didn't* get sick.

But there was more than one reason she could be throwing up.

"No way," she whispered.

Seth was putting the cap back on the gas tank when she recovered enough to walk around to the other side of the parking lot again. He hadn't seen her throw up. Crystal and Trevin looked like they were arguing in the backseat of the van.

"Ready to go?" Seth asked.

"Yeah, I just need to use the bathroom," she said. "I'm not feeling awesome."

"Take your time. I'll stretch my legs," Seth said.

Rylie ducked into the gas station and pulled a wad of cash out of her pocket. Twenty-three dollars. Would it be enough?

Her cheeks burned as she found the aisle with the condoms, headache medicine, and pregnancy tests. They had two different brands. One of them was for early detection, and the other had two sticks in it.

The one with the two sticks was a dollar cheaper, so she grabbed it. She also picked up a pack of gum and a green tea before going to the counter.

"Congrats," said the grizzled old woman behind the counter. Her nametag said "Brenda."

Rylie blinked. "Huh?"

"Congrats on the good news. That'll be twenty-one fifty." She dropped the pregnancy test into a bag.

Rylie didn't think her cheeks could have burned any hotter. "I don't think I'm really pregnant. It's just in case."

Brenda gave her a knowing look and pulled the bathroom key off of the wall. "Come on."

She set a sign on the counter that said "Out for Lunch," and then took Rylie to the bathroom and unlocked the door.

"Thanks," Rylie said.

"Hang on a second." Brenda disappeared, and came back with a paper cup from the break room. "You'll need this. You have to pee in the cup and put the sticks in it. Read the directions. They're pretty good. I've got six kids, myself."

Six kids? Rylie felt dizzy.

"I'm not pregnant," she whispered.

Brenda patted her on the shoulder, pushed her into the bathroom, and shut the door.

The light over the toilet flickered on. Rylie opened the box and read the instructions. Brenda was right—they were very clear. It would be pretty hard to mess it up.

Her heart pounded as she did her business, dipped the sticks in her urine, and set them on the edge of the sink.

The instructions said three minutes. Three minutes until Rylie would know.

She paced around the tiny, dingy bathroom with her hands jammed under her arms.

What if she *was* pregnant? A werewolf that had babies would have more werewolves. Cain was proof of that. And she had promised not to continue the species.

It wasn't that Rylie didn't want to be a mom—she just hadn't ever given it that much thought. She didn't get along with her own mother, Jessica. They had zero interests in common. And the only other mom she knew well at all was Eleanor. Hardly a shining example of motherhood.

Somehow, three minutes passed.

Rylie picked up one of the sticks and held it to the light.

There was one pink line on the right, rich and dark and thick. She grabbed the instructions. One line was just the control to show the test was working—that didn't mean anything.

But when she tilted the test, she could see another line, too. A very faint, but definitely pink, line. Right where the positive line was meant to show up.

Rylie dropped the first test and picked the second one up. The line was there too.

Her legs suddenly wouldn't support her weight anymore. She sat down hard on the toilet seat.

Someone knocked on the door.

"Rylie?" Seth asked. "Are you almost done?"

She felt like she had swallowed an entire pack of werewolves, and that they were warring in her stomach. "Almost," she croaked.

"Trevin wants another burrito. Do you want anything to eat?"

"No. I'm fine."

Except that she *wasn't* fine. And nothing was going to be fine ever again.

Rylie was pregnant.

PART FOUR

Red Rose Moon

ONE

Slaughter

Abel punched the button for the intercom into the California sanctuary for the fourth time. After the way he had left, Abel didn't exactly expect to be greeted with shouts of delight and hugs, but he also didn't expect to be totally ignored.

"Come on," he muttered, peering through the gates into the fog. The road into the sanctuary had been designed to keep people from seeing inside, and paired with the tall brick walls and barbed wire fence, it did a pretty good job of looking intimidating and unwelcoming.

Abel wasn't easy to intimidate, but he definitely felt unwelcome.

He hit the button one more time.

"Levi, you punk, I know you're there," he growled into the speaker. "Let me in!"

Still, nothing happened.

Forget this.

Abel stripped off his jacket, leaving his muscular arms and the pistols in his shoulder rig bared to the night, and threw the coat over the wire. He scaled the gate, hopped safely to the other side, and pulled the coat down with him. He grumbled as he jerked the coat closed around his black wife-beater again.

Breaking into a jog, he followed the shortcuts that he had memorized in his time living at the sanctuary, and cut a path straight toward the house. The grounds were completely silent. If Abel had been a little more morbid, he might have even thought of them as... dead.

As he approached the front doors of the sprawling manor house, a dark lump appeared in the fog. He couldn't tell what it was from that distance, but he had a pretty good feeling. He had seen a lot of dead bodies in his time as werewolf hunter, and they all kind of looked the same, after a while.

Abel kneeled next to the body and pushed it onto its back.

Eldon. One half of the resident married couple. His throat had been torn out, and he hadn't managed to heal from it—even werewolves weren't invulnerable.

So Cain hadn't been bluffing when he said that his men had attacked the sanctuary.

Abel's hands clenched into fists, and he fought not to scream his frustrations into the fog. Instead, he moved to the front doors and found them standing open; the foyer was cold and damp. It was also littered with three more bodies.

He steeled himself and went about the grim duty of finding all of the dead.

It took over an hour, but by the time he pulled the bodies into a pile outside, the fog hadn't yet receded. In fact, it only seemed to thicken, making the day seem mournfully quiet.

Once he was sure that he didn't smell any other bodies in the house, he took inventory of the ones he had piled together.

Over a dozen people dead.

He didn't know most of them—they had never come out to the Gresham sanctuary for a visit. At least one of the bodies wasn't a werewolf at all; it was a witch in Scott Whyte's coven. And, judging by all the black they were wearing, three of them were with the Union.

His wolf stirred as he pulled himself away from the pile of bodies to find wood. Usually, he didn't have to fight with his inner beast the way Rylie did, so it surprised him to feel the wolf swell in his heart. It recognized members of its pack, and it was sad. *Sad.*

"Shut up, you big sissy," he muttered to himself.

Great, now he was talking to himself, too. He was going to turn into Rylie any day now.

He lost himself in the comforting motions of hard, physical labor. Scott would have been ticked to see Abel ripping trees from the earth, but there were plenty on the property; he probably wouldn't even notice around all the dead people, if he ever came back.

The condition in which he had found the dead bugged him. Not just the indignity of letting the pack rot in the open air. It just made no sense to leave all those bodies behind. The Union liked to keep tight control of what it perceived to be its resources—which included bodies. As Abel understood it, they liked to pull things apart. Study them. Find what made them tick.

If the coven hadn't collected the bodies, and the Union had also left them behind, then that meant something must have forced the survivors away from the sanctuary. They hadn't left of their own free will.

He piled the driest wood he could find around the bodies. Just because nobody had come looking yet didn't mean that they weren't going to, and he didn't want the cops to find anything but dust.

Abel located cans of gasoline in the shed and spilled it over the bodies and the wood, his heart heavy and a knot in his throat. Fluid splashed over the slack faces of his pack. It soaked into their shirts and left them glistening.

He set the can aside, stepped back, and took out his lighter.

Everyone deserved a dignified burial. Something befitting their spirituality that would also please their families and honor their memory. But with a flickering flame dancing over Abel's chilly fingertips, he couldn't think of a single thing to say that would be good enough.

"Rest in peace," he muttered, flicking the lighter onto the pyre.

The wood caught. Fire spread. Soon, despite the fog, it was a blazing bonfire. He couldn't even make out the bodies inside. But Abel watched as it burned down, jaw set and eyes blurry.

"I'll avenge you," he told the bonfire. "Trust me. I will."

His sensitive ears picked up a distant sound—the noise of the front gate creaking open as someone forced their way inside.

Abel tensed. Someone was approaching him—someone that smelled like pack. But this person wasn't friendly. He reeked of corpse. A dead body that was much older than the fresh bodies Abel was burning. One that had already dried, decayed, and had gotten up to walk around again anyway.

He reached inside his jacket as a figure emerged from the fog, but he didn't draw his gun fast enough.

"Hello, brother," Cain said. "Let's have a talk."

TWO

I Do

Rylie was just ten miles and three long hours away from meeting her Aunt Gwyneth for breakfast. And she wasn't sleeping.

There was nothing in the hotel to disturb her: the building was silent, the temperature was comfortable, and she felt reasonably safe in bed with Seth. Trevin and Crystal were taking turns patrolling the halls, so Rylie would have plenty of warning if they were attacked.

But even with everything peaceful, her head was spinning.

She couldn't stop thinking about those two pink lines.

Pregnant.

Rylie rolled over onto her stomach, and wondered if her belly felt harder than usual, or if she was just imagining things. Neither thought helped her get sleepy.

When the clock read five, and the light outside the curtains began to brighten, she gave up on sleeping.

Rylie slipped out the door and stood on the patio overlooking the bustling street. It had snowed heavily overnight, leaving the world blanketed in white, except where the snow plows had already done their work. The trees were caked with ice.

She didn't feel cold, even though she was only wearing her underwear and one of Seth's shirts. An icicle dripped on the snow beside her foot, giving a gentle tap-tap-tap.

It was calm, beautiful, and peaceful. Impossible to tell that someone out there wanted to kill her.

Footsteps crunched on the snow in the parking lot, and a figure in a dark jacket traced a path from the door downstairs toward the trees. She could only see the top of his head, so Rylie took a sniff of the air. She picked up the smell of microwave burritos and aluminum foil. Trevin.

She watched him pace the parking lot, seemingly unaware that he was being observed, and bit her lip in disappointment. She had been hoping against hope that Abel would have come back to protect her.

Rylie felt hot just thinking about kissing Abel again. And the way that he had looked when he burst into the cabin to save her from Eleanor...

Her emotions were confusing, but it was enough to convince her that marrying Seth was a bad idea. At least for now.

Except for those two pink lines.

She slipped into the hotel room again.

Seth was buried in the fluffy duvet, and he didn't move when Rylie tracked wet footprints across the carpet to enter the bathroom. She shut the door before turning on the light.

She lifted up her shirt, pushed down the waist of her underwear, and stood with her side to the mirror to inspect the curve of her belly. It looked normal. Rylie folded her hands over her stomach and tried to imagine what was happening inside of her body.

Her mom used to breed golden retrievers, back when Rylie was in elementary school, so she was familiar with the process of producing purebred puppies that could sell for a thousand dollars a head: choosing the right stud, going to the veterinary appointments, helping the mother birth, picking out the ones with the best breed characteristics.

That was the most experience Rylie had with the birth of new life. And she suddenly had a bizarre mental image of curling up in the back of her mom's closet to have puppies, which she immediately banished. That was a really weird thought that she preferred not to entertain.

Rylie might have spent a lot of time with puppies, but as far as young humans went, she had only babysat kids old enough to be going to elementary school. Kids who were already potty trained, and could talk, and ate peanut butter and jelly sandwiches. Kids that she could stick in front of a TV while she did her homework, and gave back to their parents after a few hours.

After nine months, Rylie wasn't going to find herself saddled with puppies, nor was she going to have a child that was mostly capable of taking care of itself.

She was going to have a baby. A tiny, mostly-human baby that turned into a wolf sometimes—just like Cain.

What would her mom think? What would *Abel* think?

The door creaked, and Rylie dropped her shirt. The hem slid over her belly button.

"Hey," Seth said, stepping into the room. His face was puffy from sleep, but he smiled as he raked a hand through his hair. "Having problems sleeping?"

She gave a weak, nervous smile. "Captivity will do that to you."

He kissed the back of her neck and entwined her in a hug. Rylie watched his face over her shoulder in the mirror. "You should rest while we can. We'll have plenty of opportunity to worry later, when we head back to the sanctuary."

Rylie had already decided that she didn't want to go back to the California sanctuary. She didn't want to deal with other werewolves while she was dealing with a much bigger problem of her own.

But she didn't know how to explain that yet, so she didn't bother trying.

Rylie slipped the ring off of her right hand, pinched it between her forefinger and thumb, and stared at the glimmering rock. The ring was so perfect. So beautiful.

She just didn't want to marry Seth.

Marrying him seemed dishonest when her heart couldn't choose between the brothers. Her wolf and human sides were in constant disagreement, and it was wrong for her to be thinking of one when she was with the other. She hated herself for it.

But Seth was amazing. Wonderful. Just this side of perfect. He was willing to sacrifice everything for her—and if she was going to have Seth's baby, it should have made the decision a lot easier.

Abel wasn't going to want to have anything to do with her when he found out she was carrying his brother's child anyway.

Rylie held the ring up so that he could see it, and she tried not to shake too obviously. "Seth... would you ask me again?"

A smile grew on Seth's face. "Right now? At five in the morning, while I'm in my boxers?"

Rylie nodded silently, cheeks burning.

He dropped to his knee and took her hand in his. Seth's dark eyes were filled with heat and love. It didn't reflect the loathing she felt for herself at all.

"Rylie Gresham," Seth said, "will you do me the honor of becoming my wife?"

She swallowed hard and pressed a hand to her belly.

"Yes," she whispered, and she closed her eyes so she wouldn't have to meet his gaze while she said it.

THREE

Blessings

It turned out that Gwyneth's new address didn't belong to an apartment building at all, but a cute house in the suburbs on the north side. It had a greenhouse filled with the lush leaves of flourishing produce—Gwyn could make anything grow, at any time—and a holiday wreath on the front door.

Crystal and Trevin were having breakfast at the Denny's down the street, so Seth and Rylie approached alone, hand-in-hand. They didn't even get the chance to knock on the door before it opened.

"Look at the two of you," Gwyn said, cheeks dimpling as she took in the sight of them on her doorstep. Her gray hair was brushed out, and she wore a white blouse with clean jeans. Almost like a soccer mom.

"Gwyn!"

Rylie hugged her aunt tight. She smelled good, too—like the pleasant, buttery odor of baked bread.

She probably hung on too long, but Gwyn didn't let her go, either. When Rylie finally stepped back, Gwyn turned her attention on Seth. "You taking care of my girl?"

"Yes, ma'am," he said, grinning widely. He hadn't stopped smiling since they got into town. He lifted his broken hand. "Myself? Not so much."

"Ooh. That looks like it hurt."

She stepped aside, and Rylie immediately smelled the presence of someone else in the house. It wasn't the kind of smell that a visitor would leave behind; it was in the carpet, the furniture, the walls. Someone living with Gwyn. Her aunt had mentioned that she had a new girlfriend.

Rylie closed her eyes and took a deep breath to see how much she could learn. Nobody in the house smoked. Someone liked peach soap—that definitely wasn't Gwyn. There was also the smell of spice, herbs, and fresh soil. It was all wonderfully earthy.

When she opened her eyes, Gwyneth was giving her a knowing look. "What do you think, babe?"

Rylie blushed. "She smells good. Where is she?"

"Heather's with family this week. Come on, breakfast's in the kitchen."

Gwyn had obviously prepared for Rylie's arrival. There were steak and eggs being kept hot on a tray in the oven, and Rylie absolutely devoured them. Whenever she wasn't nauseous, she was starving—it felt like she couldn't eat enough to satisfy herself.

Seth was more polite about picking up a croissant, buttering it, and starting to eat.

"What have you kids been up to?" Gwyn asked. She wasn't eating anything. "I didn't expect you to visit anytime soon, considering how busy the sanctuary keeps you."

Rylie's cheeks were bulging, so Seth explained everything.

"It's been bad, Gwyn," he said. "We went looking for answers with Cain, and we found them. It turns out that Cain is another son of Eleanor. Different dad than I have, but..." Seth gave a casual shrug, as if it didn't bother him. Rylie could see the tension in his shoulders. "Anyway, Cain was hiding at our sanctuary the whole time. It was Vanthe."

"I should have known that guy was too helpful." Gwyn didn't look even remotely surprised. "Damn. What can I do to help? I figure you must have come here for something."

Rylie swallowed her last bite of steak and exchanged looks with Seth.

"We're not actually here because of that." Her cheeks burned as she pulled her hands into her lap and toyed with the engagement ring.

Seth fixed Gwyn with his most charming smile. "Gwyneth, I was wondering if I could—"

"Yes," Gwyn said.

He blinked. "I was going to ask permission—"

"You're asking if you can marry Rylie, and I'm telling you 'yes.'" She grinned. "Asking her family for permission? Are you a caveman? Come here, boy, come here." Seth circled the table, and Gwyn captured him in a huge hug.

"Thank you," he said.

"Nonsense. Ain't nobody I'd like to have in my family more than you."

She kissed him on the cheek.

"We were hoping to do it soon," Seth said. "We'd like to hold it at the Gresham Ranch before the next moon."

"The next moon? Why?"

Rylie bit her bottom lip and avoided her aunt's questioning gaze. "Considering everything that's happening with Cain and Eleanor, I don't think we have time to mess around," she said, trying to sound casual about it. That was the excuse she had given Seth, but it was harder to lie to her aunt.

Nothing got past Gwyn. Her gaze sharpened.

"Seth, would you clean up breakfast?" Gwyn asked. "It's your privilege as the newest member of the family, broken hand and all."

He laughed. "Of course."

Gwyneth gestured, and Rylie had no choice but to follow her out into the living room. It was decorated like a country cottage, and just as cozy as the kitchen; Rylie could easily imagine having a tea party at the coffee table. It must have been Heather's style.

She took three steps into the room before her aunt spoke.

"I'm happy to arrange your wedding, babe. You know that. But so soon..." Gwyn's gaze sharpened. "You're pregnant, aren't you?"

Rylie's cheeks flushed, and she gaped like a dying fish as she searched for words. She glanced at the kitchen door, then back at her aunt, hoping that Seth hadn't heard what her aunt just said.

How could Gwyn have known? How had Rylie given herself away?

Her speechlessness was answer enough. Gwyneth sat on the couch with a weighty sigh. "Well," she said. "Well, well."

"Oh God." Rylie sank onto the opposite chair and dropped her face into her hands. She didn't want to see the anger on her aunt's face.

"Eighteen is mighty young to start a family."

"You think I did this to myself on purpose?"

Gwyn chuckled. "You make it sound like you're trying to perform a self-amputation or something else terrible."

"*Pregnant*," Rylie whispered. It was so hard to say the word out loud. Gwyn smoothed the hair off of Rylie's forehead, and her entire face glowed with warmth and joy.

"Your daddy would have been a wonderful grandpa, and I know he'd be disappointed if I didn't spoil your baby rotten."

Rylie blinked. "Does that mean you're not mad at me?"

"Mad?" Gwyn laughed. "How could I be mad? Babies are always a blessing. Maybe it's not the right time, but it's *never* the right time. You're smart, Rylie, and Seth is a fine young man. I can't think of anyone better equipped to handle it."

Rylie hadn't even realized that she had been worried about Gwyn's reaction until that moment. She suddenly felt so much lighter.

And then her aunt spoke again.

"Have you thought about what this is going to do to you and Abel?"

Rylie smiled sheepishly. "You're way too perceptive."

Her aunt tapped a finger on her temple. "Forgot to tell you. I'm psychic."

"No, you're just old. You've seen everything."

"Not so old that I can't still kick your ass, girl," Gwyn said. "Abel's going to be hurt. I know things had changed between you two. Just make sure to be honest about your feelings, and it'll be fine."

"That's the problem, Gwyn," Rylie whispered. "I don't know what I feel."

She didn't have to say any more than that. Her aunt obviously understood.

"Everything changes when you bring kids into the picture. I think your choice has been made for you, babe." She squeezed Rylie's hand. "What does Seth think?"

"I might not have told him yet."

"Tell him. And tell him soon. Trust him—he'll be fine." Gwyn gave her a tight hug, and then gave a bright, sparkling laugh. It had been years since Rylie heard her aunt laugh like that. "Now, we better get moving. Sounds like we have a shotgun wedding to plan."

FOUR

Transport

Abel had hung out with Cain when he was still pretending to be a member of the pack, and he had seemed pretty cool. Abel had assumed that it was all pretense—there was no way that someone who sent Rylie silver bullets and wrote threatening messages in blood could be a fairly nice guy.

Nice or not, Cain *was* polite. He made sure that Abel was comfortable as his men trussed him up and put him in the back of a semi. There were even blankets waiting so that he wouldn't get cold in the shipping container. And after a few hours of driving, they untied him long enough so he could walk around and take a piss—though they never took their guns off of him, not even for a moment.

There was no mistaking Cain as nice, though. His men were afraid of him. It showed in every glance and gesture. A nice guy didn't give people a reason to fear him like that.

After their pit stop, the engine groaned to life. The semi began to move.

Cain sat down cross-legged in front of Abel once the back door of the semi was closed again. The shipping container was empty aside from the two men. "You're being awfully compliant," Cain said.

"That's because I'm thinking about how much enjoyment I'm gonna get from killing you," Abel said. And because he had spent the last two hours wearing down his ropes so that he could break free, but he wasn't quite there yet. "Where's Eleanor?"

"She's resting at home," Cain said, sweeping his coarse golden curls out of his face with a gesture that eerily resembled Seth. "She's not doing well."

"Good," Abel said.

Rage darkened Cain's features, and Abel prepared for what he knew had to be coming—the same kinds of torture Seth had endured at the hands of Cain's followers. But the other man didn't make a move to touch him.

Unfortunately, not all torture was physical.

"Eleanor never loved you," Cain said.

Abel clamped his mouth shut and didn't take the bait. His wrists, tethered behind his back, were almost free.

"I grew up alone, Abel," Cain went on. "I never knew the warmth of a mother's love."

Abel barked a laugh. "And you think you'll get it from Eleanor?"

"I already do. She's the family I've always longed for. And you—you tried to *kill* her."

"Tried? I thought we did a pretty good job," Abel said. The tension on his wrists slackened. He was free. He didn't move or show any other sign of it.

Anger flashed across Cain's face. "Seth doesn't love you, either."

"Bullshit."

"He took the woman you love."

"Seth got there first." Abel tried to make it sound like that didn't bother him, but a smile spread on Cain's lips. He knew that he had struck a nerve.

"Seth has everything. He has an education. The ability to better himself. A future. And now Rylie. How long do you think it's going to be until they get married?" Abel's hands clenched into fists behind his back. "You were the one that was there for Rylie while Seth went to college. But what do you have? Nothing. You *are* nothing."

He bristled. "I'm a hell of a lot more than that."

"Yeah? What have you got going for you? I'm dying to hear."

The problem was that Abel couldn't think of any examples. Everything Cain said were the exact things that had been gnawing at him ever since he resigned himself to becoming a werewolf.

He used to live for the goal of wiping out the species. That was so easy to focus on. So simple. All he had to do was hunt and kill.

Then he was bitten, and everything changed.

Now what did he have? A future running around on four legs every other week? It wasn't like he could get a job. The only thing he knew how to do was kill.

Cain's eyes glimmered. "You tried to murder our mother. You deserve this ruined life."

"Deserve? I don't know about that. I don't do well with philosophical thinking," Abel said. "Guess I'm not educated enough."

Cain chuckled. That was when Abel lunged.

He unleashed the full power of the werewolf's speed and strength and bowled Cain over.

No mercy. Abel went straight for the sensitive zones— driving his knee into Cain's gonads, slamming his hand into the bridge of his nose, pounding the solar plexus. He heard ribs crack. Cain didn't even have time to cry out.

But all werewolves could sponge up damage and keep going. Cain was no exception.

He flipped Abel over onto his back and squeezed his throat. Blood streamed down his lips.

Abel knocked his arms off and threw Cain across the shipping container. The impact of his body dented the metal. The shipping container rocked with the strength of their struggle, and Abel thought he felt the semi swerve.

"Come on," Cain said with his back against the wall. He snorted up a wad of blood and phlegm and spit it out again. "You're supposed to be tough."

"Tough?" Abel asked, and he laughed. It made his ribs creak.

Then he plunged a thumb into Cain's eye.

Cain roared with pain, clapping his hands over his face as he fell to his knees.

Abel scrambled to the back door and delivered a swift kick to the place he knew the latch had to be. Metal snapped. The door's springs engaged, and it rolled open.

Highway stretched behind him. They were already out of California again and across another state. It looked like the route toward the Gresham Ranch.

Cain staggered to his feet. "Don't you—" he began.

Abel jumped.

He angled for the side of the road, but his shoulder still struck pavement.

And then he was flying.

Abel had an instant to stare up at the cold blue sky and realize that he had been struck by one of the cars behind the semi.

His body bounced on a windshield. Glass fractured. He tried to grab something—anything—but the momentum pushed him off the back of the car and onto the road again.

Brakes squealed. Abel tasted rubber. Immense pressure crushed him against the pavement.

His body burned with the healing fever as soon as the injuries were inflicted, making him seize and shake. Two cars—he had been hit by two cars, and he was still in the middle of the road. But he couldn't get up. Couldn't make his shattered legs work.

He threw his weight to the side and rolled onto the shoulder just in time to feel another car blow past him. His arm slid over shattered glass, and then he was surrounded by prickly bushes and the smell of sage.

Abel was a mess of pain. One big bruise. It felt like every single bone was broken.

"Heal," he groaned to himself. "Goddammit, *heal*."

He had to get up before Cain came around for him again. Had to make a run for it, and find Rylie before she got hurt.

But he hadn't been able to eat much lately, and it made his bones knit back together too slowly. Abel gritted his teeth and tried to pop his shoulder into place. Pain scythed through his chest. He roared.

Footsteps crunched toward him.

Abel looked up, and he saw his ugly excuse of a half-brother standing over him, arms crossed and right eye a mess of blood. He was flanked by three men in black shirts. "Now, don't you feel stupid?" Cain asked. He jerked his thumb at his men. "Put him back in the truck."

FIVE

Collusion

When Gwyn and Rylie returned to the kitchen, they were both smiling. "Sunday," Rylie said. "We're going to get married on Sunday."

Seth was finished doing the dishes. He rinsed the soapy water off of his uninjured hand and dried it on a towel. "We are? *This* Sunday?"

"Yeah. Gwyn says we can have it together by then. She's going to take care of everything." Rylie's cheeks were pink.

"You're welcome," Gwyneth said as she stuffed her feet into cowboy boots, threw on a denim jacket, and grabbed her keys off the hook. "Walk us out to the truck, wonder boy."

He headed outside with his arm around Rylie's shoulders. The snow had stopped, but it was chilly, and she looked so beautiful with her cheeks rosy and hair tucked into the collar of her jacket.

"Do you want to come?" Rylie asked Seth as she climbed into the front seat of the truck.

Gwyn responded for him. "We're heading down to the dress shop and the florist. This isn't groom business. Don't worry, there's going to be plenty for him to do soon."

"I missed a call from the California sanctuary, too," Seth said. "I think I have real work to do."

Rylie leaned down to kiss him through the window. "And weddings aren't real work?"

He backed away with his hands in the air, making it clear that he knew better than to comment on that. "I'll see you soon."

She rolled up the window, and Gwyn pulled out of the driveway.

His smile faded as he checked his cell phone. The call that Seth had missed wasn't from the California sanctuary. It was from Scott Whyte's cell phone. He called him back.

"Where are you?" Scott asked without preamble.

Seth pinned the phone between his shoulder and ear, got behind the wheel, and started his car. "We're with Gwyn again. I haven't been able to reach the sanctuary for days. What happened?"

"Cain attacked us. The Union didn't even see it coming—half of their men turned around and started shooting the others. It was a mess."

Seth pounded his fist into the wheel, making pain radiate through his broken hand. "Dammit. How many casualties?"

"Too many. Stephanie, Bekah, and Levi are safe—we made a break for it as soon as we realized what was happening. Most of the pack is heading your way now."

"Did you see Abel?"

"Abel? No."

Seth jiggled his knee as he considered the situation. He had no way to find out where his brother was—either brother. But he somehow doubted that Cain would be able to resist the urge to attack Rylie's wedding.

His first impulse was to call his fiancée and tell her that they needed to delay it.

But an idea dawned on him. A terrible idea.

"Where are you now, Scott?" Seth asked.

"Not far from you."

"Head to the Gresham Ranch. We need to get everyone together there."

"Why? That sanctuary's not any safer than the one we left behind in California."

"I know," Seth said, heading for the diner where he had left Trevin and Crystal behind. "That's why we're going to lay a trap for Cain and Eleanor."

Seth told Trevin and Crystal what he had planned as they drove out of town again.

"You're nuts," Trevin said flatly.

Seth rolled his eyes. "I appreciate the vote of confidence."

"I don't know about nuts," Crystal said carefully, tapping her fingers on her chin thoughtfully. "Maybe suicidal."

"Nuts *and* suicidal," Trevin added.

Crystal poked him hard in the ribs. "Shut up. I'm just saying, there's got to be a better way to do this. Using your own wedding as a trap to lure in Cain?"

"We don't have a lot of choices left at this point," Seth said. "He's ruthless, and we've been a few steps behind him this whole time. We have to get ahead. We have to be prepared."

"What does Abel think about this?" Crystal asked.

Seth fell silent as he drove along the highway, unbroken hand clenched tight on the steering wheel.

To be honest, he wasn't sure that Abel was ever planning on coming back. Not after the last conversations they'd shared. They had been through a lot together as brothers, but the division over Rylie seemed to be the last straw—and marrying her wasn't going to make that any better.

All he said was, "Abel's got bigger worries."

Seth wasn't surprised when they reached the Gresham Ranch to find that Yasir was already waiting for him. The Union commander was alone for once—he wasn't even driving one of those black SUVs with the long antennae. He was leaning against an early nineties Ford Taurus that looked like it was held together with duct tape and hopes.

"I'm surprised you came back," Yasir said by way of greeting when Seth climbed out of his car.

"Why did you come if you didn't think I'd be here?"

Yasir shrugged stiffly. "I didn't have anywhere else to go. I can't trust any of the men on my team anymore. Half of them are tattooed with those damn apples."

Crystal and Trevin got out. Their gold eyes burned with suspicion, but Seth held out a hand to calm them. "Yasir is okay," Seth said. "Get inside and start collecting ammo. Okay?"

Yasir watched the wolves obey with his eyebrows raised. "You're leading the pack now?" he asked once they were gone.

"Not really. That's still Rylie's job. But those are the only two that I'm certain are on our side right now, and they're going to help me kill Cain."

"You've got my attention. What's the plan?"

"The plan?" Seth laughed. "The plan is that Rylie and I are getting married."

The commander folded his arms. "That's going to be a major security event."

"I know. That's why I'm asking you to be my best man. And I want you to bring guests—a lot of them."

"Have you asked your bride what she thinks about having the Union at her wedding?" Yasir asked. Seth answered with a guilty grin. "So this will be covert."

"It's better than waiting for Cain to come and kill us. Worst case scenario? We can have a dozen armed men in the audience ready to take him down. Best case scenario, your men get to enjoy an open bar."

"There's only one problem with that," Yasir said.

"The traitors."

He nodded. "Right. Even if I only bring men that I trust to the ceremony... I trusted Stripes. You understand what I'm getting at? I don't know if there's anyone in the Union that's safe to bring."

"That's why your people won't be the only ones prepared to fight," Seth said.

Yasir's expression changed from one of caution to something more appreciative.

"This could be a bloodbath."

"If that's what I have to do to secure safety for Rylie, then let it be a bloodbath." Seth held out his uninjured hand. "Will you stand with me?"

Yasir shook. "I would be honored to be your best man."

SIX

Traitors, Liars, and Floral Arrangements

It turned out that telling Gwyn about her wedding and pregnancy wasn't going to be the hardest part of Rylie's day. It was trying to get a dress fitted without having to run to the bathroom to throw up.

"You okay, babe?" Gwyn asked from outside the stall.

Rylie groaned as she flushed the toilet. "No. I'm dying."

Her aunt chuckled. "I stayed with your daddy for a few weeks to help around the house while Jessica was pregnant with you, and she did the exact same thing all nine months."

All nine months? Just the mention of it made Rylie want to throw up again.

She sat in front of the toilet for another minute, and nothing happened, so she gave up waiting. "I thought it was supposed to be *morning* sickness," she said, getting up and wiping her mouth with a square of clean toilet paper.

"Sure. Morning, afternoon, and evening sickness. It's a good sign, though. Means that the baby is healthy."

Rylie pushed open the stall door, and Gwyn gave her a gentle hug.

"*I* don't feel healthy," Rylie said.

"Yeah, I bet you don't. Come on. We'll just tell the tailor to use the measurements from your prom gown."

Rylie nodded gratefully, and returned to the dressing room to change out of the bustier and underskirt into her street clothes again.

Her pocket vibrated as they headed to the parking lot. It took Rylie a minute to remember that she was carrying Gwyn's cell phone.

It was Seth.

"Bekah and Stephanie are in town, and they're heading your way," he said when she answered. "Where are you?"

Relief swamped Rylie. She had to stop and hold onto the light post to keep from falling over. Bekah and Stephanie were coming—that meant that they were okay. Even though she still felt nauseous, she suddenly felt much better overall.

"We're just leaving the dress shop," Rylie said. "We're going to go to the florist next."

"Already done with your measurements? That was fast."

Rylie worried her bottom lip between her teeth. "Yeah. So... um, everything is coming together. What's going on with you?"

"Just starting to get the ranch ready for the wedding this weekend." Seth's voice sounded weird. Rylie frowned. Before she could ask him what was wrong, he added, "Do you mind if I invite some of my friends?"

She blinked. "Friends?"

"Yeah. Some other hunters I've gotten to know over the years."

Rylie hadn't known that Seth had any friends. He never mentioned them. "Of course I don't mind," she said. "That sounds nice."

"Good. I'll let Bekah know where you are. See you tonight?"

"Sure," she said.

"Love you, Rylie." He hung up.

Bekah and Stephanie caught up with them while Rylie was throwing up in the bathroom of the florist's shop. She had been feeling pretty good until they walked through the door and the powerful perfume of blossoms smacked her in the face.

It wasn't the smell itself that made her sick, so much as the fact that it reminded her of Pagan, and Seth getting tortured. Either away, it was enough to send her running again.

When she emerged, Gwyn was embracing Bekah, and Stephanie was peering closely at a bouquet of flowers with plump, drooping leaves.

Bekah squealed when she saw Rylie.

"Oh my gosh!" She flung her arms around Rylie's shoulders. "I'm so glad to see you alive!"

Rylie returned her hug with a weak smile. After throwing up four times that day, she couldn't seem to work up the energy to return Bekah's enthusiasm. "I'm glad to see you're alive, too. What happened at the sanctuary?"

Bekah gave her a quick overview—the way that most of the Union team assigned to protect them had turned against the werewolves, and how quickly everyone scattered.

"We've been prepared for this for a while," Stephanie said. She was a tall, elegant woman with strawberry-blond hair that had never been very friendly, although she managed a small smile for Rylie. "We had escape routes planned. The number of traitorous Union members seemed to shock everyone, though. Except me."

"Why weren't you shocked?" Rylie asked.

Stephanie gave a delicate sniff. "I never trust the Union." She was a doctor by trade, but also a witch in her family's coven—and apparently, she had run across the Union more than once before.

The florist came out of the back room holding a binder thicker than a family Bible, and they all stopped talking. He beamed at all the women standing in his shop. Rylie could practically see the dollar signs in his eyes.

"I can put a rush order on any of these for you, of course," he said smoothly, setting the binder on the table by the window.

"I'm sure you can," Gwyn muttered. Rylie stifled a giggle.

It felt strange to be flipping through pictures of floral arrangements while Bekah continued to whisper about the night that the California sanctuary was attacked. Rylie was feeling queasy again, but she didn't think it was the pregnancy this time.

"Eldon?" she whispered back. "And his wife?"

"Both of them dead," Bekah said grimly.

Rylie stared at the pictures without really seeing them.

She had failed to protect her pack and let them down. Now a few more were gone.

How many werewolves did that leave? Fifteen? Seventeen? Their endangered species was dwindling fast.

Rylie pressed a hand to her stomach.

But not dwindling as fast as it would have been, otherwise.

"Tell me what happened with Cain," Bekah urged, drawing Rylie from her reverie.

Gwyn gave them a sharp look. "I don't think we need to talk about that today. We should focus on happy things. Like how these lilies and the winter berries would look together. Stephanie?"

The doctor's lips pinched together. "Lilies? Really? Those are funeral flowers."

While Gwyn and Stephanie argued, Rylie filled Bekah in on the events of the kidnapping in a low whisper.

When she got to the part about Eleanor, Bekah's voice rose to a shriek. "Eleanor's *resurrected?*"

That got Gwyn's attention. "Resurrected?" she asked, mouth falling open.

"Like a zombie." Rylie was surprised at how shocked her aunt looked—almost like she might fall over. She reached out to grab her arm. "Are you okay?"

Gwyn shook herself. "I'm fine. Used to be, I didn't even believe in ghosts, much less werewolves. Now zombies?" She glanced at the counter. The florist was in the refrigerated back room again, but he was still too close for comfort. "But this isn't the time or the place to talk about it."

Bekah gave a sullen nod and sat back.

"I like roses," she added helpfully.

Rylie nodded. "Roses are fine."

At least *one* thing was settled.

As soon as they got into town, Scott Whyte sent Levi to find him supplies for a ritual. In truth, Scott wasn't planning on performing any rituals, but he had business to attend to. Private business. And he didn't want his adopted son knowing about it.

Scott got a room at the local motel and locked himself inside.

He set the box he was carrying on top of his desk before drawing the curtains to block out the orange glow of sunset in winter. People were walking outside, enjoying the unseasonably warm evening, and he didn't want anyone to catch a glimpse of what he was doing.

The lockbox was enchanted. Only his hands could undo the latches and lift the lid.

Scott reached inside to remove his prize—the tiny skull in a glass ball, which he had brought with him from California.

Someone knocked on his office door.

"Just a minute," Scott said, sliding the box underneath the desk.

He unlocked the door, and Gwyneth Gresham walked inside.

"Gwyn," Scott said, occupying himself by setting his suitcase on the bed and unzipping it. "What a pleasant surprise. I thought we were meeting later."

She tipped her hat. "Sorry to drop in. I've been in town all day to help Rylie plan her wedding, and after everything she told me this afternoon, I thought a visit might be prudent."

"Oh?" Scott asked. "What did she tell you?"

Gwyn paced around his desk to the window, peering out the curtain. "A few things. Mostly, we've been talking about the wedding a lot."

He sat down again and swiveled his chair to face her. A frown touched the corners of his mouth. "What does that have to do with the wedding?"

"Nothing. Everything." Gwyn waved her hand through the air. "The kids are pretty tough, and they've bounced back from the attacks ready for another fight. The wedding thing, though—that's exciting. Really exciting. I think it's going to be the party of the decade."

"Are you saying that you need wedding help?"

Gwyn smiled faintly and let the curtains fall shut again. "That's all right. I don't think we need your help on much of anything anymore."

Scott got the feeling that they were having two separate conversations, about two totally different things. There was menace in Gwyn's tone, despite her casual stance.

"If you don't have any specific need, Gwyneth, I'm going to have to ask you to leave. I have a few things I need to do before I can meet you at the ranch tonight."

He busied himself with unpacking, and hoped that she would get the hint.

Something clicked behind him.

Scott turned slowly, although he already knew what that sound had to be. Gwyn had pulled a gun out of her denim jacket, and aimed it straight at his forehead.

"What are you doing?" he asked, eyes widening.

Gwyn squeezed the trigger.

SEVEN

Brother's Keeper

Abel woke up feeling like he had been run over by a car or three. Of course, that was probably because he had.

He opened his eyes to find that he was strapped to the ground by ropes at his wrists and ankles. They were tethered to stakes buried deep in the ground.

Looked like his day wasn't about to get any better.

Craning his neck around, Abel took a quick survey of his situation. He was outside, on top of a hill looking down on gently rolling pastures under a clear night sky. A mobile home stood at the bottom of the valley, just a few hundred yards away.

It was hard to tell in the dark, but the land looked a lot like it did around the Gresham Ranch. He didn't recognize any landmarks, but he couldn't have been far. Maybe just a hundred miles or so.

The screen door on the mobile home creaked as it opened and swung shut again.

Cain headed toward him, whistling a cheerful tune. He was showing no signs of injury from their earlier fight. Even his eye had healed cleanly. Abel growled and strained against his bindings.

"Evening, bro," Cain said, sitting next to him. He was holding a plate of grilled meat, and the smell of steak wafted over the air. "How do you feel?"

"Like I jumped out of the back of a semi," he croaked. Taking the smallest breaths made it feel like a broken rib was digging into his lungs.

"Yeah. Not your best move." He cut a piece of the steak and held it over his face. "Want a bite?"

Screw dignity. Abel strained his head forward, caught the meat between his lips, and pulled it off the fork.

As soon as he swallowed, warmth rippled down his skin. That was why he hadn't completely healed yet—it had been too long since he last ate.

Cain fed him a few more bites. Abel tried not to enjoy it *too* much.

It wasn't long before his strength had returned enough to soothe the worst of his breaks and bruises. And then he felt strong enough to talk. "I'm guessing this means you're going to sacrifice me to bring back Mom," Abel said, twisting his wrist in the ropes.

"So Rylie and Seth told you about that." He held out another bite of steak. Abel ignored him. Cain ate it instead, chewing loudly.

Abel scowled. "I can't believe that everything you've done—stalking Rylie, threatening us, attacking the sanctuaries—has all been about bringing Eleanor back."

"Not *all* about that. The revenge is a big part, too. You starting to feel better?"

"A little."

Cain drove the fork into Abel's side. The tines scraped against his ribs.

Abel roared and arched his back.

"How about now?" Cain twisted the fork once before jerking it free. It wasn't silver—the wound began stitching back together immediately.

"Go suck yourself," Abel groaned.

He knew that was pushing it, so he wasn't surprised when Cain drove the fork into his ribs again, before the last wound had even healed.

His screams echoed off of the rolling hills.

"Funny," Cain said, licking the fork clean. "Seth didn't make a peep when we tortured him. I guess he really is the better brother."

That hurt worse than a thousand forks.

"Kill me now. I don't care. Just stop *talking* at me."

"I can't kill you yet. I have to wait for my necromancer to get here, and *then* I can kill you." Cain finished off the steak using the bloody fork and sat back with a sigh.

But Abel knew that wasn't going to be the end of it. He could tell by the sadistic glimmer in Cain's eye, and the way his lips peeled back from his teeth when he smiled.

"You should just be grateful that Rylie got pregnant, or she would be in your position right now," Cain said.

Pregnant?

Abel twisted in his ropes to glare at his half-brother. "What the hell are you talking about? Rylie's not pregnant."

"Whoops. Guess I just let that puppy out of the bag. Didn't she mention it to you?"

He was bluffing. He had to be. Rylie *couldn't* be pregnant—it wasn't physically possible.

"Female werewolves can't have babies," Abel said.

"True. Most female werewolves can't. They miscarry every time they transform. But some—like Alphas—have enough control to stay human. Since they periodically go into heats, where they must couple with their chosen mate, they can breed."

"Chosen mate," Abel echoed, unable to keep a scowl off his face.

So Seth was going to be a dad, and he'd have a kid with the girl Abel loved. Great. Just freaking great. That was going to make family reunions fun.

Cain leaned over him. "You know that werewolves only mate with other werewolves, right?"

"Sure. Tell that to Rylie."

"Let me show you something, Abel," Cain said. "I have some pictures. Do you like pictures?" He stood up, and Abel craned around to snap at him. Unfortunately, Cain stayed just out of reach.

He ducked into the mobile home and returned a moment later with a camera.

Cain turned it on and clicked through some of the pictures.

"Funny thing about children fathered by a werewolf, like I was—we're completely in control of our wolves and don't have to change on the moons. Which means that I could watch what everyone else was doing at the sanctuary."

He angled the camera. Abel recognized the two wolves in the picture, even though the quality wasn't very good. There were only so many sleek golden wolves that ran around the Gresham sanctuary with hulking, black-furred werewolves.

The first picture was of the two of them fighting. Judging by the color of the sky, it must have been the night of the awful barn fire.

Cain clicked through a few more. He stopped on a picture by the pond. Abel wasn't sure what he was looking at for a moment, and then it dawned.

He and Rylie had been mating on the nights they transformed.

His mind raced as he tried to remember the last time that he had seen her change into a werewolf. She had changed several times after that particular night—but he was pretty sure that she hadn't shifted since the night that they kissed. Which was long enough for her to get, and stay, pregnant.

Abel remembered how right, how *normal*, it had felt to push Rylie against the wall of his bedroom and claim her lips with his.

It was because he had already claimed her before.

Abel's mouth hung open as Cain moved back, turning the camera off.

"It's convenient," Cain said. "It means I don't have to lower myself to breeding with a human woman. Rylie's child will share Eleanor's genetics, which means *my* genetics. And they'll be born like I am: pure. It saved her life, at least for now." He gave a thin smile, but it wasn't a happy one. "I can't wait to meet my nephew."

Cain drove the fork into Abel's side one more time, and left him groaning on the ground. The screen door whined shut behind him.

Abel couldn't heal around the foreign body, and the pain burned through his bones. Yet that didn't bother him so much as the news he had just heard.

Rylie was pregnant with Abel's baby.

EIGHT

Necromancy

"How are you feeling?" Seth asked, stroking a hand down Rylie's side.

They were in bed together at the Gresham Ranch after a long day of arrangements, from flowers to the marriage license and picking a dress, and Rylie was exhausted. She thought that she could sleep for weeks if given the opportunity.

But there wouldn't be enough time for that. Sunday was just two days away now. The vendors were already beginning to deliver their decorations, and she still had a million other things to prepare, too.

"I feel good," she lied, snuggling under his arm. "All this planning is kind of making me go out of my mind, though."

He kissed the top of her head. "It'll be over soon. And then you'll be Mrs. Rylie Wilder."

She tried the sound of that name aloud. "Rylie Wilder. I like it."

They rested together for a few silent minutes, and Rylie felt herself beginning to drift off to the sound of Seth's heartbeat. But she woke right up again the next time he spoke.

"I asked Yasir to be my best man."

Her eyes opened. "Yasir? Really?"

Seth's gaze was focused on the ceiling. "He's been a good friend to me."

"But what about Abel?"

"There are two big problems with that. First of all, we don't even know where he is. He hasn't called, he hasn't left us a note…"

The reminder stung. Rylie burrowed her face in Seth's shoulder. "And what's the other thing?"

He traced circles on her bare ribcage. "Do you really have to ask that? Abel loves you. He wouldn't want to go to your wedding anyway. Especially not when I'm the groom."

She thought about kissing Abel, and her cheeks got hot. *Love* wasn't the word she would use for what they shared.

"He doesn't love me," Rylie protested, sitting up and hugging the sheets around her chest. She had been trying to stay covered all night so that Seth wouldn't notice the faint curve to her belly.

He raised his eyebrows. "Do you seriously think that? Really?"

A dull thud shocked through the house—the front door opening.

Someone screamed. It sounded like Bekah.

Seth bolted out of bed, pulling on his pants as he ran to the hallway. Rylie was just a few steps behind him. She whipped a bathrobe around her shoulders and knotted the belt at her waist.

She stared at the tableau in front of her, unable to make sense of what she was seeing.

Gwyn stood in the doorway, holding an old revolver that looked like it might have belonged to Abel. Bekah was shrieking, hands clapped to her face. Levi was halfway to turning into a wolf.

And then Rylie's gaze dropped, and she saw why.

Scott Whyte's body rested at Gwyn's feet with a gunshot wound in his forehead.

It took time for Levi to change, which gave Seth the advantage in reaction time. He grabbed a shotgun out of the unlocked case on the wall, pumped it once, and turned on the werewolf.

"Don't move," he said, and Levi froze.

"Oh my God, Gwyn," Rylie said. "What's going on? Did you kill him? What—why—?"

Gwyn kicked Scott over. Considering his mass, he should have been a lot harder to budge, but the man was totally limp. She never lowered her aim from his body. "He's not dead. Trust me. Or at least... he's not dead for good."

Seth moved forward and pressed his fingers to Scott's throat without dropping his aim from Levi.

No heartbeat.

"What the hell is going on, Gwyn?" Seth asked.

"It would be easier for me to just show you," she said.

She knelt beside Scott, unbuttoned his shirt, and pushed it aside. There was a tattoo of a bleeding apple on the left side of his chest.

Bekah cried out again. "No!"

Seth was only distantly aware of Levi changing back to his human form behind him.

"What do you kids know about Scott Whyte?" Gwyn asked. Nobody answered. She looked between their shocked faces and sighed. "You don't get to be high priest of a coven unless you're strong. Scott likes to pretend that he's a healer. That's a pretty special talent right there. But it's not as special as the truth. He's a necromancer."

Seth lost his balance and sat down hard. He carefully placed the shotgun beside him.

Slowly, everything fell into place.

In order to bring Eleanor back from the dead, Cain would have needed a necromancer. But he was a werewolf, not a witch. And if Scott had the bleeding apple tattoo...

"So you killed him," Levi said. He was pale and shaking. Almost the exact mirror of Rylie.

"It's not that easy." Gwyn stepped inside and shut the door behind her, blocking out the cool night. "Necromancers can't die the first time. He'll be back soon. Give it a few hours."

Bekah turned her tearful face up without releasing Scott. "How can you possibly know that?"

"Because," Gwyn said with a grim smile, "Scott brought me back from the dead months ago."

Gwyn put Scott Whyte's body in the cellar beneath the ranch house, called Stephanie at the hotel, and then brewed a strong pot of coffee. Rylie sat at the kitchen table next to her aunt, struggling not to cry.

"It was the disease," Gwyn said, taking a sip from her steaming mug. Even though the entire pack was there— Seth, Bekah, Levi, Trevin, and Crystal—the silence in the kitchen was deathly. She addressed Crystal and Trevin directly. "You probably don't know this, but I had AIDS, and I wasn't good about taking care of it. I was hospitalized a few times."

"But you got better," Rylie interrupted.

Her aunt patted her hand. "I died, babe. Heart failure." She sighed. "I woke up in the hospital immediately. Scott had given me a charm bracelet before—said it was a Christmas present that would help heal me. But all it did was bring me back when I died."

"So you're like Eleanor," Seth said.

"I reckon so."

"No way. She's all rotten," Rylie protested.

"He must have brought her back from the grave after she'd been decaying for a while. I was fresh. See, if I break or tear something, I don't heal. But as long as a necromancer keeps fixing me, I could live like this forever. I was grateful for Scott's gift. It let me stay with you, babe." Gwyn smiled fondly at Rylie and patted her hand. "But I didn't know that Scott had... other plans."

Bekah gave another ragged sob. Levi hugged her tightly. "He would never work for Cain," Levi said fiercely. "I don't believe it."

Rylie rounded on him. "You think Gwyn is lying?"

"No. I saw the tattoo. But it must be something else. Blackmail, maybe." Levi pounded a fist on the table, making the coffee mugs jump. "You didn't have to kill him!"

Gwyn didn't rise to meet his anger. She took another sip of coffee and set it down again.

"No," she said softly. "I didn't. Frankly, I don't know if he'll be able to keep me running now that I killed him, so it would have been in my best interests to do nothing. But I couldn't let that traitor run free. He was going to sacrifice Rylie to resurrect Eleanor."

Rylie couldn't hold it back anymore. A hot tear slid down her cheek.

It was Crystal who spoke. "So you're going to die anyway."

Gwyn just pushed Rylie's mug closer to her. "Drink up, babe."

She stared at the black fluid. A disjointed corner of her brain wondered if she should drink that much caffeine when she was pregnant. Rylie brought the mug to her lips, but didn't drink before setting it down again.

"What are we going to do about Scott?" Trevin asked.

Seth pushed his chair back and stood.

"Get answers."

NINE

The Day before the Wedding

Despite his exhaustion, Abel couldn't sleep. It wasn't even that he still had a fork buried in his ribs—after a couple of hours, it turned to nothing more than a numb spot on his side. And it definitely wasn't fear, because he wasn't afraid anymore, either.

The thought that kept him up was Rylie. She was out there somewhere, growing his baby in her womb, and thinking of it filled him with possessive heat. The urge to claim her, and beat all other claimants away.

He couldn't sleep. Couldn't let his guard down. Couldn't get sacrificed to bring his bitch of a mother back to life.

A rumbling growl rose in Abel's chest and rolled through his throat. His muscles tensed as he strained against the ropes, twisting his wrists and arching his back to put all of his strength behind trying to snap them again.

He had been trying every five minutes ever since Cain left him, and made no progress. But he *had* to get free. That singular need drove everything else from his mind.

The night wore on, long and slow. The dawn was broken with the sound of Eleanor's shriek.

"What do you *mean*, he's gone missing?"

Abel jerked in his ropes, twisting around to see where her voice had come from. He had smelled her, and known that she had to be close, but his mom hadn't come out to taunt him.

Now Eleanor and Cain were yelling at each other.

"He was supposed to be here last night, and he never arrived!" Cain's voice filtered through the window, only a fraction quieter than Eleanor.

"You didn't have someone *watching* him?"

"Of course I did," Cain snapped. "But he hasn't reported in lately, and——"

He fell silent. Eleanor must have said something, but it was too quiet for Abel to hear what she said.

Abel finally stopped fighting. He didn't know *who* was supposed to have arrived—the necromancer? But an aura of anger radiated from the mobile home, and he was certain that something had gone wrong. Really wrong.

"It's not safe to keep Abel much longer," Cain finally said. "He's dangerous."

Eleanor's response chilled Abel.

"Fine. I'll kill him."

Trevin, Crystal, and a few of the other werewolves that had survived the attack on the sanctuary were getting set up for Rylie's wedding. The arch and chairs had arrived, the baker's truck was rolling up the driveway, and things were starting to look like a real wedding.

Despite the light dusting of snow, the news report was good—the next day was supposed to be in the high forties and only a little overcast, with no actual falling snow.

Perfect for an outdoor wedding in winter.

"What are you going to do if the weather gets bad?" Yasir asked, handing a box of ammunition and an empty magazine to Seth. They were on the other side of the property getting ready for their part of the wedding.

"Wear a warmer jacket," Seth said. Loading a magazine was tricky with a broken hand, but he had practice at it. "We can't do this inside. It has to be outside, where we have more room to maneuver. How many men will you have?"

"Two full units are on their way," Yasir said. "Over a dozen men. Considering my batting average as of late, I'd say at least five or six of those aren't going to try to kill us."

He popped the magazine into the bottom of his gun.

"Not bad odds," Seth said, giving Yasir a slanted smile.

"What are you guys doing?"

Rylie came down the hill, wearing a white tank top and a dusty pair of jeans. It looked like she had been hard at work getting everything arranged.

Seth stepped in front of the car so that she wouldn't see the guns they were assembling in the trunk, but Rylie didn't need her eyes to tell what was going on. Her nose wrinkled as she sniffed.

"We're preparing," he said.

She frowned. "You're armed."

Seth looked to Yasir for assistance, but the other man seemed to be pretending to be deaf.

He didn't bother trying to hold Rylie back when she stepped up to look in the trunk. They had several fully automatic weapons and a few smaller, easy to conceal guns spread in front of them, like a miniature armory.

Rylie pulled a face. She must have smelled the silver bullets. "Do you think Cain is going to attack the wedding?"

"I just want to be prepared," Seth said, voice level.

Her eyes flicked to Yasir. "Is that why your 'hunter friends' are coming? Are they Union?"

"Rylie…"

"The Union tried to kill me," she said.

"To be fair, they've tried to kill most people at one point or another," Seth said. Rylie didn't seem to think that it was funny. He wrapped her in his arms. "I'm just trying to keep you safe. That's all. Nobody is going to hurt you." She sighed and didn't respond. Seth was pretty sure that meant she didn't forgive him. "Did you need something?"

"Stephanie sent me," she said. "She wanted me to tell you that Scott came back from the dead."

Seth met Stephanie at the cellar door, and they entered together.

"Back from the dead" was an interesting description—and pretty appropriate, considering that Scott had a permanent hole in his forehead. There was no mistaking him for alive. Not the same way that Gwyn had always looked lively and bright.

"I'm sorry," Scott said as soon as they descended the stairs. He was sitting against a few boxes in the corner, and he looked horrible.

"Why, Papa?" Stephanie asked. There was a softness to her voice that Seth had never heard before. "You betrayed us. You're working for Cain."

"The Apple," he whispered. "I had no choice."

Seth stepped forward. "You mean that tattoo—right? What is the Apple?"

Scott gripped his daughter's hand. He reached up to touch her cheek, and she closed her eyes. "I'm sorry, Steph," he said. "I'm so sorry. I never wanted you to think so badly of me."

"What is the Apple?" Seth pressed.

"The mark of Cain." He choked on the words. "It's hard to explain how I got involved with the Apple, but it was long before either of you were born, and I hope you can trust me when I say that I never thought that it would involve hurting people. I *haven't* hurt anyone. But I had obligations. There was no choice but to resurrect Eleanor."

"There's always a choice," Stephanie said.

Scott's brow wrinkled, making the skin around the bullet wound pucker. "I don't consider letting Cain kill my children a choice." He gave a rattling sigh. "I don't have the answers you want. I'm sorry."

He sounded like he meant it. Seth paced away from him, trying to calm his pounding heart.

If they couldn't trust Scott, who *could* they trust?

"Do you know anyone else with the Apple?" Seth asked, even though he suspected that he knew the answer.

Scott shook his head. "Please let me out of here. I need to attempt to heal myself."

"Will you die if you don't?" Stephanie asked.

"No, but—"

She stood and straightened her blouse. The look she gave her father dripped with disdain.

"Consider it a lesson," she said. She turned to Seth. "Let's let him think on this. We have to finish getting ready for your wedding."

TEN

Sacrificial Wolf

Eleanor came to kill Abel that night. She carried a knife the size of her forearm in her left hand, which was not her dominant side. When she circled around him, Abel saw why. The opposite shoulder terminated in a stump of bone, gleaming a dull shade of gray in the moonlight.

It was starting to snow again, so she was careful navigating the hill to his side.

He studied her every movement as she approached. Even dead, Eleanor was smart. If she dropped her guard for an instant, he was going to have to act fast to get free. He still wasn't sure how—after hours of fighting against his ropes, all he had gotten were sore wrists and not an inch of slack, and his anger had faded into something more like grim resignation.

"Eleanor," Abel said when she finally stood over him. She reeked of death and soil. After a beat, he changed it to, "Mom."

"Don't call me that," she snapped.

Eleanor jerked the fork out of his side. Abel's cry echoed off the hills. She flung it down the hill, and the fork disappeared into the bushes.

He sagged, panting and shaking as the healing fever swept over him again. Snow drifted through the air, landing on his chest and melting into tiny puddles. It didn't melt when it landed on Eleanor. Her hair was crunchy with ice.

She waited to move again until he was totally healed, and then she lifted the knife. The sour tang of silver's stench filled the air.

"Let me go," Abel said.

Her eyes narrowed. They had sunk deeper into her skull, like she was beginning to shrivel. "I don't talk to animals. Especially not the ones on the butcher's block."

She struggled to lower herself onto her knees. It was strange seeing her fight against her own body's mobility. Alive, Eleanor had been graceful and strong. As a corpse, she was in shambles—and getting worse.

Once she was closer, Abel could see that her arm wasn't the only thing missing. Her throat had collapsed. Her hair was missing on the left side.

Eleanor slid a hand over his chest and rested her fingers on his heartbeat. He realized with a jolt that she was trying to find his heart, because her right eye was glazed and blind.

"Wait," Abel said.

She didn't respond. Having found his heart, she positioned the point of the knife over his chest.

Eleanor was going to kill him. Just like that.

His heart raced, and his breath caught in his throat.

"Rylie's pregnant with your grandbaby," he blurted.

Eleanor froze. The knife drew back, but his pulse didn't slow again.

Her chin tipped down so that she could focus her one clear eye on him. The look she gave Abel was pure venom. "Who?" she asked, hatred dripping from that one word. "Seth?"

"Me," Abel said. His heart skipped a beat again, but it wasn't with fear this time.

Eleanor's eyes slid shut, and a shudder rippled through her broken body.

She had spent her entire adult life trying to wipe out werewolves to fulfill her husband's legacy. She knew as well as Abel did what her grandchild would be like.

"It doesn't matter anyway. Cain's going to kill her," she said, but she sounded worried. "He won't let that devil spawn walk the Earth."

The knife hung at her side. She hadn't moved to stab him again.

Abel tried to catch her gaze, hoping she would hear him. Really hear him. And he prayed that she still had enough of a brain to understand. "You got to have wondered why he let her live at the cabin. Why not kill her when he had the chance?"

Eleanor leaned closer. The hole on her upper chest was glistening, and he realized that there were maggots squirming inside the dried flesh. Abel's stomach flipped. "Cain let her live because he was saving her for me. To bring me back."

"He let her live because he smelled that she's pregnant. He had seen her mating with me. He wants to bring the werewolf species back—and he wants them to be pure." Abel spat out the last word.

He could practically see the cogs turning in Eleanor's head as she considered his claims. He saw the instant that she realized he was speaking the truth.

"Every fruit born from my womb is a piece of useless garbage," Eleanor said. "Failures. All of you." There was a strange, hollow tenor to her voice. Like she was repeating something that had been recorded before, instead of speaking something new.

Abel hadn't expected his news to make her love him in the way that she never had before, but it still didn't feel good to hear those words from her shriveled lips.

"Mom," he whispered.

Eleanor lifted the knife again. He tensed.

But she brought it down on the ropes, cutting his wrists free.

"Run, boy," Eleanor said.

"What are you doing?" he asked, rubbing his raw wrists.

"You promise me something," Eleanor said in a low voice, quiet enough that Cain wouldn't be able to hear it inside the mobile home. "Promise me that if I let you go, you demons are done. That you'll die out."

Abel frowned. "That was always the plan. Ever since that night on the mountain."

"Good," she said, her dry voice rattling in her chest. "So run. My other son has betrayed me, lied to me, and he's going to answer for his sins."

Eleanor cut Abel's ankles free as well. He got to his feet, and she didn't stand. He wasn't sure that she could.

He gazed longingly at the empty fields bathed in moonlight. The white swells were so tantalizing— freedom, just a few steps away. All he had to do was start running.

He took a step, and then stopped. Looked back at his mother's corpse.

Abel's heart ached. "I can take you with me," he said. "I can find someone to fix you. It's got to be possible."

She sneered. "Run!"

The arrangements were complete, and Cain was just hours from victory.

He reclined on the floor of the mobile home's empty living room, hands folded over his stomach and eyes closed. The walls were covered in maps, reports of Rylie's movements, pictures of the Gresham Ranch. He even had a few photos of the wedding decorations that had been set up earlier in the day.

Eleanor had taught him her Process for tracking prey, and his eyes were everywhere. Even now, his men were watching the Greshams.

But Cain was resting, and enjoying the anticipation.

Trying to organize a movement wasn't easy, yet he had claimed dozens of men as his own—men who bore the mark of the Apple, but would listen to everything he told them. Now, after so many months of stalking, he was going to have his retribution.

Abel would die tonight. Seth would die tomorrow. And he would claim Rylie—and her unborn infant—as his own. He wanted to savor the victory.

Cain smelled Eleanor's approach before she entered again. It was hard not to smell her coming now. Without Scott's spells to maintain her, she was decaying.

He didn't open his eyes. "Mother," he said, allowing himself a smile. "Was it as good as you imagined to kill Abel, so many years after he betrayed us?"

She didn't reply.

He finally looked at her. Fluffy snow was stuck to her hair and the layers of her black dress. Her destroyed eye pointed toward the wall, while the other focused on him.

And she looked *pissed*.

Cain sat up. "You killed him, didn't you?"

Eleanor raised the knife. The blade was unbloodied. "Tell me why you let that blond whore live."

"Tell me you killed Abel," he said, getting to his feet. His moments of languorous peace were shattered. "Mother. I need to hear these words from you."

"She's pregnant," Eleanor said, advancing on him at a limp. One of her legs dragged underneath her.

"That doesn't change anything—"

"You want her baby to live!"

So Abel had told her. Cain cursed himself inwardly. He hadn't thought that Abel would tell Eleanor, much less that she would actually listen to him—Eleanor's mind seemed to be rotting along with the rest of her body.

"I knew I should have taken care of this myself," he said, reaching for the knife.

Eleanor lunged. Silver flashed through the air, and he felt the bite of the metal burying into his bicep.

Cain roared and ripped the knife out of his arm. Silver didn't sting a natural-born werewolf the way it did the impure, but that didn't mean that the injury didn't hurt like hell.

He flung the knife aside.

"What's wrong with you?" he demanded, grabbing Eleanor's remaining arm as blood cascaded down his elbow. "I'm your *son*."

"You're a waste of breath." She spat ichor into his face. It splashed like acid on his cheek. "You're just as bad as Abel and Seth."

Hurt and betrayal crashed over him. Cain closed his eyes, took deep breaths, and tried to calm his anger.

He had spent his childhood raised in foster homes, knowing that his mother was out there somewhere. He had spent so many days dreaming of her. What she would be like. Longing for her love.

When he learned that she had been killed, he had abandoned everything to find a necromancer to resurrect her, and then dedicated months more to tracking down her killers—Eleanor's other sons, the useless bastards.

He had thought he was finally happy.

And now she spit on him.

"I think that you're having a bad night," Cain said slowly, carefully. "We need—"

"You deserve to die," she said in a dry voice. Each syllable was slower than the last.

She swiped at him with bony fingertips, and it was too easy to step back and dodge her.

"I'll find Scott," he said. "He needs to heal you."

"You don't deserve my blood," Eleanor hissed, taking the knife from the floor and rounding on him again.

"Mother—"

"I'm going to bleed it from you."

"Mother!"

She swung with the knife, and he wasn't so shocked that he couldn't dodge her blow. Cain instinctively knocked her arm aside with his. There was a dry crack when his elbow drove into her flesh. One of the bones in her forearm fractured and jutted from the skin.

"Bleed," Eleanor said. Even her good eye was empty of consciousness now, too. The rage had taken her somewhere else. Somewhere inhuman.

Cain felt panic swell in his chest. "Don't make me hurt you, Mother. Not now. Not when we're *so close*."

But she only kept advancing on him.

He threw open the front door and dropped down the steps. The stakes that had bound Abel to the ground were little lumps under the snow, but his body was gone.

She had freed him.

"What have you done?" he asked. He heard her taking slow, careful steps out of the trailer behind him.

And then he felt a blazing point of pain erupt between his shoulder blades.

Cain reacted on instinct. He swung as he turned, lashing out with both fists. They connected with Eleanor's skull and sent her crashing to the ground.

He watched in horror as she fell.

The dry ligaments that barely held her together snapped free when she struck. A horrible shriek filled the air—one leg was twisted underneath her, her spine was twisted at an impossible angle, and her face was screwed up with pain. She shouldn't have been able to hurt. Scott told him that zombies didn't *feel* things the way live humans did.

"No!" Cain cried. "I didn't mean to—"

"Failure," Eleanor hissed through her gritted teeth. Her eye glistened at him in the moonlight. "*Failure.*"

His protests fell into silence as he stared at the broken fragments of his mother. Any living human in that state wouldn't have been able to speak. Yet even now, she stared at him with hate.

Calm settled over him, and a grim certainty that robbed him of his panic.

"You're just having a bad day," he said gently, even as his heart was breaking. "I know that the Greshams have Scott. When we kill them all at the wedding tomorrow, he'll fix you. But for now, you're... you're *unwell*, Mother."

She hissed and wailed as he carefully picked up the pieces of her body, took her behind the mobile home, and placed her inside the trunk of his car. Her body fit in there neatly, folded in half.

"You animal bastard," Eleanor said.

Cain shuddered. Wiped his cheeks dry.

"I'll fix you, Mother," he promised, voice a low whisper.

He slammed the trunk shut.

The rising sun broke over the horizon, glowing through a crack in the clouds.

Just a couple more hours until the wedding now.

ELEVEN

To Have and to Hold

The phone rang six times, and then clicked over to voicemail—the exact same way that it had the last twelve times Seth tried to call.

He swallowed against the lump in his throat as he heard the recording of his brother's voice.

"This is Abel. Leave a message."

Beep.

Seth had hung up every other time he called, but he was out of time. The wedding was due to start in an hour. He couldn't keep hoping for Abel to answer.

"Hey, man," he said, clearing his throat as he paced in his bedroom at the Gresham Ranch. "This is—it's me. We've got to talk. I keep trying to reach you, but…"

But what? Seth sighed.

"I'm marrying Rylie today. I was hoping you'd be here, but I understand why you're not answering, and why you wouldn't want to come."

Could he leave it at that? It didn't feel like enough. There were still a thousand things that he wanted to say.

"I wasn't bluffing," Seth said. It came out before he could even think to stop himself. "When I called Scott at the California sanctuary, and asked him to let you know that I love you. It wasn't a bluff. I do love you, bro. And I don't think I've told you that enough. I hope you'll come back soon."

Feeling strange and awkward, Seth hung up. He set the phone on his table and stared at it.

It had been almost a week since he last heard from Abel. Every day hurt a little more than the one before. He thought that they were friends, as well as brothers—and good enough friends that they wouldn't let something like a girl get between them.

"I guess I was wrong," he muttered, facing the mirror.

Seth was already in his rented tuxedo. He wore a white suit with a red vest underneath. It matched the theme of the wedding—Gwyn had given him the vest with a wink and told him that he would match Rylie somehow.

The bowtie hung loose around his neck. He had already tried, and failed, to get it to tie about a hundred times.

"One hundred and one times is the charm," he said, working on the knot again.

There was a brief knock at the door, and Yasir entered. He cleaned up pretty good. Black suit, no tie, dress shirt with the button open at the neck.

"Need help?" Yasir asked.

Seth dropped his hands. "Hell yes. Save me from this unholy thing." The commander took over, standing behind Seth to quickly tie it in a neat bow. He made it look so easy. "Is that suit Union issue?"

Yasir laughed as he turned Seth around and brushed the hair off of his shoulders with brisk motions. "Believe it or not, yes. We do covert ops sometimes. There's even a whole department for espionage."

"Nice," Seth said, reaching up to fiddle with the tie.

Yasir grinned. His gold canine glinted in the light. "Nervous?"

Seth braced his hands on the windowsill to stare out at his wedding. Bekah, Trevin, and Stephanie were in hyper-party mode, and they whirled around getting everything right at the last minute—the chair drapes, the red ribbons, the roses, the table of gifts. There weren't many presents. Half of their guests were plants from the Union, and the other half were werewolves; they didn't have actual friends to invite.

There were snow flurries that morning, so they had put an awning over everything and draped fairy lights on it. It looked like a huge gazebo. Really pretty.

And in about an hour, he was going to meet Rylie under it and promise to love her until the day they died.

Hopefully, that wouldn't be tonight, too.

"Nervous?" Seth echoed. He gave a small laugh. "No way."

But he didn't feel right going into battle without his brother at his back, either.

Yasir gave him a hard pat on the shoulder. "Let me show you what we've got out there."

They headed out into the snow. The heavy clouds and absent wind made everything warm, even as the daylight faded, like a pleasant autumn day that was a little icier than usual. The winter berries and roses were beautiful splashes of red against the white of the snow.

It was easy to pick out the Union, because they were the only men in black nearby. The suits really were Union issue. They were all dressed the same.

They milled around the back of the gazebo together under the watchful eye of Levi, who was getting the sound system ready nearby. Seth noticed that their jackets bulged under the arms.

"Subtle," Seth said.

Yasir shrugged. "It doesn't have to be." He pointed at the man on the far left. "That's Grant. He's an ordained priest. He can officiate the ceremony for you two."

"Actually, I was hoping I could do the honors."

Seth turned. Someone had let Scott Whyte out of the cellar, and he wore a neat suit and bowler hat low on his brow that concealed the bullet wound. Levi hovered a few feet behind him, looking worried.

"What do you want?" Yasir asked sharply.

"Wait," Seth said, putting a hand on his best man's arm to keep him from drawing his gun.

"I realize what a betrayal it was to cooperate with Cain's demands and bring back Eleanor," Scott said, holding his hands out to show them that he was unarmed. "But I hope you understand why I did it."

"Cowardice?" Yasir suggested.

Scott gripped his heart, as if the word wounded him. "Love," he said. He caught Seth's eye. "I'm not the only one who has done stupid, misguided things to protect his family."

Seth rubbed his chin thoughtfully.

"If you're seriously considering listening to him, I have to protest," Yasir said. "This is a bad idea. We need someone we can trust at the altar."

"I already have you," Seth said.

Levi stepped up to his father's side and placed a hand on his shoulder. He was a lot taller than Scott, which made him fairly imposing. "He can't do any damage if all of us are watching him. And he knows he's made a mistake."

Scott extended a hand. After a moment, Seth shook it. "I look forward to the ceremony," Seth said.

Yasir gave a snort of disgust and walked away. The other men from the Union followed him. They didn't go far—just to the gazebo to sit down. Many of the werewolves were already seated. The time for the wedding was approaching quickly.

"Thank you," Scott said.

Seth fixed him with a hard look. "You're not forgiven. I'm sorry, Scott, but it's going to take more than words to regain my trust."

"What do you expect from me?"

"There was a way to bring Eleanor back from the dead," Seth said, lowering his voice. Levi leaned in to listen to him. "After all of this is done, I want you to bring Gwyneth back instead."

The witch looked startled. "But it requires sacrifice."

"I know," Seth said. "I know."

Music started playing from the speakers by the gift table. It wasn't the processional yet, but it was a warning that they only had fifteen minutes left. Seth stepped away.

"I'll have Stephanie check on Rylie," Levi said.

Seth led Scott to the altar and took his position beside a disgruntled-looking Yasir. He swallowed his nerves, checked his cell phone, and saw that Abel still hadn't called back.

"Almost time," he whispered.

The music started playing. Rylie could barely hear it from her tent outside the house, but it still made her heart leap into her throat.

"But I'm not ready!" Rylie gasped, pulling her garter belt over her stockings.

She pulled shoes on, but her fingers were shaking too much to get the straps around her ankles. Gwyn laughed and took care of it for her. "Relax. The wedding's not going to start without you. Trust me."

Rylie gnawed on a fingernail. "What if we get attacked during the ceremony? What if we *don't* get attacked during the ceremony? Oh my God, what if I trip while I'm walking down the aisle?"

Her aunt grabbed her shoulders. "Breathe in. Breathe out."

"I am breathing! I couldn't panic if I stopped!"

"You're not going to trip and fall. You're a werewolf, babe. You're the epitome of grace. Remember?"

"Oh," Rylie said. "Yeah. But what about—"

"Cain and Eleanor? Don't worry about it." Gwyn jerked her thumb at the table that was occupied by a space heater and parts of Rylie's wardrobe. "I've got a shotgun under my wrap. And I have an extra weapon, too."

She pulled a glass ball out of a box on the table.

"What's that?" Rylie asked, curiosity winning out over her fear. She leaned in closer. It had a tiny animal skull inside.

"This is what Scott used to resurrect Eleanor," Gwyn said. "If she shows up, I'm pretty sure I can use it to get rid of her."

Rylie opened her mouth to argue, but Stephanie Whyte stuck her head through the flap, interrupting them. "Almost ready?" she asked. Little white flowers were pinned in her strawberry blond hair.

"Almost," Rylie said with a weak smile.

Stephanie stepped in and fluffed out Rylie's skirt. "Lovely," she said fondly. And then her voice hardened. "My father's officiating, but there are Union soldiers out there. I saw them myself. You'll be safe."

"Stephanie," Gwyn snapped. "Is this the time?"

Rylie pressed her hands against her stomach. She wasn't sure if that queasy feeling was morning sickness or nerves. "It's good to know. It's not like we aren't preparing for trouble, too." Rylie hesitated, and then asked, "Any sign of Abel?"

Stephanie frowned. "No. Were you expecting him?"

Expecting? No. Hoping? Maybe a little bit.

Rylie shook her head.

"I'm going to take position," Stephanie said. "I'll be watching you from the back." She squeezed Rylie's arm encouragingly. "You look great."

And then she was gone, and Rylie still had to get her dress done up the back.

"Hurry," she urged Gwyn, sucking in her stomach.

"The dress is just a little snug." Her aunt grunted as she forced the sides of the fabric together. Her fingers were cold against Rylie's skin.

Rylie pressed her hands against her lower belly. It seemed a tiny bit bigger than when she had first tried on dresses. "I can't be growing *that* fast. Do I look pregnant?"

"You've changed sizes since prom. That's all. *There.*" Gwyn finally secured the hook and sighed.

Rylie twisted and turned to study herself in the mirror. Bekah had already done her hair in loose curls down her back, with smoky eye shadow and pink lip gloss. All of that looked good. And the dress was gorgeous, too—it had demi-sleeves, a red sash at the waist, and a heart-shaped cutout at the small of her back. But all Rylie could think about was the shape of her belly.

"You don't look pregnant," Gwyn said, noticing her paranoia. Moonlight filtering through the gaps in the tent shimmered in her eyes. She fidgeted with Rylie's sleeve, trying to smooth the satin flat.

"Why are you crying?" Rylie asked.

Gwyn picked up her shotgun and started loading it with silver bullets. "It's just—you look beautiful, babe. I wish your dad was here to see the way you look tonight."

Rylie swallowed around the lump in her throat. It was a horrible thing to think, but she had always been kind of glad that he died before she became a werewolf. He never knew that his baby girl had become a killing machine and leader of a monstrous race. And it also meant that he couldn't walk her down the aisle in front of enemies.

Her aunt jacked a round into the chamber. Propped the gun against her shoulder.

"You ready?"

Rylie closed her eyes and imagined everyone waiting for her to step outside.

Werewolves on one side.

Plainclothes Union army on the other.

Scott Whyte waiting to officiate the wedding.

And who knew how many men loyal to Cain would be hiding in the crowd?

The processional music started to play.

Whether or not Rylie was ready, it was time to walk down the aisle.

She picked up the bouquet and used the blossoms to conceal the claws that had already replaced her fingernails. Her inner wolf was stirring. It was afraid, and ready for a fight.

Gwyn cradled the shotgun in her arm and draped her wrap over it. Rylie took a deep breath, nodded once, and stepped outside for the wedding.

TWELVE

Forever Hold Your Peace

Abel had been running for hours, but he just wasn't fast enough. The hills and plains and farms were long and unending. Rylie was still too many miles away from him.

He was out of his mind with adrenaline and fatigue. He couldn't feel his bare feet, couldn't feel the muscles in his legs, couldn't feel his hands or nose or cheeks because of the cold wind blowing past him. All he could think about was *her*—and the wolf's overpowering need to be with Rylie.

Abel couldn't let Cain get to her first. She was his mate. He *needed* to protect her.

So he pushed through the exhaustion, pushed through the snow, and kept running.

The hills turned into a blur around him. Daylight faded into evening. He only knew that he was crossing a highway when the thin snow under his feet suddenly turned to pavement.

A car skidded in front of him. Abel barely dodged it.

He glimpsed the driver as the vehicle passed—it was Cain, gripping the wheel in both hands with fire in his eyes as he tore down the road. He didn't even notice that he had almost hit someone.

Abel stopped to look around. The stretch of road was familiar. He recognized the sign for the Batemans' farm, which was just down the road from the Gresham Ranch.

He was almost there. And so was Cain.

The melodious tones of a three-piece orchestra drifted through the air, and Rylie felt like she floated down the aisle on a sea of music. She was hyper-aware of the people watching her—Levi in the back row, and Stephanie behind him; all the men in black suits were on the other side. Their staring eyes drove straight through her skin and made her gut cramp.

Her fingers tensed on Gwyn's arm. She almost stopped walking. "I think I'm going to be sick," she whispered to her aunt.

"You're going to be fine, pumpkin," Gwyneth said. "I promise."

That was the name that Rylie's dad used to call her. Hearing it again reminded her of him, and his reassuring smile, and it filled her with warmth.

Rylie swallowed hard and kept walking.

She brought her gaze up the aisle. Bekah had spread rose petals over the snow where Rylie was meant to walk, and her path through the audience was marked with crimson ribbon. Snowflakes caught on her veil so that she could see the tiny crystals just beyond her nose.

Her gaze focused on who was waiting for her at the altar—and the rest of the world dropped away.

Seth's hands were folded in front of him, and the sight of him in his suit made her heart give a funny flop. His shoulders and chest were broad, filling out the tuxedo until it looked like he strained the seams. The white material offset his dark skin. That charming, slanted smile made his face glow—and glow for *her.*

Rylie hesitated a few steps away, heart beating in her chest like a caged animal.

Ever since she had first seen Seth, she had known that she loved him. But she had been such a different girl then. So much younger. Rylie was a different person, and she didn't know if the change was for the better, but Seth was the same.

He still loved her. It showed in his eyes, his smile, the way he held himself. He didn't care that she had killed more than a dozen people while sick with silver poisoning. He didn't care about her position in the pack. He only cared about the woman he had loved for years, and in his eyes, she felt like all her sins were forgiven.

Rylie faced her aunt, who used one hand to lift the veil. Gwyn was still cradling the shotgun under her wrap.

She bent down, and Gwyn kissed her cheek. "Love you, babe," she said.

Rylie gave a tearful smile. "I love you, too," she whispered back.

Gwyn stepped away, leaving Rylie nothing to do but take Seth's outstretched hand. His fingers were warm. She wished that she could kiss him now, instead of waiting for the end of the ceremony. She could have used the comfort.

"You okay?" he whispered as everybody in the audience sat.

Rylie nodded, unable to speak.

His hands tightened on hers.

"Dearly beloved," Scott said to her left, "we are gathered here today to celebrate the union of Rylie Gresham and Seth Wilder in holy matrimony…"

She was so on edge that she barely heard him. Blood roared in her ears.

Rylie thought she was going to faint.

Her wolf was struggling to emerge from within, making her gums ache and fingertips itch. She could smell the pack surrounding her, the stink of gun lubricant and silver bullets, hear distant footsteps on snow…

Wait. Footsteps.

Rylie's ears perked up, and she tuned out the drone of Scott's voice so that she could listen closer.

It sounded like someone was approaching. Running hard. Panting, gasping, staggering.

A faint breeze lifted, making her veil flutter behind her. Rylie let her eyes close so that she could take a sniff of the masculine smell of sweat and gunpowder.

"Will the bride please repeat after me?" Scott said, stirring Rylie from her daze.

She opened her eyes. Seth was looking worried.

And then his eyes focused over her shoulder.

"It can't be," he breathed.

Rylie gathered her skirts and turned, but she already knew who was approaching the gazebo.

Abel sprinted up the snowy hill. He was in a black tank top and jeans, completely unarmed, and looking exhausted. His foot caught on a rock under the snow, and he spilled onto the ground.

She sucked in a gasp. "Abel!"

Everyone in the audience stirred, craning to see him. Rylie heard guns drawn from holsters, safeties released, the soft growl of werewolves on the alert.

Rylie didn't even realize that she was running until she reached Abel's side. She dropped beside him.

"Oh my God," she said, hands hovering over his body. She wanted to touch him, but he was looking so pale—was he injured? "Abel, what are you doing here? What's wrong?"

He shoved himself over to roll onto his back. Every breath tore from his throat and made him grimace. "Rylie," Abel gasped. "Cain—"

Seth crunched through the snow to them. "Your timing sucks, man," he said, grabbing Abel's arm. "Are you okay?"

Abel gripped Seth's shoulders and stared in his face. "Cain is coming."

A gunshot split the air, and someone in the gazebo screamed.

Thirteen

Until Death

Seth released Abel and whirled, drawing a handgun from inside his tuxedo.

It was chaos in the gazebo. Guns fired, people shouted, and Rylie couldn't see what was happening. From the number of weapons firing, there had to be a lot of enemies—but through the tumult of bodies, it was impossible to tell who was attacking who.

"Stay here," Seth said, launching up the hill again.

Rylie choked on a sudden surge of bile, clapping her hand to her mouth.

"You okay?" Abel asked, his fingers wrapping around her wrist. His touch was warm and familiar. Her wolf was dizzyingly happy to see him alive, and Rylie found herself leaning into his shoulder.

"I thought you were gone," she whispered once she was certain that she could speak without vomiting.

He cupped her face in his hand. "I would never leave you behind, Rylie. You're my pack. My mate."

Seth's shout echoed over the hill. Rylie's head jerked up, and her wolf senses focused on him instantly.

He was firing from the hip at a moving target. A blur darting over the hill.

Cain.

Nerves swamped Rylie, and she gripped her stomach with a groan. "Abel..."

"I know," he said.

She stared at him. "You know?"

He covered her hand with his, and warmth spread through the gentle curve of her belly. For a moment, Rylie heard nothing—no shouts, no gunfire, no chaos. The world was reduced to the place just below her navel, and the feeling of Abel's skin.

"How can you already know?" she asked. "I haven't even told Seth yet."

Amusement flicked through Abel's eyes. "Cain told me. You can't fight like this—we have to get you out of here."

She nodded mutely, and he pulled her down the hill, tripping on her long skirts as they ran. Rylie grabbed fistfuls of the material and hiked it to her knees, but running was still too hard.

They left the gazebo behind them quickly, but not quickly enough. When Rylie glanced behind, she saw three of the black-clad Union men separate from the others.

Bullets pinged into the snow around them, sending up white puffs.

"The Apple," Rylie gasped. "They're coming for us!"

Abel growled. "They can't have you."

Even though it looked like he had totally exhausted his strength in running, he still wrapped an arm around her and pulled her out of the way just in time for another smattering of bullets to hit the ground.

He scooped her off the ground, skirts and all, and ran faster.

Rylie gave a cry of surprise. "Wait—"

"Shut up," Abel said, hauling her down the road toward the remnants of the barn.

There wasn't much of the building left, but there were two half-walls, and it was enough to shelter them. Abel jumped behind it. Bullets smacked into the other side, making the wood crack.

He set her down on the dry ground.

"What are we going to do?" Rylie asked. "We can't leave them behind! What about Gwyn, and Seth, and...?"

"Seth's fine," Abel said, glancing around the corner before facing her again. "Change me."

"What?"

"You can't wolf out. You'll lose the baby. But you're still Alpha—so *change me*."

Rylie reached out a shaking hand and brushed Abel's forehead. She focused all of her energy on him, and her wolf gladly rose to meet his.

It was easy to draw out his beast with the adrenaline roaring through her, and he changed in a rush of fur.

Seconds later, a massive black beast stood over her. He was the size of a small horse, and a thousand times more imposing.

Rylie smoothed her hand over the ruff of fur at his neck. "Be careful," she said.

Abel jumped around the wall.

She watched through a crack in the boards as he rushed on the Union soldiers. She couldn't see much, and she was glad for it—their screaming was horrible, and every time a gun fired, she feared that it would mean Abel's end.

But he was a blur as he leaped through them, growling as he ripped into the men with his teeth and claws.

Rylie seriously doubted there would be any survivors.

Seth took cover behind the presents' table to reload his gun. The rush of adrenaline made everything around him brilliant with clarity.

More than half of the Union men had turned on them when Cain attacked. Yasir's estimate of having five or six people on their side had been seriously optimistic. And what was worse, it looked like some of the wolves had turned traitor, too.

Seth jammed the magazine into his gun and rose, bracing his arm against the table to aim.

It was hard to tell who to shoot. Everyone was tangled in a knot of spraying blood and screams.

His gaze zeroed in on Stephanie Whyte. A werewolf had his hands around her throat.

Seth let out a breath, took aim, and fired.

A silver bullet buried in the shoulder of Stephanie's assailant—one of the traitorous wolves, who was named Manny. He grabbed his arm with a cry of surprise, then rounded on Seth as Stephanie fled.

Seth fired again, and again. Two more to the chest.

Manny fell, most likely dead.

He didn't let the kill distract him. He swiveled, knocking a box of china off the table. It shattered on the ground next to him.

Cain stood at the end of the aisle.

"Hello, brother," he said.

The werewolf moved too damn fast. One second, he was a few feet away, and the next, he was on top of Seth. The handgun flew from his grip and bounced across the snow before he could even think.

They wrestled, knocking over the table and rolling out from under the shelter of the gazebo. Snow fluttered around them.

Seth's skull rang as Cain punched him hard, right in the jaw.

"Sorry to crash the party," Cain growled, "but I think my invitation must have gotten lost in the mail."

Twisting free of Cain, Seth clambered to his feet and searched for his gun. He didn't waste breath on banter. Cain was too strong for him—much too strong.

The gun was a few feet away.

Cain jumped, and Seth rolled under him, avoiding the blow.

His unbroken hand fell on the gun. He aimed and fired.

The shot went wide.

Cain smacked the gun out of Seth's grip and punched him—hard.

He flattened on the snow, and the werewolf straddled his body.

"This is for our mother," Cain growled, drawing back his clawed hand and aiming for Seth's heart.

A gunshot cracked just behind him.

Red fluid fountained from Cain's shoulder. Another gunshot, and it poured from his chest. He looked down as though shocked by the wound.

Yasir walked up behind him and pointed his gun straight down at Cain's skull.

"Watch out," the commander told Seth, and then he fired a third time.

The bullet exploded from his skull and hit the snow right next to Seth's head. Cain's face blanked. He slumped to the side.

Seth pushed Cain's limp body off of him with a shout and scrambled to his feet.

"You almost hit me!"

"But I didn't," Yasir said, turning to pop off a couple more shots at the crowd. His aim was fantastic—he had once been a military sharpshooter, and every bullet hit a traitorous Union member. Two men fell.

Seth couldn't argue with his reasoning. He crouched beside Cain to inspect the wounds.

It seemed too easy. Three shots, and the half-brother that had menaced Rylie for weeks was gone. "Guess I shouldn't complain," he muttered with a scowl at all the blood. It had ruined his tuxedo.

He grabbed his handgun and stood beside Yasir.

There wasn't any fight left to speak of. Everything had sorted itself out in the fastest, bloodiest way possible—the beautiful gazebo was strewn with bodies, and only a few werewolves were left standing. Seth could see Stephanie hiding behind the altar with Scott.

There was no sign of Rylie or Gwyn.

Yasir holstered his gun. "Seven of them," he said, his eyes skimming the bodies. "Seven of my men turned on us."

"Seems like the Union's got a pretty big loyalty problem," Seth said.

The commander barked a laugh and headed for the bodies. Seth moved to follow—but an arm wrapped around his throat, strong and unyielding as an iron band.

He was jerked back against a muscular body. He thrashed hard, but couldn't break free.

"Cain!" Yasir shouted, spinning to face him again.

"Drop your gun! One move, and I pop off his head," Cain said. His deep voice thrummed in his chest and vibrated through Seth's back. "You want this guy alive? I want Rylie."

Yasir was frozen with his gun half-drawn.

"Don't," Seth squeezed out, his vision dimming.

"I shot you in the head," Yasir said, eyes narrowed. "I used silver bullets."

"Guess you don't know much about natural born werewolves," Cain said. "Rylie. Now."

Seth tried to shake his head, but he was confined too tightly.

Cain's arm tightened.

And then a black mass shot over the hilltop and crashed into them both.

Seth bowled over, thrown by the momentum of being struck by a wolf. It ripped him free of Cain's grip and knocked all the breath out of his lungs. He sprawled on the snow, gasping for oxygen.

His vision blurred, but he could just make out the huge wolf that was Abel clashing with Cain. Even as a human, Cain was powerful—more than a match for Abel. Having a hole in the side of his head didn't even faze him.

But then Cain made the mistake of trying to shift. His skin rippled, his knees popped, and he fell to all fours.

A moment of vulnerability was enough. Abel pinned Cain to the ground, jaws buried in his throat, and he bit down.

Cain cried out.

Seth got to his feet, dizzy and unsteady. Yasir grabbed him before he could fall over. "I've got you," he said.

Together, they went to Abel's side. He had a half-human, half-wolf Cain held down with his teeth and one massive paw. He couldn't seem to finish shifting with Abel's teeth in his neck.

Seth patted Abel on the shoulder. It wasn't enough to show his gratitude, but he had to try.

The wolf shied away from him.

Biting back his annoyance, Seth focused instead on Cain. "Give it up. You're alone, and you're not getting out of here with Rylie."

"Oh, I'm not alone," he said in a rasping gurgle, almost a growl. Blood bubbled in his furry throat. "You might have won this battle against me, but you're going to lose the war, little man. I let Eleanor out, and she's finishing off your wife as we speak."

Seth stared. "*What?*"

"If I can't have my pure race, nobody can," Cain hissed.

And then the blood loss was too much. His eyes glazed over, and he passed out.

Seth wiped the sweat off his upper lip with his sleeve. If a gunshot wound to the forehead hadn't killed Cain, then a combination of blood loss and strangulation wouldn't, either.

But he couldn't linger and keep trying to kill Cain. Not if Eleanor was after Rylie.

Abel had already made his decision. He released Cain and tore down the hill in a black blur.

"I'll watch Cain," Yasir said, pushing Seth's shoulder. "Find Rylie. Go!"

Rylie hugged her knees to her chest and shivered in the snow. It was quiet out on the ranch now, but she didn't know if it was safe to emerge.

If her side had won, wouldn't someone come looking for her yet?

She was so busy arguing with herself over the idea of leaving that she almost didn't notice when something else shifted in the burned remnants of the barn.

Eleanor dragged herself out of the shadows of what used to be a bedroom, and staggered toward Rylie.

Her right leg was missing below the ankle, and her spine was weirdly bowed, like it could no longer support her weight. But she *could* support a huge knife. It had a spiked blade that looked like it would hurt going in, and be impossible to remove without serious damage.

Rylie struggled to stand in her dress. "Eleanor?"

The woman limped toward her. "Did you do it?" Eleanor asked. Her words were jumbled, a little too fast. "Did you lasso my boy at long last?"

Fear made Rylie's heart pound. But she couldn't lose herself in the comfort of the wolf's merciless anger, even though it tried to rise within her—Abel had said that shapeshifting would make her lose the baby.

But she also couldn't fight Eleanor as a human, unarmed and alone.

She backed away slowly. "Wait," Rylie said, swallowing down her wolf. "Don't—"

Her foot caught on the train of her dress, and she tripped backwards. She landed hard on her butt. Her temple smacked into a broken board, sending her head spinning.

Eleanor lurched forward.

"Temptress," she whispered, ichor dribbling down her lip. "*Whore.*"

Kicking her feet free of her dress, Rylie struggled to stand again. But Eleanor was strangely fast, for a woman who was falling apart. She lifted the knife.

Rylie was going to have to change. She *had* to.

She pressed a hand to her belly. "I'm sorry," she whispered, closing her eyes.

A shotgun blast rang out.

Eleanor shrieked, and Rylie's eyes flew open.

Gwyn stood a few feet away, gun braced against her shoulder. She had blasted away part of Eleanor's ribcage.

The knife slipped from Eleanor's fingers and bounced across the burned ground.

"You keep the hell away from my niece," Gwyn said.

"You can't kill me," Eleanor said scornfully. "I'm as immortal as you are!"

Gwyn lowered the shotgun and pulled something out of her pocket.

The animal skull.

Eleanor's eyes widened as Gwyn lifted the tiny animal skull over her head.

"Immortal? I don't think so. You've already walked this earth about thirty years too long, Eleanor."

"It will kill you, too!"

But Gwyneth brought the skull crashing down on the wall. The bauble shattered. The skull exploded into a thousand fragments.

"No!" Rylie screamed.

Her cries mingled with Eleanor's. It shook dust from the crumbling rafters of the barn.

Seth's mother collapsed in an instant, as if she was nothing more than a bag of bones. But the life—and the anger—remained in her face. Her one good eye stared up at the rafters.

"Monsters," Eleanor whispered.

Then she was gone.

FOURTEEN

The Reception

As soon as Rylie was sure that Eleanor's remains were done twitching, she ran to Gwyneth. "Oh my God," Rylie breathed, grabbing her aunt by the shoulders to look at her. "Are you okay?"

Gwyn chuckled. "I'm fine, babe."

"But the skull——"

Gwyn patted her back. "I was brought back by a charm, not black magic. I knew I'd survive breaking the skull."

"Did you? Really?"

"Well... no." She winked. "But I had a pretty good feeling."

A laugh burst out of Rylie's chest—one that was more relief than actual happiness. She threw her arms around Gwyn and squeezed her tightly. But not *too* tight.

"I'm so glad you're okay," she whispered against her aunt's shoulder.

"Well, I'm not totally unscathed." Gwyn drew back and turned to show Rylie a wound on her back—a circle of human teeth over her ribcage. "A couple members of the pack sided with Cain, and they fight nasty. Good thing I'm already dead, or the next three months sure wouldn't be fun."

Rylie clapped her hands over her mouth. "Oh no."

"It's all right. Just a flesh wound."

"But you can't heal that!"

Gwyn shrugged. "You're okay, and the baby's okay. That's all that matters."

She looped her arm around Rylie's shoulders and steered her out of the barn.

A black wolf came rushing down the hill and stopped just in front of Rylie. Abel butted his broad nose into her side. His hot breath snuffled over her hands and neck.

"I'm fine," Rylie said, pushing his head down. He laved his tongue over her face, and she giggled. "Seriously, I'm *fine*."

Abel touched his nose to her belly, as if to make sure that was also okay, and her smile faded a fraction.

"Yes," Gwyn said. "That's fine, too."

Rylie stroked her hand over his massive head and released the transformation. Abel shifted back quickly. He stood naked and steaming in the snow. "Eleanor?" he asked.

Gwyn jerked her head toward the barn. "Dead. For good this time, I think."

"Rylie!"

Seth was just a few yards behind his brother. Gwyn released her, and Rylie pushed past Abel to run to him as best she could in all of her skirts.

He caught her up in a hug, and Rylie buried her face in his neck.

She might not have gotten married, but she had survived—and so had the baby. Seth and Gwyn were safe, Abel was home, and Eleanor was dead.

She couldn't ask for anything more.

Yasir loaded Cain's unconscious form into the back of a van with the surviving Union traitors. There weren't many left—Levi had gone wild with fury, and it was only because of Bekah's intervention that any survivors were left at all.

"What will you do with Cain if he can't die?" Seth asked Yasir, keeping an eye on the twin werewolves still wrestling with each other at the bottom of the hill. It looked like Bekah was starting to wear Levi down.

Yasir slammed the door shut and locked it. "The Union has a special prison. And now that we have control of Cain, the traitors shouldn't be a problem——I hope. I'm going to take him straight to HQ until I can get him to give me the names of all of his followers."

"You don't think this is over?" Seth asked.

The commander shook his head. "Not even close."

He climbed into the van and drove away. Seth watched them go, and he felt a little bit less safe than he had before speaking to Yasir.

Abel sat down at a chair next to the toppled table of presents. He pulled a box into his lap and opened it.

"China set," he said. "Nice."

"Those aren't for you," Seth said.

His brother ignored him. He dropped the china, grabbed another bag, and ripped out the tissue paper. "Who the hell gave you a fishbowl?"

Seth rolled his eyes and decided not to remark on it.

The rest of the surviving pack members were helping clean the bodies and tear down the decorations, which had been thoroughly destroyed in the fight. But all Abel seemed to want to do was be annoying.

"Did you get my message?" Seth asked. "I left you a voicemail."

"Naw. I lost my phone somewhere between getting kidnapped and fork torture. Why? What did you say?"

Seth swallowed hard. "Nothing. Never mind."

"Are they gone?" Rylie asked, emerging from the house. She had changed from her dress into a pair of jeans, but her hair and makeup was still perfect. She looked incredible.

He caught her hand and pulled her against his chest.

"They're gone," Seth said firmly. "You're safe."

She sighed and leaned against him. "That wasn't what I expected to happen when I said we should get married."

He rubbed his hands over her shoulders. "Well, we still have the license. All we need is a ceremony."

Abel stood up.

"No," he said.

Seth lifted his eyebrows. "No?"

"No," Abel repeated, pushing his way in between them. "You can't get married."

"Abel..." Rylie said warningly.

Seth reached out to take her hand. "It's okay, Rylie. Abel knows that you've made your choice. He's not going to do anything stupid... right, Abel?"

His brother's golden eyes glimmered. "That's the thing. She *did* make her choice, and she can't marry you. Rylie is pregnant with my baby."

AUTHOR'S NOTE

SM Reine is a writer and graphic designer obsessed with werewolves, the occult, and collecting swords. Sara spins tales of dark fantasy to escape the drudgery of the desert where she lives with her husband, the Helpful Toddler, and a small army of black animals.

Enlist in the Army of Evil!

Be the first to hear when a
new book comes out! Visit
smarturl.it/armyofevil

Made in the USA
Middletown, DE
25 September 2015